THE
VULGAR
BOATMAN

The Vulgar Boatman

A
BRADY COYNE
MYSTERY

William G. Tapply

CHARLES SCRIBNER'S SONS
NEW YORK

Author's Note:

For their help and support in the preparation of this manuscript, I wish to thank Rick Boyer, Charlotte Wade, Cindy Tapply, and Betsy Rapoport. Each has a singular expertise which I value. All are people I trust. I am blessed.

And the way led on to the waters of darkest Acheron.
A whirlpool thick with gray mud spits
and boils and belches forth its slime.
Here the boatman keeps his watch on his dear waters,
Charon terrible in his filth: the scraggle of beard
all yellow-white and tangled: eyes like points of flame:
a stained cloak knotted hangs from bony shoulders.
It is he who pushes with the pole and watches the sails,
his cargoes of bodies fill the rusty bulk year after year.
Aged now himself, but the green old age of a god within him.
To him the crowds of eyeless dead flow like a gentle current:
matron ladies and their lords, bodies of
great-hearted heroes, boys and unwed girls,
the young burnt of the pyre before their parents' eyes
You know, you who have seen in early autumn forest,
the leaves in their numbers glide and fall, or in windstorm
rafts of birds in thousands, massed to flee
over winter-grey ocean to lands of sun.
How the dead beg and plead for passage,
stretching out their hands in longing for the further shore;
But he is the mournful captain who chooses these and those
and others he pushes and keeps away from the shore.

—Virgil, *the Aeneid* (Book VI)
translated by Michael M. Fiveash

THE
VULGAR
BOATMAN

one

WHEN TOM BARON CALLED ME, HE did not beat around the bush. This was unusual, since he had earned a reputation for excellence in misdirection and evasion during his current gubernatorial campaign.

"I gotta see you, Brady," he said.

"Is this something political, Tom?"

"It's not political. It's personal. It's something for my lawyer."

"Because if this is political, I already told you. I want nothing to do with your campaign. I'm not even going to vote for you."

"I told you. It's personal."

I lit a cigarette and swiveled around to look out my office window at the rooftops of Copley Square. The sky over Boston was clear and blue. Indian summer. The frost would soon be on the pumpkin. Next thing, it would be nipping at my nose. Or was it toes? Whatever, an attorney with well-ordered priorities should be casting dry flies to rising brown trout someplace like the Deerfield River on a day like this.

I rotated my chair again in an effort to put the temptations of the great out-of-doors behind me. A futile try.

"You there, Brady?" said Tom.

I sighed. "Yeah, Tom. I'm here. What do you want to talk about?"

"Not on the phone."

"Why the hell not? My lines are secure, believe me. Your opponent got something on you, is that it? You want to bring suit against the Democratic party? Looking for the *Globe* to make a retraction? Hey, I loved that cartoon on the editorial page this morning. See it? They had you dressed in an animal skin. You looked a lot like Fred Flintstone, actually, and you were swinging around this big club at a bunch of dinosaurs. The dinosaurs were labeled 'Big Government' and 'Drug Kingpins' and 'Welfare Moochers.' It was beautiful."

"I didn't find it that funny," said Tom primly. "But that's not it. I told you it wasn't political."

"They're doing a real number on you, pal."

"Screw them. Hey, I really gotta see you. You still my attorney, or what?"

"Sure. I'm your attorney."

"You still handle my personal stuff, right?"

"Yup."

"And you make house calls."

"I do. That is part of my charm."

"That's your main charm," he said. "Look. We're having one of our frank-and-bean fundraisers this evening in the old hometown. Why don't you come to it, and we can get together afterwards?"

"You want me to pay twenty bucks for a plate of beans?"

"For you, Counselor, it's on the house. I'll throw in a speech for good measure."

"You do that, I won't know which gave me gas."

"You'll be there, then."

"I'm a lawyer. It's a tough job. But I'm a tough guy."

"Terrific."

"Look, Tom. What the hell is this all about, anyway?"

"Can't tell you. See you tonight. Elks lodge in Windsor Harbor. Be there around six-thirty."

Windsor Harbor, Massachusetts, Tom Baron's hometown, was about an hour's drive from my office in downtown Boston. I persuaded Sylvie Szabo to go with me. I thought she would find Tom Baron's frank-and-bean dinner in the local Elks hall entertaining.

"Tom Baron," I told her as we drove, "is trying to combat the Republican fat-cat image. He wants people to think he's down-to-earth, old-fashioned, approachable, plain folks."

"But Tom Baron *is* a fat-cat Republican," observed Sylvie.

"True enough. But that isn't important. What's important is the image."

"American politics is amusing," said Sylvie.

"Well, I think you might find this evening amusing, anyway."

"Should I vote for this Tom Baron?"

"If you believe in the great American Dream, you probably should. If you believe that any poor boy can make good, and that the only enemy of progress is big government and individual sloth, yes, Tom Baron is your man."

Tom Baron, I went on to tell Sylvie, grew up in little Windsor Harbor on the Massachusetts North Shore in the days before it had been condoed and yuppified. Tom's father had scratched a meager living out of a nine-hole golf course along the rocky seacoast. Tom had earned a degree in agronomy from UMass, paying for his tuition by mowing his father's fairways and selling golf balls in the pro shop. When he graduated, he married his high school sweetheart and took over the club. He pursuaded his worn-out parents to retire to Florida and within three years Tom turned developer. He carved up the hundred or so acres of fairway and rough into house lots, built expensive homes on them, and made his first few million. It was rumored that Tom had smoothed over any uneven spots by spreading around incentives among key members of the Windsor Harbor planning board, board of selectmen, and zoning board. This was never proven, although several of those officials ended up living in Tom's development, having received favorable mortgage rates from the banks where Tom did his business.

"This," Sylvie interrupted, "is the American way, no?"

"It is, yes."

"So your Mr. Baron is a crook, then?"

"Being a crook is not necessarily the American way, Sylvie."

"I am hopelessly confused," said Sylvie, pretending to pout.

I exited Route 128 onto 1A and stopped at a red light. I leaned over and kissed the top of Sylvie's head. "You are the least confused person I know," I said into her hair. "But you do seem to have a lopsided way of looking at politics."

"I lived in Hungary for fourteen years," she said softly, her head bowed while I nuzzled the nape of her neck. "I see American politics differently from you. In America, the politicians care what the people think. That is not a bad thing."

"Well, I'm not so sure it's a good thing," I murmured. The light changed and I put my BMW through its gears. We were into the country-side now, winding through apple orchards and pastures and woodlands painted crimson and gold. We crossed several little tidal creeks. The smell of salt air wafted in through the sunroof.

This was Baron country. After he'd made his fortune out of his father's golf course, Tom had taken up buying and selling North Shore properties in a big way. I handled most of his contracts, cleared the deeds, researched the laws, and in general kept him on the proper side of the fine line. What he managed to accomplish over martinis was his own business. At least, that's the way I rationalized it. He was a tough, hardheaded businessman. He broke no laws. If he had, I would have defended him. And then I would have cut him loose, because if he broke a law it would have meant he had failed to follow my advice. But he never did. He was a good client. He also happened to pay me a lot of money.

He was also a pretty good guy and, as often seems to happen between me and my clients, we had become friends. When I was still married to Gloria, we'd take our sons, Billy and Joey, for Sunday afternoon picnics with Tom and Joanie and their boy, Buddy. Tom had a boat, and we'd cruise out to the Isle of Shoals or up into the mouth of the Merrimack. Sometimes we'd find the bluefish running, or maybe a school of mackerel, and the boys would haul them in.

Tom was also a helluva golfer, a talent he claimed was useful in his business activities. He gave me two strokes a side, and he usually beat me anyway.

After Gloria and I split, I steered clear of social get-togethers with Tom's family. Joanie kept inviting me for dinner, and I kept finding excuses. I knew that Joanie and Gloria kept in touch, and I sensed that we would be awkward. There had always been a vague chemistry between Joanie and me, harmless enough when we were both married, but nothing I wanted to let loose after my divorce.

When Tom decided to heed the blandishments of the Republican party to run for governor, he asked me to serve on what he called his "brain trust." I declined instantly. A man had to draw the line somewhere.

"Politics," I told Tom gently when he asked me, "just isn't my thing."

A more accurate truth was that Tom Baron's politics in particular wasn't my thing.

His "just plain folks" campaign was the butt of jokes in what he referred to as the "liberal press," which included both Boston newspapers. The small-town weeklies were generally kinder to him. The campaign was the brainchild of his campaign manager, Eddy Curry, who claimed to be a student of the American political scene. "It's the old log cabin and hard cider theme," he told me once. "Abe Lincoln splitting logs. JFK playing touch football with Bobby and Teddy, or at the helm of old Joe's schooner, squinting saltily into the sun. Ike in hip boots trying to catch a trout. Right? We've gotta personalize our man, see. I mean, Tom is a wealthy fella. But we've gotta package him as a regular guy. One of the boys. Republicans like to hold their fundraisers at the Ritz or the Parker House, right? Five hundred, a thousand bucks a plate. Lobster, shad roe, shit like that. Black tie, right? Okay. So we tip it over. The Ritz? We line up the local Sons of Italy hall. K of C. Rotary. Elks. Go to the small towns. Let the press take its best shot. Most of the people don't trust the press anyway. Lobster? Prime rib? We serve baked beans and franks and brown bread. Mother's apple pie for dessert. And we wheel out old Tom, he tells a few jokes, lets the folks see that he ain't any bigger than life, knock off a few homespun truths, two or three eternal verities. He's glib enough. Handsome fella to boot. He'll go over good. After the speech, we clear away the tables and bring out the jug band. Let Tom do a couple riffs on the bass fiddle. Tap a keg. Turkey in the straw. Hee-haw. Beat the Democrats at their own game. We'll sell this sucker. Folks don't wanna know that the twentieth goddamn century has arrived, never mind it's practically over. They wanna think that if they work hard they'll earn something for it, roughly what it's worth, and when they earn it the government ain't gonna take it away from them and then turn it over to shiftless minority types who'll use it to buy the house next door and screw up their property values. The demographics are with us on this. The liberals have had their day in the old Bay State. Now it's Tom Baron's turn."

Tom had kicked off his campaign with one of his frank-and-bean shindigs at Windsor Harbor the previous May. Ostensibly, he was campaigning for the primary election in September. Actually, though, he had that all sewed up, since he had the endorsement of every important Republican in the Commonwealth, and now the polls showed him a scant seven percentage points behind his probable November opponent, Governor McElroy himself, the Democratic incumbent. Eddy Curry found the nineteen percent undecided in the polls particularly encouraging.

Sylvie put her hand on my knee. "If you are so cynical about your friend Mr. Baron, why are we going to see him?"

"Because he is still my client, and he is my friend, and because he has a problem."

"But must we go and eat this awful food?"

"Tell you what," I said. "For putting up with all this—and with me in general—you don't have to clean your plate. We'll take a detour on the way home and have dinner at Gert's. Ever had monkfish?"

"It does not sound pretty."

"It's downright ugly. Maybe the ugliest fish in the sea. Also maybe the most delicious. Fortunately, they don't serve monkfish faces in restaurants. We'll have the monkfish at Gert's, carafe or two of her nice house white, then we'll go back to my place and . . ."

Sylvie's hand began to slither up the inside of my thigh. "And what, Bradee?"

I grabbed her hand and moved it to her lap. "I'm driving," I told her.

"And don't try to seduce me with your Hungarian accent, either. You know perfectly well and what."

She squeezed my hand and laid her head on my shoulder. "I will try the monkfish, then. As long as I don't have to eat any beans."

The parking lot beside the Windsor Harbor Elks lodge was nearly full. I found a slot between a Toyota and a Ford pickup. There weren't any other BMW's there.

Inside, the big room was lined with long narrow tables covered with paper tablecloths. I estimated that there were fifty tables, each of which would seat ten or twelve people. At twenty bucks per, that would clear the Tom Baron for Governor coffers around ten grand before expenses. Not much, by current standards. But Tom had plenty of other sources. Money wasn't the point of these events.

Sylvie and I stood in the doorway. She grabbed my hand and whispered, "Do we really have to do this?"

"Hey," I said. "It'll be fun."

People were milling about. Many had already laid claim to seats. The place was filling up fast. "We should find a seat," I said to Sylvie.

Eddy Curry pushed his way through a knot of people and extended his hand to me. "Brady. Damn glad you could make it. Our candidate has been asking for you."

"I'm here," I said. "Sylvie Szabo, this is Eddy Curry."

Curry looked Sylvie up and down. She was well worth examining. She grinned at him and held out her hand. "Mr. Curry," she said, "Brady tells me you are a politician."

Curry took her hand. "Yeah, I suppose you could say that."

"That," said Sylvie, still smiling, "is unfortunate."

Curry shrugged. "If that's your opinion, Miss, I guess it's my loss."

He was a big man, soft and fat, his neck bulging over his shirt collar, his forehead perpetually damp, the armpits on his shirts ringed. He had achieved the reputation as the shrewdest campaigner in the state, and when the Republican bosses summoned Tom Baron, they insisted that Eddy Curry run the campaign.

Curry, as far as I could tell, had no particular loyalty to Tom. For that matter, he evinced no loyalty to the Republicans, either. His loyalty was to the game, to the tricks and ploys and tactics, to the winning.

And to the enormous fees he commanded, too.

"Can I see Tom?" I asked him.

"Not until after the speech. He's getting ready to come out now."

"Psyching himself up, huh?"

"Yeah. Like that. Look. Everyone's finding seats. Whyn't you and the lady grab a chair and enjoy yourselves."

"Fat chance of that."

Curry grinned. "How'd you like to do this five, six times a week? Tom'll catch you later, okay?"

He slapped my bicep and waddled off into the crowd. I took Sylvie's hand and we wended our way to a distant table where it looked like we might have a little privacy.

No such luck. Our table filled rapidly with people who all seemed to know each other. They were friendly enough, calling me and Sylvie by our first names, actually "Brad" and "Sylvia," but it was close enough. The meal was served family-style—a big vat of baked beans, a platter of hot dogs, several baskets of steamed brown bread, jars of catsup and mustard and relishes. Paper plates, plastic flatware.

The guy seated next to Sylvie, an emaciated old fellow with thick suspenders and big wattles hanging from his chin, loaded up Sylvie's plate with beans and franks despite her protests. Several of our tablemates made jokes about flatulence. Their wives all giggled pinkly. They seemed to be having a grand time. Clearly, Tom Baron was a prince of a fellow to make all this revelry possible.

The man with the suspenders kept touching Sylvie. She was wearing her long blond hair in a braid, and this old guy liked to tug it and make a sound like a train's whistle. "Woo, woo," he'd hoot, and then he'd look around expectantly to see if anyone besides himself was guffawing. Sylvie rolled her eyes at me. I grinned back at her. I knew she could take care of herself.

"C'mon, little lady," wheezed the old guy. "Eat them beans. Put some meat on your bones." He poked her ribs, very near her breast. "Yep," he opined, looking around and nodding. "Need to put some meat on you."

After a few minutes of this, Sylvie leaned close to the guy and whispered into his ear. He listened for a moment, his grin transforming itself into a frown, and then his head jerked back as if she had slapped him. He stared at her briefly, his mouth agape, and then shoved back his chair and fled.

Sylvie arched her eyebrows and shrugged at me.

"What'd you say?" I asked her.

She leaned across the table to me. "I just asked him if he wanted to get laid. I guess he didn't, huh?"

A gang of volunteer waitresses cleared away the debris of the meal and slid paper plates of apple pie in front of us. We passed around big stainless steel pitchers of hot coffee for our Styrofoam cups. From the head table came the whine and hum of the amplifier. A voice said, "Can I have your attention, please?"

The conversational din gradually died, and all heads turned to the front. A guy with slicked-back black hair and sideburns was standing at his place at the table, holding a hand mike. "Probably the head Elk," I whispered to Sylvie. "Guy with the biggest rack."

"Folks," he said, and he frowned at the feedback from the system. "Folks, Tom Baron is back where he started. Back here with his good friends and neighbors in Windsor Harbor."

There was a ripple of polite applause. One man yelled, "Baron for governor!" Louder applause.

"Absolutely right, friend," said Sideburns, warming to his task. "Tom is on his way. But he never forgets his roots. And it's my pleasure tonight to give you our native son, and the next governor of the Commonwealth of Massachusetts, Tom Baron."

He stepped aside as Tom made his way to the microphone. The two men shook hands ceremoniously. Around me, folks were standing up, clapping their hands, whistling, and calling out, "Way to go, Tom," and, "Hey, Big Tom." I glanced at Sylvie, who looked at me and shrugged. We both stood up. Neither of us applauded.

Tom Baron had the look, no doubt about it. A thick unruly head of black hair, with just the right touch of gray at the temples. Solid jaw, fierce gray eyes, a lanky, Lincolnesque frame.

All politicians have a Speech. It's the same one, and they deliver it over and over again, substituting the names of local politicians and appropriate anecdotes. Tom Baron's speech touched on hoary old themes dear to the hearts of politicians—the identification of the speech-giver with the good folks in the crowd, the sanctity of God, community, and family, the virtues of hard work and law-abiding behavior, the evils of drugs and promiscuous sex. Tom, to his credit, made it sound new and sincere, and even a hardened cynic such as I was touched momentarily by the possibilities of renewing the American Dream under an administration headed by Tom Baron. His powerful voice rose and fell in hypnotic rhythms, carrying the hometown folks on its waves, and when he finished, the applause thundered and rolled through the room.

Sylvie leaned across to me. "What did all that mean?"

"I don't know." I shrugged. "But he said it awfully well, I thought."

Up front, Tom beckoned to his wife, Joanie, who had been sitting at the head table with him. She rose with a great show of reluctance and stood beside him. She was a fading blonde, perhaps thicker-waisted than in her cheerleading days, but still photogenic. A definite asset. Tom threw an arm around her shoulder. She gazed fondly up at him. He bent and kissed her cheek. The folks in the Elks lodge applauded this move with renewed enthusiasm.

After a few minutes, Sideburns reappeared. Once again he and Tom shook hands. Tom handed him the mike and returned to his seat. Sideburns continued to stand there, beaming. Gradually the noise died down.

"Okay," he shouted. "Let's have music."

Everybody stood up and began milling around. Tables were shoved against the walls to clear the way for dancing. I grabbed Sylvie's arm and steered her outside.

We sat on the front steps of the Elks lodge. I smoked a cigarette. Sylvie sat close to me. "I'm hungry," she said.

"Soon as I talk to Tom, we can go."

The September night air promised frost. A half-moon hung over the big maples that rimmed the town common. Sylvie put her head on my shoulder. "Pretty," she said. "My village in Hungary, it was like this in the fall."

"And now you are living the American Dream."

"It was all silly, what he said. But I do believe it, in a funny way. I cannot be too cynical." Sylvie's voice was soft. "What I came from, I cannot dislike what he was saying. Here, at least, it is possible."

"But it is more possible for some than for others."

"Ah, you are such a cynic. I don't know what I see in you."

Loud voices seeped over us as the door behind us opened. I turned around. Tom Baron was standing there. He sat down beside me.

"Gimme one of your butts, will you?"

I took out my pack of Winstons and shook one loose for him. "What a rat race," he said. "Gimme a light."

I held my Zippo for him. He inhaled deeply and sighed.

"Sylvie Szabo, Tom Baron," I said.

Tom barely glanced at Sylvie. "Yeah, nice," he said. "So what'd you hear in there? What do the simple folks say?"

"Lots of jokes about farting. Beans the musical fruit. Like that."

"Ah, Coyne," said Tom, smiling. "I can always count on you for necessary deflation. They're having a good time, though, huh?"

I shrugged. "What's this all about, Tom?"

He pulled back from me gently and moved away from the light that spilled out of the Elks lodge windows. I followed him. We leaned against the hood of an ancient Cadillac parked in a shadow.

Tom sighed and flicked away his half-smoked cigarette. "They found the body of a high school girl in the woods behind the school this morning.

Kid named Alice Sylvester. She was strangled, they think. This was a real popular kid. Cheerleader type. Honor Society. Small town like Windsor Harbor, Brady, something like this is a big tragedy."

"Big tragedy anywhere," I observed.

"Yeah, right. Thing is, this girl, this Alice, she was Buddy's girl friend."

"That has to be rough on the kid," I said. I took a hard look at Tom. I realized I had missed his point. "What are you saying?"

He gazed away at the dark sky. "For all I know," he said slowly, "Buddy was with Alice last night."

"What do you mean, for all you know. Didn't you ask him?"

"I couldn't."

"Why the hell not?"

"Buddy didn't come home. We haven't seen him."

Tom started pacing back and forth in front of me. I went to him and put my hand on his shoulder. "What exactly are you trying to say? Do you think your son killed the girl?"

He shook his head at the night. "I don't know what to think, Brady."

"I mean, I know Buddy has had some problems. But I wouldn't think he was a murderer."

"I didn't say Buddy was a murderer," said Tom softly, not looking at me. "Hell, I don't think he is. In my heart, I know he's not. But my head —ah, shit, you know what I mean. All I'm saying is, this is a problem. I don't know how to handle it."

"What have you told the police?"

He turned to face me. "Nothing. I called you."

I nodded. "But they haven't come knocking at your door?"

"No."

"And you haven't reported that Buddy is missing?"

"He's not exactly missing. He just didn't come home last night. Hell, he's eighteen years old. He comes and goes. He's stayed out all night before."

I took out my Winstons again and offered one to Tom. He shook his head impatiently. I lit one for myself. "I want to know what you think," I said.

"Well, I don't think Buddy killed his girl. That's one thing. Hell, he loved that girl. He really did."

"Those," I observed, "are the people who kill each other."

"I don't really need your cynical homilies, Counselor. You're not exactly making this easy, you know."

"I wasn't trying to make it easy. I think you ought to assume that Buddy is in trouble."

"You don't think I thought of that already?"

"There's another thing," I said.

"Yeah. I know what you're going to say. Something could've happened to Buddy. Right?"

"Right. Either way, we should've talked to the cops a long time ago. You have already screwed up. A felony has been committed. You possess relevant information."

Tom's laugh was sudden and harsh. "No shit, Counselor. Relevant information, indeed." His tone shifted abruptly. It became soft, hesitant. I sensed a rhetorical trick, but it was still effective. "Look," he said. "This is, ah, delicate, Brady. Sensitive. You understand, I know."

"You're saying that these events are inconvenient. They do not serve to advance the cause."

Tom straightened and moved several steps away. I held my ground and waited. After a moment he came back to stand in front of me. "Brady," he said. "We've known each other for a long time. You don't have to treat me this way. I don't have to tell you everything that's whirling around in my head. You know me. I shouldn't have to apologize for myself."

"You want a lawyer or a friend, Tom?"

He stared at me. "You are one tough son of a bitch when you want to be. Okay. Fair enough. If I gotta choose, right now I think I want a lawyer."

I touched his shoulder. "You don't have to choose, old pal. But be straight with me, okay?"

He nodded. "Look," he said, "I don't want you to get the wrong idea. I am upset about the girl. I didn't know her well. But I liked her. I liked what she seemed to be doing for Buddy. And, hell, I'd be upset anyway, a thing like this. And I'm worried about my son. Very worried. Whether he did this or not, I realize that he could be a suspect. And I'm not stupid. I know something could've happened to Buddy. It's—I've tried not to think about that. Joanie's been ever so cheerful. I know she's had the same thoughts I have."

"Look," I said.

Tom held up his hand. "Right. I know. We should've talked to the cops right away. I knew that. You're right. As usual, Coyne, God damn you." Tom jabbed me lightly on the bicep. "But listen. You have to understand about the campaign, too. It's important to a lot of people, Brady. It's bigger than just me. It's—"

"Ah, bullshit!" I thrust my face close to his. "Don't you give me that kind of shit. That's Eddy Curry talking. That's not Tom Baron."

Tom pulled back from me, but he returned my stare. "It's the truth," he said simply. "Whether you think it's dumb or not, there are a lot of people who care a lot about this campaign, who have invested time and money and commitment, too. It's not just my power trip, Brady. That's why this thing has to be handled . . . discreetly, know what I mean? Yes, you do. Look. If Buddy's not involved, not guilty of something—and you know as well as I do that he's not—then there's no reason why his name—my name —should be dragged through the shit. You do see that, don't you?"

I nodded. "In theory, yes," I conceded. "Except this isn't theory, and it doesn't work that way."

"Helluva good way to ruin a candidate, Brady, you gotta admit that."

"Shame on you," I said. "Only Eddy Curry would think of that."

He shrugged. "Just a thought. A touch of scandal and this campaign is gonzo."

"I've heard of dirty tricks, but this is a crazy thought."

"Those Democrats, they're known for dirty tricks."

"Politicians are known for dirty tricks. But we're not talking about a dirty trick, here. This is murder. So get off that kick."

"Yeah, stupid," he mumbled.

"Besides," I added. "It really is possible something happened to Buddy. And here you are, performing for the home folks as if nothing has happened. You've got your priorities fucked up, my friend."

He looked at me for a moment, then shrugged. We wandered back to the lodge and Tom slumped on the steps beside Sylvie, who seemed to be savoring the night air. Tom turned to her and said, "What do you think, Miss?"

"You should do what Brady tell you to do," she said promptly.

He grinned up at me. "Hell, I know that. That's why I called him."

"Then let's get going," I said.

"Where?"

"The cops. Where else?"

He shrugged and stood up. I extended my hand to Sylvie, who got up and put her arm around my waist.

Tom said, "Hang on just a minute, okay? I gotta go back inside, tell Joanie and Eddy that I've gotta take off."

He went back in. Sylvie hugged me and put her cheek on my shoulder. "Does this mean no monkfish?" she whispered.

"Afraid so, hon. This might take a while."

two

WE PARKED IN THE LOT BESIDE THE Windsor Harbor police station. The building was a flat-roofed cement-block structure. All function, no form. Floodlights were mounted up on the corners to illuminate the area. Good way to discourage prowlers, burglars, rapists, and other criminal types who might want to hang around there.

Sylvie decided to stay in the car and listen to my collection of Miles Davis tapes while Tom Baron and I went inside. A young, red-headed cop who sported a bushy mustache and a big expanse of sunburned forehead was perched behind a glass partition in the cramped entry area. When he saw us come in, he leaned down to speak through the slit at the bottom of the glass.

"Hey, Mr. Baron. How you doin'?"

"Great, Pete. Never better."

I imagined Tom's hand twitching out of frustration because he couldn't reach over the partition to shake the cop's hand.

"How's the campaign?"

"Good, Pete. Looking real good. Listen. Is the chief in?"

The cop frowned. "Matter of fact, he's over at the hospital. We had a bad thing last night—don't know if you heard. Anyhow, he's getting the word from the medical examiner. He oughta be back soon. You want to wait?"

Tom glanced at me. I nodded.

"Well, sure," he said.

We sat in molded plastic chairs and shared what was left of my pack of Winstons. I scrutinized the wanted posters on the bulletin board. All the criminals with their portraits up on the wall looked sinister as hell. I found that vaguely comforting.

The phone rang a few times. Although I couldn't hear what the desk cop was saying, I had the impression he was talking to a girl friend. I was sure it wasn't a wife. A pair of uniformed policemen wandered in. Tom greeted them warmly. They both claimed they intended to vote for him.

We had been there for more than an hour when the police chief came in. He glanced our way, hesitated just an instant, then said, "Hi, Tommy."

"Harry," said Tom. He darted a quick look at me, then he said to the other man, "Got a minute?"

The chief touched his steel-rimmed glasses. "Matter of fact, I do," he said. He glanced inquiringly at me.

"Oh, ah, Harry Cusick, this is Brady Coyne. Brady's my attorney."

Cusick extended his hand to me. "Good to meet you," he said. To Tom he said. "Good move."

"Huh?" said Tom.

"Bringing your lawyer. Come on in."

Tom and I followed the chief through a door that buzzed when he approached it. We went down a short corridor to Cusick's cramped office. He settled behind his desk, and Tom and I arranged ourselves in straight-backed chairs in front of him.

Cusick was wearing a rumpled summer-weight suit. The collar of his shirt was open and his tie was pulled loose. He pushed his glasses up onto his forehead and rubbed his eyes with his knuckles. Then he peered at Tom.

"I just finished telling two very nice people that their beautiful daughter had been murdered. Her windpipe and larynx were crushed. She died in great agony. They are not taking it well."

Tom and I looked at him. He smiled bleakly at us.

"This is not my favorite part of the job. We don't have much of this in Windsor Harbor. I came to this town to get away from this sort of thing. I have some preliminary results from the medical examiner." He shot a look at Tom. "Maybe you're interested?"

Tom nodded.

"I had to tell these parents that their daughter had engaged in sexual intercourse within an hour of her death, one way or another."

"What is that supposed to mean?" blurted Tom.

"Obvious." Cusick shrugged. "Somebody screwed her either before she died or—"

"Jesus!" breathed Tom.

"The M.E. thinks it happened before she died, actually. There was evidence that she was, ah, sexually aroused herself."

"Not rape, then," I said.

"Probably not. She was fully clad when she was found. The other thing I had to tell these nice people was that their little girl had significant traces of cocaine in her bloodstream. These folks did not like to hear any of this. But I had to tell them. And I had to ask them questions, of course. I couldn't allow them to grieve, to feel their anger and their loss. My job is to ask the questions. So I did." He looked down at his desk and touched the edges of some papers that were lying there. He looked up at Tom. "Why are you here?" Cusick asked him.

"I guess you probably know, Harry."

Cusick nodded. "Alice Sylvester's parents said they thought she was with Buddy last night."

"I don't know whether they were together or not. They might have been."

"I have to talk to Buddy."

"I don't know where he is."

"What do you mean?"

Tom took a deep breath, either to gain some patience or to steady his nerves. He let it hiss out slowly. "He never came home. I don't know what to make of it. Normally, of course, I wouldn't give it a thought. He's eighteen, he's got a job, he's pretty much on his own. But this . . ."

"You should have told me this before now."

"What? That my son didn't come home last night? That he was friends with a girl who got killed?"

Cusick nodded. "Yes. Of course."

Tom spread his hands. "Yeah. That's what Brady told me."

"Where do you think Buddy went?"

"I haven't got the foggiest, believe me. He didn't show up for work. He's got a car, money, credit cards. He could be anyplace. He didn't tell us." He hesitated, looked at me, and continued, "But the other thing is, Harry, if he *was* with the girl—"

"Alice Sylvester," said Cusick. "Her name was Alice. A pretty, bright girl."

"Yes. I'm sorry. If he was with Alice, and if Alice was killed, well . . ."

"Something could have happened to Buddy, too. Yes. I thought of that." The chief unhooked his glasses carefully from his ears and placed them on his desk. Without them he looked much younger. His pale eyes showed intelligence and sympathy. "We've known each other a long time," he said softly, studying Tom's face.

Tom nodded. He did not return Cusick's gaze.

"But we haven't been friends," continued the policeman.

"No. No, we haven't."

"But that is not important here," said Cusick. "Look. I won't try to bullshit you, even if, under the same circumstances, you'd probably try to bullshit me. Mr. and Mrs. Sylvester think Alice was with Buddy last night. I don't have to tell you the implications of that."

"They think Buddy killed her," said Tom tonelessly.

"We'll check it out," said Cusick. "See if anybody saw either of the kids. If they *were* with each other, we will bring Buddy in and read him his Miranda. Okay? If it looks like they weren't together, we'll still want to talk with your son, just like we'll be talking with lots of other people. I don't think I need to tell you that if you hear from him, or if he shows up, it's in his best interest to get himself here pronto." Cusick peered at me. "With a lawyer would be a good idea."

Tom looked up at him. "Sure. That all makes sense. But the other thing—"

"The other thing," said Cusick quickly, "is that we will put out an APB on Buddy. Is his car registered in his name?"

Tom nodded.

"Okay. And I want you to bring me a recent photograph of him."

"Okay."

Cusick picked up his glasses and began to polish the lenses on his handkerchief. He cocked his head. "How's Buddy been doing with his problem?" he said in a new, gentler voice.

"He's clean," answered Tom after a moment. "I'm sure of it. He's a new kid, really. Since the problem. Since he got back. He's held the job at the computer store since he got out of school. Up and out of the house on time. They seem real pleased with him. He's been pretty agreeable around the house. Getting along with me and Joanie again. He's talking about college next year. And the girl—Alice—she's been real good for him. A serious, adult relationship. We didn't see that much of her. I don't know, I think he's still a little distrustful of us, but it's been getting better. He wants to separate things in his life. He's talked about that. It makes it easier for him to cope. Work, family, friends, each in their own little slot. But, anyway, since you arrested him, Harry, and since his probation and everything, I really think he's seen the light."

Harry Cusick was studying Tom as he talked, a small frown wrinkling his forehead. When Tom finished, Cusick nodded slowly. "That's been my impression, too. But like I told you, Alice Sylvester used cocaine last night. You can see what my question is."

"If they were together . . ."

"Right."

"Buddy's clean. I'm positive."

The chief shrugged.

"Look," said Tom, hitching himself up on his chair so that he was leaning over the desk. "When you busted Buddy two years ago and prosecuted him, I can't tell you how wrong I thought you were. He was sixteen years old. A kid. He got in with the wrong crowd. He needed help and support, not courts and probation."

"He was old enough to know better, and he was connected," said Cusick. "He was selling cocaine to high school kids. He refused to give us names. I wanted to prosecute him as an adult. I thought he should have spent time in prison, to tell you the truth."

Tom glanced my way. "Brady got us a good lawyer. It would have ruined my son to go to prison. He's not a tough kid. Anyway, like I said, he's done the rehab. He's finished his probation. He's reformed himself. What I started to say was that when you arrested him instead of bringing him home to his parents, I swore to myself that I'd get you. I could do that."

Cusick nodded. "Hell, yes. I know that."

"But you didn't care."

The chief shrugged. "It's not that I didn't care. I like my job. But I gotta do it, or I wouldn't like myself."

"What I'm trying to say, Harry, is that you were right in what you did. And even if you weren't, I admire you for doing it."

"Correct me if I'm wrong, Tom, but what you're trying to say is, find your son for you."

Tom nodded. "That's too. But I meant what I said. I do admire you."

"If Buddy was with Alice Sylvester last night, we will have probable cause to get a warrant. We'll search his car. We'll take blood samples. We'll do forensics on his clothing. We may arrest him. He will need an attorney. Nothing that has happened before this, no threat or promise you can make, will change that. Do you understand?"

"Of course."

Cusick looked at me. "Mr. Coyne?"

"You're right," I said. "Although if it comes to that, you better make sure all the T's are properly crossed."

The chief grinned. "You can count on that. I am one helluva good T-crosser and I-dotter." He hooked his glasses around his ears and stood up. "Tom, run home and get me a photograph of Buddy, will you?"

Tom and I stood up. "I'll do everything I can," he said.

Cusick came around his desk and moved to the door with us. As we started to walk out, the chief said, "Ah, Tom. One thing."

Tom turned. "What's that?"

"I want you to know I appreciate it."

"What, my coming here?"

"No. You had to do that. No, what I appreciate is that you didn't ask me to hush this thing up. A man in your position . . ."

Tom's smile was forlorn. "Hey. I hope you won't make a circus of this. But somehow I never thought you would. If Buddy's name gets drawn into this thing . . ."

"No promises," said Cusick. "But I'll keep it in mind."

The air outside was downright cold. A cloud bank had skidded in, obscuring the moon.

"Fall's coming," said Tom.

"Feels like it's here."

He put a hand on my arm. "Brady . . ."

"I'm with you, Tom. I'll do what I can."

"I'm not ready to drop the campaign. I've got to keep it going. But I want this handled right. Can I count on you?"

"When Buddy shows up, I'll be there."

"I'm concerned about the press."

I shrugged. "You want a free government, you've got to have a free press. You've been saying stuff like that yourself."

"I don't want my son tried and convicted by the Boston *Globe.*"

"Sometimes it happens that way. It's the price."

"When it's the son of a political person . . ."

"What do you expect me to do, Tom?"

"Two things. First, I want to be able to funnel inquiries to you."

"That makes sense. I'm your attorney. What's the second thing?"

"Help me find Buddy."

"That's the police's job. They're good at that sort of thing."

"Harry Cusick's a good cop, don't get me wrong. But he's still a cop. I want Buddy found. I want to know what he did last night, why he disappeared. If he's found alive, I want him home. If something's happened to him . . ."

"You want a private detective, then, not a lawyer. I know a few."

Tom put his hand on my shoulder. "I am the Republican candidate for governor. I want this kept in the family. Am I asking too much?"

"You're asking for something I have no expertise in."

"Look," he said, his voice low and intense. "Give me a day. One day. Give me tomorrow. I'll give you some names, some places. If you strike out, Joanie and I will be climbing the walls by then anyway."

"I dunno, Tom."

"One day, Brady. Please."

I shrugged and glanced up at the dark night sky. The breeze smelled damp. "Doesn't look like tomorrow's going to be much of a day for fishing. Okay. One day. I'll come by the house first thing in the morning. You and Joanie get together tonight. Write down everything you can think of. Buddy's friends. Places he hangs out. Anyplace you can think of he might go. Teachers, employers, whoever knows him. I'll see what I can do for you."

Tom sighed. "I appreciate it, friend."

"Don't expect miracles."

"I expect discretion and intelligence."

"Discretion, at least, I am good at."

Tom pumped my hand and climbed into his new Buick. I got into my BMW. Sylvie was slouched in the seat, snoring quietly. I leaned over and kissed her ear. Her arm crept around my neck and hugged my face against her breast. "Is it time to eat the fishes with the ugly faces?" she mumbled sleepily.

"Too late," I said, extricating myself from her embrace. "Gert's is closed. We're going home. I'll cook us something."

I started up the car and backed out of the lot. Sylvie's hand crept into my lap like a shy puppy. "I do have great appetites," she whispered.

"We'll see how many of them we can satisfy."

"Promise?"

I picked up her hand and gave it back to her. "I solemnly promise."

three

THAT INFERNAL ALARM CLOCK IN-
side my head jangled me awake at five-thirty the next morning, as it always
does. Sylvie was sprawled on her stomach beside me, clutching her pillow
over her head as if to keep away the sounds of artillery fire. When she was
awake, she was gay and vibrant. When sleeping, however, the demons of
her childhood flight from Hungary still tortured her.

I snuggled against her and lifted up the pillow to kiss her cheek. She
moaned and twitched. Her leg kicked convulsively.

I rolled out of bed, stretched and yawned, and slipped into my jeans and
sweatshirt. The coffee machine in the kitchen, on its own alarm system,
had already begun gurgling. I retrieved my morning *Globe* from outside
the front door of my apartment and took it to the table by the glass doors,
leading out to the patio. Outside, six stories down, the gray ocean of the
Boston harbor spasmed and kicked as restlessly as Sylvie slept in the other
room. Hard raindrops ticked against the glass.

The story was buried on page seventeen. The headline read: "Body of
Merit Scholar Found in Windsor Harbor."

> The body of seventeen-year-old Alice Sylvester, a senior student at Wind-
> sor Harbor High School, was discovered by Windsor Harbor police early
> Tuesday morning.
>
> According to local police, the honor student had been strangled. Her fully
> clad body was found in a thickly wooded area near a parking lot by the high
> school.
>
> The little North Shore community of Windsor Harbor is the hometown of
> Tom Baron, the Republican candidate for governor.
>
> Windsor Harbor Police Chief Harry Cusick said, "The young lady was

murdered. It appears she was strangled. We have no suspects at this time, but we are pursuing several leads. We have no further comment, pending a full report from the Medical Examiner."

Gubernatorial candidate Baron, in a prepared statement, said, "The death of a young person is always a tragedy. Our prayers are with the family and friends of Alice Sylvester. This will hit our community hard. We trust the police will exhaust every resource to bring to justice the individual who committed this awful, senseless crime."

I got up, poured myself a mug of coffee, and brought it back to the table. Then I reread the brief newspaper item. In Tom Baron's "statement" I detected the fine hand of Eddy Curry. There was no mention of Buddy Baron. So far, at least, the press had not caught on to the possibility of a link between Buddy and Alice Sylvester.

I flipped through the rest of the paper, sipping my coffee, listening to the storm rage outside, and resenting the promise I had made to Tom Baron. I did not relish playing detective, even just for a day.

I solved the chess problem and had just begun to study the daily bridge hand when Sylvie staggered out of the bedroom. She had pulled on one of my T-shirts. It was big for her, but not by much.

I cocked my head and regarded her. "Fetching," I said.

She yawned and stretched. The T-shirt rode up. More fetching yet. "I smelled coffee," she mumbled.

She poured herself a mugful and sat down across from me. She propped up her chin with the palms of both hands.

"Isn't that cold?" I said.

"What?"

"The vinyl of the chair where you're sitting?"

Sylvie giggled. I got up and poured myself a second mug of coffee. When I returned she was reading the article on Alice Sylvester's death.

"You will solve this crime, no?" she said.

"Probably not," I answered, setting fire to my first cigarette of the day. "That's not my job. But I will see if I can track down Buddy Baron."

"That may be the same thing."

"Maybe. I doubt it. Wouldn't you like to put some clothes on?"

"First I will drink my coffee. Then you and I will have a shower. Then I will get dressed."

"You will drink your coffee while I take my own shower," I said.

"Brady is a poop."

"This is true."

After I showered, shaved, and dressed, I went back to the kitchen.

Sylvie was at the stove, tending an omelette. I sat at the table to watch her cook. I thought of Julia Child and the famous chefs of Chicago and New Orleans and the other public television cooking series. I had my own idea for a can't-miss series: The Great Bareass Cooks of America.

Sylvie would be a star.

After we finished eating, I knotted my tie and retrieved my raincoat from behind the sofa. It was a bit rumpled, but what the hell. It was going to get rained on anyway.

Sylvie followed me to the door. "When will I see you?" she said.

"I'll call when I can. Don't you dare straighten things out before you leave. The last time you did that, I lost my sneakers."

"I put them in the closet."

"They belong in the living room. Under chairs. Who'd ever think to look in the closet?"

I arrived at Tom Baron's house in Windsor Harbor a little after eight. Tom and Joanie built their place on a high bluff overlooking the Atlantic, where the ninth fairway of Tom's father's golf course used to be. It's a long, low, rambling place, with lots of glass and fieldstone and cedar sheathing. You could putt on the rolling sweep of lawn.

Joanie answered the door wearing a floor-length burgundy robe made of some kind of clinging silky material. She had done her hair and her face. Her brittle smile looked as if it might shatter.

"Brady," she said. "Please come in. Tom's gone already. Some sort of breakfast thing in Greenfield. He left something for you."

I stepped into the foyer and Joanie helped me out of my wet raincoat. She ushered me into her kitchen, part of a big open area that included the dining room and one of the living rooms, walled in on three sides by floor-to-ceiling glass. The view of the ocean was spectacular.

She sat me at the kitchen table and poured two cups of coffee. Then she produced a bottle of brandy. "Little snort?" she said.

I shook my head. "Don't need it."

"I do," she mumbled, dumping a healthy slug into her cup.

"No word from Buddy, then."

She sipped her coffee and gazed out at the storm-chopped sea. "No. Nothing. Brady, I'm so grateful that you're going to help."

"I told Tom that this isn't my line. I'll see what I can do."

"You'd think he'd at least call his mother."

I shrugged.

"Unless," she continued, "something's happened to him." She peered up at me hopefully.

"I'm sure he's fine," I answered automatically.

Joanie sighed. "Let me get what Tom left for you."

She got up and swished into the other room. It didn't look as if she was wearing anything under her robe.

She was back in a minute and slid an envelope onto the table. I ripped it open.

Brady:

Only names I can come up with—

Dr. Larsen, principal at W. H. High School. Knew Buddy pretty well, also Alice and others. Gil Speer, computer guy at the school. Only teacher Buddy liked. Or vice versa. Bob Pritchard, Buddy's boss at Computer City. Middle-aged hippie type. Knows the scene, I think. Mr. and Mrs. Sylvester, Alice's parents, who probably won't want to talk to you and I wouldn't even try.

Good luck. Call me tonight.

T.B.

I folded the note and tucked it into my shirt pocket. To Joanie I said, "Didn't Buddy have any friends?"

She touched her hair with her hand. "Boys he went to school with. They're all off to college now. With all his trouble, he's been avoiding them anyway. When he wasn't working or home, he was with Alice." She hesitated. Her voice shifted gears. "He was—he had become quite reclusive, Brady. A loner. He was depressed. It was natural, I guess. We tried to get him to therapy. It was recommended. Even Tom saw the need for it. But Buddy refused. He said he was all right, that he could work things out for himself. But I don't know."

I reached across the table and touched Joanie's hand. "What are you saying?"

Her eyes brimmed. "I guess I'm saying that I don't know what Buddy might do. Might have done. He's a stranger to me. Tom thinks he knows his son, but he doesn't. Buddy's been through a lot. He's fragile. You don't want to touch him, because you think he might crack. Do you understand?"

I nodded slowly. "Joanie, do you think Buddy could have hurt Alice?"

She flinched when I said it, but she met my eyes and nodded.

"In the sense that I don't know what he's capable of anymore, I guess I think so. He was wound real tight. He could have snapped. Then . . ."

"Joanie," I said after an awkward moment, "what else do you think he could have done?"

She sighed deeply and took a big gulp of brandy-laced coffee. "As you know, he had a drug problem. I mean, sure, he got caught selling it. But his problem was using it. Marijuana. LSD. Cocaine. Whatever he could find, I guess. He did rehabilitation, as the court ordered. Afterwards he went to those meetings. Every single night. But there was a black part of Buddy where he wouldn't let me in. Maybe he let Alice in there, I don't know. But not me and not Tom. He spent a lot of time in his room. Not listening to that awful music, not reading. Just lying there, staring at the ceiling. Sometimes he seemed on the verge of talking about it. But then he'd pull back. There was no anger, none of those overt behaviors you might expect. That we were told to expect from him. But no joy, either. Just this awful, passive blackness. To answer your question, I think he was capable of hurting himself more than hurting somebody else. That's what worries me. And if he did hurt Alice . . ."

She didn't need to finish. I sat there, smoking a cigarette and sipping my coffee while Joanie Baron composed herself.

After a few minutes she looked up at me and made her mouth smile. It was not particularly convincing, but I pretended it was. I stubbed out my cigarette and stood up.

"I best get on with my sleuthing," I said lightly.

Joanie followed me to the door, retrieved my raincoat, and held it for me. As I turned to open the door, she put a hand on my arm. "I really appreciate this, Brady," she said.

"Don't get your hopes up, Joanie."

"Just the same, thanks." She reached up on tiptoe to kiss me. As she did, she leaned her body against mine, confirming my observation that the sheer robe was all she had on. I moved my mouth away from hers, giving her my cheek to kiss. She stood back from me, an odd smile on her face.

"You don't wanna comfort the grieving mother?" she said.

"Cut it out," I said harshly.

"Yeah. Shit. Dumb old broad. I'm sorry."

"C'mon, Joanie. Buddy's okay."

She pushed me toward the door. "Go. Before I do something stupid." I went.

My first stop was not on the list Tom Baron gave me. I pulled into the lot beside the Windsor Harbor police headquarters and skipped over the puddles to the door. A different cop was behind the glass wall. I asked for the chief and gave him my name, and he got on the intercom. A minute later Harry Cusick came out.

He grinned at me and extended his hand. "I thought I might be seeing you again," he said.

"I just wanted you to know that I'm going to be around town today, and to ask you to keep me informed on the Buddy Baron situation."

"Gonna play a little cops and robbers, huh?"

I smiled and shrugged. "You might call it that."

"We're just a small-town police force, Mr. Coyne," he said. "But we're pretty good at what we do."

"I have no doubt," I said. "I don't really expect to accomplish anything, to tell you the truth. Maybe it'll make Tom and Joanie Baron feel a little better." I shrugged apologetically.

"It's a funny thing about lawyers," said Cusick. "They're always telling the cops how to do their job. But when you take a look at who screws things up, more times than not it's the lawyers."

"Readily granted. I'll try to stay out of your way."

"That," he said, "is more than I have any right to expect. Look, why not check in with me in the afternoon. We can compare notes."

"You're willing to do that?"

"Sure. We're all after the same thing here, aren't we?"

"Probably not. But we're in the same ballpark. If you can tell me how to find—" I pulled out Tom's note and scanned it "—ah, Computer City, I'll be on my way."

"Bob Pritchard has neither seen nor heard from Buddy Baron," said Cusick.

I nodded. "Sure. You've been there already."

"Of course."

He gave me the directions and I jogged through the rain to my car.

Computer City occupied a corner of a recently refurbished brick building in what passed for downtown Windsor Harbor.

The walls of the large room were lined with multitiered desks, on which were displayed several different models of home computers. Chairs in front of each one invited the potential customer to sit and peck at the keyboard. One of the chairs was occupied by a bearded young man, who glanced up at me.

"You don't wanna buy a computer," he declared.

"That is one helluva sales pitch," I said.

He grinned. "Gets 'em every time."

"I'm looking for Bob Pritchard."

"How come?"

"I want to talk about Buddy Baron."

"See?"

"Huh?"

"I was right. You don't want to buy a computer. I can tell instantly who's a customer and who's getting in out of the rain. Save myself a lot of time that way. I'm Pritchard. Pull up a chair."

I did. I glanced at the screen of the computer monitor. It was covered with columns and rows of figures. He hit a few keys, and the columns and rows moved. "Spread sheet," he said. "You wanna keep your books up to date, just get one of these suckers. Everything on one little disk. No more file cabinets full of documents, no big ledgers, drawers crammed with scraps of paper. Neat and tidy."

"I'm getting in out of the rain, remember? I've got a computer in my office. My secretary is a whiz at it. I don't know diddly about it, myself. Don't really want to."

He nodded. "Lot of people, they get a certain age, they don't like to deal with new technology. It scares them. Makes them feel old, outmoded." He cocked his eyebrows at me.

I shrugged. "You're probably a better salesman than I thought at first."

He grinned. "So who're you?"

"My name's Coyne. Brady Coyne. I'm Tom Baron's attorney."

He nodded. "Ah."

"I understand Buddy has missed work."

"He was out yesterday. Hasn't showed up today yet, either, as you can see."

"And he didn't call?"

"Nope."

"Has he ever done this before? Not come to work, not called in?"

"Nope."

"Am I boring you?"

"Nope." He smiled again. "The police asked all these questions already."

"Can you think of any questions they should've asked that they didn't?"

"Now that," said Pritchard, "is a good question. The cops did not ask me that question. And the answer is, yes, there are a few questions I'd expect someone to ask."

"Like?"

"Like, had Buddy really kicked cocaine."

"Has he?"

"Yes. I'm sure of it. And I should know."

"You've been there," I said.

"Yes. I've been there and back."

"Is that why you hired Buddy?"

Pritchard made a wry face. "No. I didn't know that when I hired him. If I had known that, I would have thought twice. Bad risk. Drug addicts are always bad risks. No, I hired Buddy because Tom Baron asked me to, and you don't say no to Tom Baron too easily in this town. Not that he twisted my arm. Still, you like to get along with old Tom. Anyway, when Buddy found out what I'd been through, he started to open up to me. We talked about it a lot. He's a surprisingly strong kid. Tough-minded, I mean. He messed up, but he cares about himself. He's been straight for a long time. More than a year clean. A long time for an addict. He's been through the worst times. There is a time, you know, and it comes about nine months after rehab, when you don't think you can take it any longer, when you feel like giving up. People go one of three ways then."

"What ways?"

"You either go back to the drugs or you push through it. Those who push through it, many of them, they get pretty mystical about it. They go up on the mountain. They see burning bushes. The skies open up. They hear voices."

"They get born again, you mean?"

"All kinds of born again. Born again Christian, born again Buddhist, born again Existentialist, for God's sake. Same thing happened to me, in a way."

Pritchard grinned at me, and I returned his smile a bit uncomfortably.

"Yep," he said. "A born again cynic. That's me. It's a theology that works good for me."

I nodded. "That's two. You said there were three ways someone could go. What's the third?"

Pritchard scratched his beard. "The third way is, you kill yourself."

"Buddy . . . ?"

Pritchard shook his head. "Not Buddy. I don't think so."

"He's been missing for about thirty-six hours now."

"Something might've happened to him. But he didn't kill himself."

"The police mentioned to me that when Buddy was arrested, he refused to cooperate with them. Has he—?"

"No. I didn't ask, and he didn't say. I don't know who supplied him. It's not a question I would ever ask."

"Do you have any thoughts?"

He ran his forefinger over his mustache. "Specifically, no. But I'll tell you this, and it's no secret. It had to be local. Somebody in this town. And I'll tell you something else, if you promise not to press me for details."

"Okay," I said.

"It's this. Whoever was supplying Buddy is still in business."

"Selling coke to kids?"

"Crack, now," he said. "Cocaine for smoking. Evil stuff. Addictive as hell. Someone's wholesaling crack to kids, so they can retail it to their friends."

"Mr. Pritchard," I said. "A teenage girl was killed night before last. A teenage boy is missing. If there's something you know . . ."

He held up his hand. "There isn't. Believe me. I just know the scene in general. I know what's going on. If I knew who it was, I would tell the cops. I'd tell them in a minute. No problem. But I don't. All I know is, Buddy isn't involved in it."

I nodded. "Any other questions I should've asked?"

"One."

"What?"

"Would Buddy kill Alice Sylvester?"

"How would you answer that, if I'd had the wit to ask it?"

"I'd say no. But I'd say he might've had reason to be pissed off at her."

"Then I'd ask what that reason was."

"And I'd tell you that she wasn't the Miss America candidate that everyone is making her out to be. And, no, I would not elaborate on that."

"You wouldn't."

"No."

"Slandering the dead?"

He shrugged.

"There's one other question that occurs to me," I said.

"Go ahead."

"Can you think of anybody who'd want to hurt Buddy?"

"Sure."

"Will you tell me who?"

"I don't know who. But if you can find the person who set him up in business two years ago, you'd have a good candidate."

I nodded. "I suppose I would."

"Assuming," he said, "that something happened to Buddy."

"Yes."

"Which," he said, "isn't a bad assumption."

"That's what I'm afraid of," I said.

four

I HAD A CUP OF COFFEE AT A DOWDY little hole-in-the-wall restaurant a few doors down from Computer City and used the pay phone to make an appointment with Dr. Larsen at the high school. The place was empty. I sat by myself at a table by the window and watched it rain until it was time to go.

Windsor Harbor High School was just outside the center of town. A long curving drive ascended a slope to the sprawling flat-roofed brick building. I parked near what looked like the front entrance. Three boys were standing under the overhang smoking cigarettes. When I got out of my car they hastily cupped the butts in their hands.

The principal's office was just inside the door. A white-haired woman was sorting papers behind a chest-high counter. I gave her my name and told her I had a nine-thirty appointment with Dr. Larsen. This seemed to fluster her, and she consulted with another woman who was seated at a desk, typing. She, in turn, jerked her head at a third woman, who was talking into a telephone. Finally the white-haired woman came back, smiling triumphantly, and beckoned me to follow her.

I went around the counter, weaved among some desks, and was ushered into an office. My guide cleared her throat and mumbled, "Ah, Dr. Larsen . . ."

A woman was working at a computer terminal, her back to us. She turned and smiled. "Yes?"

She was, I guessed, thirty. She had long blond hair, worn loose around her shoulders. She had elegant cheekbones, a dimple in her chin, and when she stood up I observed that her aquamarine knit dress complemented both her eyes and her figure.

I had for some reason assumed that Dr. Larsen would be gray, overweight, and male.

"I'm Brady Coyne," I said. "I have an appointment."

Her smile faded instantly. To the white-haired woman, who hovered uncertainly by my elbow, she said, "Thank you, Emma," and Emma scurried away, closing the door behind her.

Dr. Larsen gestured at a chair and said, "Won't you sit down?"

I sat, and she sat beside me. "Dr. Larsen—" I began.

"Let me be candid with you, Mr. Coyne. Somebody from Tom Baron's organization called me this morning. I have been instructed to cooperate with you. I don't mind cooperating. I would have cooperated in any case. But I don't like being instructed. Bullied. The students and staff at my school are very upset about what happened. This is a new experience for all of us. I am trying to help everybody deal with this reality. But I do not want policemen and private investigators prowling around in my school, asking questions and disrupting things. And, for heaven's sake, don't call me 'doctor.' My name is Ingrid. I was hired because I have a doctorate in education, and the school board thinks it's classy for me to be called 'doctor.' I do not happen to agree."

"Well, then, Ms. Larsen—"

"Ingrid will be fine." She permitted herself a small smile.

"Okay. Ingrid, then. I'm not a cop and I'm not a private eye. I'm an attorney. I'm not investigating anything. I'm trying to find Buddy Baron. Tom Baron says you might be able to help."

"Well I certainly haven't seen Buddy lately."

"But you knew him."

"I knew him. He graduated last June, after a fashion."

"What do you mean by that?"

"Buddy earned a bunch of phantom graduation credits from a drug rehabilitation place in Pennsylvania last spring. I always liked the boy, and I know he had lots of academic potential. But except for computers, he had no interest in school. His record reflected that. One of my jobs is to be sure that a Windsor Harbor High School diploma means something. Under normal circumstances, Buddy Baron would have been required to return here for a semester before he could have qualified. Certain individuals thought these were not ordinary circumstances." She shrugged. "I'm a public servant. So I made an exception of Buddy. He graduated."

"Look," I said. "I don't want to snoop around or anything. I'm just trying to get a line on Buddy. He's been missing since the girl was killed. She was his girl friend."

She peered at me. Three parallel vertical lines were permanently etched between her eyes. Ingrid Larsen, I guessed, frowned a lot. "How do you expect me to help you, Mr. Coyne?"

"Brady is fine. I don't really know. Tom Baron said you might be able to."

"Tom Baron is not a magic word in this office."

"I understand. I didn't mean—"

"You're his attorney, right?"

"Right."

She nodded, as if that proved something.

"Look," I said. "I'm sure that a pretty young woman has to be tough as nails to get to be principal of a high school. You don't look right for the job. Maybe a guidance counselor, health ed teacher. But not a principal. I reckon your authority gets challenged all the time. Overtly, covertly. And I bet you stand up to it. You're tough. Why are you smiling?"

She shook her head, grinning now. "Keep going."

I shrugged. "I imagine you take real pride in standing up to the Tom Barons of this world, and I'm sure you resent the hell out of all the local power brokers who try to tell you how to run your shop. Small town like Windsor Harbor, everyone's attended a school one time or another, everyone knows how to run one. What've you got, a plumber for chairman of the school board?"

"Housewife, actually," she said, still grinning. "Former social worker."

"God help us," I said. "Listen, Ingrid. I'm not any of these people. I'm just this lawyer from Boston who's looking for a missing boy who might be in a lot of trouble. I'm no threat, believe me. Okay, you don't want to help, then fine. I'm not going to go running to Tom Baron or the school board, tell them to cut your chalk budget in half or something. I'll just muddle along, and maybe I'll find Buddy anyway, and maybe I won't. You mind if I smoke?"

"Yes," she said absently, brushing a strand of hair away from her face. She stared at me for a moment. "You're quite disarming, actually, Brady. And somewhat persuasive, in a subtle sort of way. But you still haven't told me how you expect me to help."

"You knew Buddy."

"A little."

"Would he kill Alice Sylvester?"

"Wow! What a question."

"Thank you. Throwing in questions like that is a trick of the trade."

"I figured it was. The answer is no. But then, I can't think of anybody on earth who would kill anybody. But it happens, doesn't it?"

"Yes. Often."

She shook her head thoughtfully. "No," she said. "Not Buddy. Unless . . ."

"Unless he was back on drugs," I said.

She shrugged. "Yes, that's what I was thinking. Not that I know much about that."

"Me neither. Okay, then. Who would kill her?"

"What does this have to do with finding Buddy?"

"It's complicated."

She frowned. "Yes," she said. "I see what you're getting at. Harry Cusick asked me that question, too."

"The chief was here?"

"Yesterday."

"What'd you tell him?"

"The same thing. I don't know any killers. Alice is—was—a terrific student. A good school citizen. Honor Society her junior year. Tennis player. Student Council. All those things. A little wild, maybe. But not the sort of girl you'd expect to get involved with a boy like Buddy Baron."

"How so, wild?"

Ingrid Larsen frowned again. "Boys. Parties. That's all."

"What about drugs?"

"Alice? I have no idea, really. I wouldn't think so."

"But she was Buddy's girl friend."

"Maybe he thought so. But she was very popular. I somehow doubt if she was committed to him, if you follow me."

"I think he was committed to her," I said.

"Well, there's an issue for you right there."

"Jealousy."

"She was a vivacious, attractive girl."

Harry Cusick had told me that the coroner found evidence of cocaine in Alice Sylvester's blood and semen in her vagina. I wondered if he'd told Ingrid Larsen that. "Can you think of any boys other than Buddy who were interested in her?"

"Cusick asked me that, too."

"How did you answer him?"

"I refused to speculate for him."

"You probably wouldn't speculate for me, then."

"Definitely not," she said.

I was getting nowhere. I took out the note that Joanie Baron had given me. "I'd like to talk with Gil Speer," I said.

"This interrogation has ended, then?"

I shrugged. "Unless you can think of something."

"You really need to sharpen your technique, Brady." She smiled. "You don't handle hostile witnesses that well, do you?"

"Are you hostile?"

"I'm trying to be."

It was my turn to smile. "I don't do that much trial work."

"It shows." She stood up. "Well, come on. Let's find Gil Speer."

Ingrid Larsen and I followed several long corridors to the far end of the building before we arrived at the computer wing. Whereas the interior of the main part of the building featured gray cinder block and beige tile, the big computer room gleamed with chrome and glass and oak paneling. A perfect reflection of contemporary educational priorities.

A computer-generated sign on the door curtly instructed all comers to "Keep the Door Shut." When Ingrid and I went in, I knew why. The temperature was at least five degrees cooler and twenty points drier in that room than in the rest of the school. In New England public schools, only computer types enjoy the benefits of air-conditioning. For the comfort of the machines, not the people.

The main room was about four times the size of an ordinary classroom. Glass walls partitioned off several smaller adjacent rooms. There was a row of carrels along one wall. An enormous mainframe computer dominated one end of the room. And everywhere there were chrome desks with terminals, monitors, disk drives, and printers. The air in the room seemed alive. I was aware of an almost inaudible electronic buzz, the energy of all that machinery crackling in my brain.

Ingrid Larsen touched my elbow and pointed across the room to a young man who was bending over the shoulder of a girl working at one of the terminals.

"That's Gil Speer," she said. "The one indispensable man in this school system. He put all this together. Wrote the grant proposals, handled the bids, and designed all the programs. He also created the computer curriculum. All the work of the school is done here. Records are stored here. Student grades, attendance, transcripts, payroll, budgets, the works. Gil can make all these machines jump through hoops. He's also a brilliant teacher."

Speer was singularly unimpressive to look at: short and pear-shaped, with thin, sandy hair retreating from his pink forehead. I guessed he was still in his twenties. Steel-framed half-glasses were perched low on his nose. He was wearing blue jeans and a dress shirt with the cuffs rolled up to his elbows. Computer geniuses evidently dressed by their own code.

Ingrid led me over to Speer. He glanced at us, said, "Oh, hi," and bent back to the girl he was helping.

"Okay, see, at line seventeen. Now, in BASIC it's one thing, but you're using FORTRAN, so—"

The girl looked up at him. Her smile dazzled. "I get it. I do. Don't tell me anything else."

Speer patted her shoulder. "I'll make a first-rate hacker out of you yet, Christie."

"I'm getting there, huh?" she said.

"You're getting there, kid."

Speer straightened up and turned to us. "What's up?"

"This is Mr. Coyne," said Ingrid. "He's interested in talking with you about Buddy Baron."

Speer squinted at me. "How come?"

"Can we go someplace private?" I said.

Speer appealed to Ingrid. "Jeez, can't this wait?" He waved his hand around the room at the flickering monitors and the students hunched over them. "Really, Ingrid," he said. "We've got about fifty things going on here."

"I'd appreciate it, Gil. It shouldn't take long."

He shrugged. "You're the boss." He went over to a boy who was watching a printer clack out a long strip of paper and spoke to him. The boy listened intently, then nodded. Speer came back to us. "I put Allen in charge. He's very advanced. Okay, Mr. —what was it?"

"Coyne," I said.

"Well, okay. Come on in here."

I turned to Ingrid. "Thanks," I said.

"I've got to get back to my office," she said. "Why don't you drop in on your way out?"

"I will if I can find my way back," I said.

She smiled, waved her hand, and left. Speer led me into a small glass-partitioned area that was devoted to storage. The walls were lined from floor to ceiling with cardboard boxes. A table and a few chairs stood in the center. We sat down.

"Okay, Mr. Coyne. What do you want to know about Buddy Baron? I hardly know the boy, actually."

"Exactly how well do you know him?"

He held his hand over the table, palm down, and rocked it back and forth. "I know him the way I've known lots of kids. Every year I know a hundred or more kids. They add up after a few years. Why? What's up with Buddy? He in trouble again?"

"I don't know. He's been missing since night before last."

"Missing?" Speer arched his brows and lowered his head to peer at me over the tops of his glasses. Then he made a long, exaggerated up-and-down motion of his head. "Ah. I get it. Alice Sylvester. Right? You think he had something to do with that, right?"

I shrugged. "He's missing. I'm trying to track him down. That's all."

"You're a cop."

"No. I'm Tom Baron's attorney. He's worried about his son."

"With good cause, I should think."

"You think—?"

"Hey. I'm just a computer freak. No shrink. You don't care what I think."

"Sure I do."

"Well, I don't have any interesting theories, Mr. Coyne."

"You don't know where Buddy is, do you?"

"How should I know that?"

"I don't know. Any ideas?"

He shrugged. "Buddy Baron took a few courses from me. From what I understand, computer was the only thing he liked or did very well at. But I've had lots of better students than he ever was. We weren't what you'd call close. He came in, worked on problems, I helped him, and when the bell rang he left. There was a while, back before his trouble, when he was coming in quite a lot after school. But even then, he was a dilettante. He fooled around with a lot of things, but he never really dug in. No, I don't have any thoughts on where he might be. I'm sorry if he's got problems, but I don't see how I can help."

"He did get a job at a computer store."

Speer grinned and squinted myopically at me. "It's a selling job. Perform little demonstrations for the customers. Requires no expertise. Surprised he held the job."

"Why?"

He shrugged. "Not the salesman type, ask me. Shy kind. Not aggressive at all. Never spoke unless spoken to. Not that self-confident. Easy to understand, I guess, with an old man like Tom Baron."

"What about Alice Sylvester?"

He cocked his head. "What about her?"

"She and Buddy were going together."

"I wouldn't know about things like that."

"Did you know the girl?"

He nodded. "Sure. She was taking an intermediate programming course. Took the introductory course last year. Did very well. Not what you'd call gifted, but very competent. A good student. Not necessarily brilliant, but she knew how to study, quick learner, could psych out the teachers. An achiever. Hard to picture her with Buddy."

"What are the chances of looking at those kids' records? Buddy's and Alice Sylvester's?"

He shook his head. "I don't have the authority."

"Does Ingrid Larsen?"

He shrugged. "She's my boss."

"Will you ask her?"

"Sure. Why not. You want that now?"

"Yes."

"Hang on, then."

He got up and went back into the big room. Through the glass wall I watched him pick up a phone and talk into it. In a couple of minutes he was back. "Come on with me," he said.

I followed him out into the big main room. He found an unoccupied desk with a computer and sat down at it. Then he began pecking rapidly at the keyboard. In a moment the printer began clattering. In about ten seconds it stopped, and Speer ripped off two sheets of paper. He handed them to me.

"I think Ingrid is bending the rules a little, letting you have these," he said.

They were copies of the two kids' high school grades. I scanned them quickly. Buddy Baron's record was comprised mostly of C's and D's, although I noticed that he earned B in his computer courses. Alice Sylvester had nothing but A's and B's—and very few B's.

Beside each course appeared the name of the teacher. I thought I might find that helpful. I folded the two transcripts and tucked them into my jacket pocket.

I thanked Gil Speer for his help, gave him my business card in case he should think of anything, and left the computer room. Out in the dreary school corridor, the air felt hot and damp, reminding me of the storm that still raged outdoors.

I found my way back to Ingrid Larsen's office. Emma seemed confused by my reappearance, but I persuaded her to allow me passage to Ingrid's sanctuary. She was on the phone when I walked in, but she smiled and waved me to a seat. After a moment she hung up and looked at me. "So?"

"So I didn't learn much. But I suppose I didn't expect to. I appreciate your letting me have these." I showed her the transcripts.

"Oh, you can't have those," she said. "I told Gil you could look at them. Figured he'd pop them up on a screen. I didn't think he was going to make hard copies. You can't keep them. Heavens, those are confidential as hell."

I smiled at her mixture of mild expletives. "Okay. I can't see how they'd help anyway. If I need to talk to teachers or something, you could help me, right?"

"Sure." She held out her hand and I put the transcripts into it.

I stood up. "I don't want to keep you. Just to say thanks for your cooperation."

We shook hands formally, and I left. Outside the rain was coming down in angled sheets, driven by an insistent wind, and I sprinted to my BMW. I had a serious dilemma: It was noon, and Gert's was a fifteen-minute drive from the school. I could pay my respects to Harry Cusick before or after I replenished the inner man.

I decided I'd do better with the chief on a full stomach.

five

PAPER-THIN FLOUNDER FILLETS DEEP-fried in an egg-and-beer batter. Tossed salad of mixed greens with a little oil, vinegar, and lemon juice. A cup of rich, spicy espresso. Gert had not lost her touch.

I virtuously passed up the Indian pudding with vanilla ice cream for dessert.

Outside, the rain continued to slant down from a slate-colored autumn sky. I lingered at my table by the window, mourning the end of summer and trying to decide if I really owed Harry Cusick another visit. He'd suggested I drop in. It hadn't sounded like a command appearance. I decided to call him.

The cop who answered put me through to the police chief. When he came on, he said, "Well, Mr. Coyne, what'd you find?"

"Nothing. Don't you ever sleep?"

"Busy, busy, busy. No line on Buddy Baron, huh?"

"Uh uh. How about you?"

"No, nothing on the boy. Interesting developments on the girl's murder, though. Curious?"

"Hell yes, I'm curious. Most of the time policemen don't want to share stuff like this with laymen like me."

"Well, I figure we're on the same team."

"I have a feeling there's more to it than that," I said.

I heard him chuckle. "Maybe there is. Why don't you come on over. We can chat for a few minutes."

"If we can do it right now. I've got to get back to the office this afternoon."

"Tell you what," said Cusick. "I'll be here waiting for you."

"It's important, then."

"Yes."

Fifteen minutes later I was sitting in Harry Cusick's office. The chief kept a neat desk, which set him apart from all the other cops I knew. A single manila folder rested on top of the blotter. Cusick was fingering the edges of it.

He squinted at me through his steel-rimmed glasses. "I have issued a warrant for the arrest of Buddy Baron," he told me.

"You've learned more than I have, then."

He nodded. "Alice Sylvester's parents told me that she was supposed to meet Buddy the night she died."

"Supposed to?"

"He wasn't in the habit of picking her up at the house. Something about his not wanting to confront her parents, who, I gather, did not entirely approve of him."

"Understandable."

"Mm," he said. "So Alice would walk out and Buddy would meet her somewhere. She always told her folks what she was doing. And that's what happened the other night."

"So say her parents."

Cusick nodded. "So they say. Anyway, as you are about to point out, that by itself would be considered hearsay. Good reason to talk to the boy. Not a good enough reason to arrest him."

"But," I said.

"But, there's a waitress at Brigham's who saw them together."

"Aha."

"They had hot fudge sundaes. Each of them paid for their own. They left the girl a fifty-cent tip. Alice Sylvester was wearing blue jeans, a pink blouse, denim jacket. She had a white bow in her hair. Like that singer."

"Madonna," I said. "She's got a new look now. The new Marilyn."

Cusick arched his eyebrows at me. "If you say so. Buddy Baron was wearing gray corduroy pants and a blue sweatshirt. Got the picture?"

"Your witness seems reliable."

"She knew both kids. Talked with them a little. Said they seemed depressed, or grouchy, as if they were arguing."

"Sounds bad."

"There are compelling conclusions to jump to," said Cusick. "I am always reluctant to jump. On the other hand, everything points in one direction."

"If I find Buddy, I know what to do," I said. "But I don't intend to keep looking. It's not in my job description. I talked to a few people today. You got there before I did, and you probably learned more."

"Well, if you're the family lawyer . . ."

"I wouldn't necessarily be defending Buddy."

He nodded and picked up the folder. He extracted a sheet of paper, pushed his glasses up onto his nose with his forefinger, and frowned at what he was reading. "Some things about the case do bother me," he said slowly. "I've got this final report from the medical examiner." He ran his finger down the page. "This, for example. I think I may have mentioned to you that the girl had had sexual intercourse shortly before she died. But I didn't know this when I spoke to you." He peered up at me over the tops of his glasses. "It would appear that Alice Sylvester had had sexual intercourse with two different men."

"At the same time?"

He peered at me to see if I was joking. He evidently decided I wasn't. "More or less. Within an hour or two of each other, at most. See, they can type semen. Like blood. Same process exactly. Antigens, whatnot. Type A positive, Type B, and so forth. This girl had two different types in her."

"Everybody says this was a real nice girl," I said.

"According to the M.E. this was not rape."

I nodded. "So what do you make of it?"

He shrugged. "I guess I'd like to know who the second one was, since he'd be the last one to have been with her."

"Not necessarily."

He stared at me for a moment. "Of course. We're just developing hypotheses here. Anyway, some other things. Whoever killed her did it with his hands. Crushed her larynx and trachea with his thumbs. There were bruises on her face and throat. And he repeatedly banged the back of her head against something hard while he was doing it. There was significant damage to her cervical vertebrae and major trauma to the back of her head. Fracture of the skull." He glanced up at me from the paper he was holding. "I'm summarizing what it says here."

"Sparing me the technical words. Thank you."

He nodded without smiling. "You get the picture. This was vicious. Whoever did it was trying to kill her, and didn't stop until he had."

"During intercourse, do you think?"

He shook his head. "Probably not. She was fully dressed when we found her body. She was even wearing panty hose under her jeans. Her clothing wasn't torn. Nothing inside out or backwards. No, I'd say she dressed herself afterwards. Doubtful if the murderer would dress her again after killing her. Not typical, anyway, though there are all different kinds of nuts around. You figure, if a guy was careful enough to get her all dressed again, logically he would have tried to hide the body. But Alice Sylvester was found on the grass right beside the parking lot. As if she'd been dumped out of a car. We looked for a rock or something her head could've been banged against. There would've been a lot of blood. We didn't find anything. I figure she was killed inside the car and then rolled out onto the ground. We find the right car, we'll find blood inside of it."

I sighed. "This is not a heartwarming tale."

"There's more," said the chief. "I mentioned, I think, that the M.E. found traces of cocaine in her blood. This report—" he shook the paper he was holding "—says that there were also traces of coke in her lungs. Congested mucous membranes. Inflamed trachea." He arched his eyebrows at me.

"Crack," I said.

He smiled thinly. "You are really up to date, Counselor. Right. Cocaine that is smoked. Possibly free-base, but most likely crack. This stuff is starting to find its way up here from New York. A little shocking for this sleepy little seaside community." He grimaced at his own cynicism. "You figure Roxbury, Dorchester, Lawrence, Lowell—"

"Actually," I interrupted, "you figure Wellesley, Winchester, Concord. What I hear, this is upper-class dope. Sexy. Prestigious."

"Cocaine, yes," said Cusick. "Crack, not necessarily. It's cheap, for one thing. And just deadly as hell. In any case, Windsor Harbor is not exactly your hub of the drug underground. But if nice high school girls like Alice Sylvester are getting ahold of crack, we've got more of a problem than one murder."

"Windsor Harbor is a seaport," I suggested.

"A very minor seaport, Mr. Coyne. A few sport fishing craft, lots of sailboats and runabouts. Nothing commercial."

"You don't need anything commercial to haul this stuff."

"He nodded. "I've thought of that, believe me. Matter of fact, I talked with a guy at the Coast Guard this morning. Guess what he said?"

"He said it's a long coastline."

"That," said Cusick, nodding, "was the essence of it. Of course, if we can come up with any good leads, they'd be delighted to seize a vessel on the high seas for us."

"And accept full credit."

"Sure. Anyhow, that's all conjecture. Point is, the girl was smoking this stuff, had sex with two guys, and then got herself strangled to death. And I need all the help I can get."

"Well, I'll cooperate, don't worry about that. I really find it hard to believe that Buddy Baron . . ." I let my voice trail off. Harry Cusick regarded me benignly. "Not that I knew him that well," I added.

The chief stood up dismissively. "You just never know," he said gently.

We shook hands and I left. I played Vivaldi on my tape deck on the way back to Boston. I had my seasons mixed up. It seemed like the dark pit of a dead, frozen winter, with the cold rain angling out of a black sky, and the slick roads littered with fading leaves, and young people getting murdered in a nice little town like Windsor Harbor, Massachusetts. I was eager to get back to the sanity of my law office.

I nosed my BMW into my reserved space in the parking garage and took the elevator up to my office. Julie, my secretary, was working at the computer keyboard, listening through earphones to a tape I had dictated for her. I still missed the cheerful clack, clatter, and ding of the old typewriter. She looked up at me, crossed her eyes by way of greeting, and said, "Well, look who's here," without missing a beat at the keyboard. "Be with you," she added, and returned her attention to the tape.

I poured myself a mug of coffee and took it into my office. A place for rational analysis. Legal theory. Precedents, hoary old Latin terms, statutes and torts and contracts, all the good stuff that was evolved to enable attorneys to maintain an abstracted distance from the human pain and inequity the law is supposed to mediate. In one corner of my office, I have two shoulder-high file cabinets crammed with abstractions. Two shelves of weighty tomes full of more abstractions. Thousands of little legal pigeonholes, each with its unique shape, into which real flesh-and-blood people are supposed to be fitted.

The fit never seems perfect.

Those volumes and file cabinets are full of laws. But they're not the law. That's why they put people into offices like mine, along with the files and the books. Laws are like automobiles: They need lawyers to make them go.

Julie scratched on my door with her fingernails.

"Abandon all hope, ye who enter here," I said.

She came in and stood in front of me, looking slim and Irish and gorgeous as usual. She carried a sheaf of papers in her hand.

"Care to discuss business, or do you want to bag the rest of the day?" she said.

"What I want to do and what I've got to do are two different things."

"Fishing trip got rained out, huh?"

"Yes, but that's not it."

"Something heavier than getting rained out of a fishing trip? Want to talk about it?"

"Yes. But not now. Come in. Sit down. Fill me in."

Julie took the chair beside my desk. Up close, I could see the spatter of freckles across the bridge of her nose, the last vestiges of her summer tan.

She took the top sheet of paper from her pile and looked at it. "Mr. Paradise called. Three times. You have to call him back."

"My kind of law," I said. "He's got a new invention, no doubt. Frank Paradise is my favorite client. He never calls me for anything bad. He's always excited when he calls. Frank is a helluva guy. What else?"

"Doctor Adams. He left a message, and I quote: "The blues are going bananas off Plum Island. Interested?" " Julie frowned. "This must have something to do with fishing."

"Right," I said. "Bluefish. Doc wants to go fishing."

She sighed. "Sometimes I feel more like a social secretary than a legal one. Mr. McDevitt wants to play golf. He told me he thinks he's cured his slice. In vast and totally incomprehensible detail. He used the word 'pronate' several times. Mentioned his 'V's' often, too, and where they should be properly aimed."

"His grip," I said. "Charlie is messing with his grip again."

Julie shrugged. "I just take the messages. But he was very agitated. He said, and I'm quoting again now because he made me write it down, he said, 'It's a matter of great urgency that we convene on Friday.' That's the end of the quote."

"He said 'convene'?"

"Of course. I am very precise about such things."

"Of course you are. Friday, huh. How's my calendar look?"

"You always keep it clear on Friday afternoons. Golf, fishing, Hungarian ladies . . ."

"Hmm," I said. "Charlie's afraid he'll forget his new grip. Okay. Anything else?"

"I took the liberty of making a ten-thirty for you tomorrow. Mr. and Mrs. Fallon. A referral from Doctor Segrue."

"Divorce?"

"*Au contraire,*" said Julie, smiling. "They want to have a child."

"I'm not a sex therapist."

"A classic understatement," said Julie, rolling her eyes. "Somehow I didn't get the impression that they were looking for that. Mrs. Fallon was understandably reluctant to discuss it with me. But, frankly, my dear, I am curious as hell, so after you see them . . ."

I reached over and patted her arm. "You will hear all, I promise."

She grinned. "Okay. And that's it. I took care of everything else."

"I must say, it's a pleasure working for you," I said. "Now leave, so I can do what you've assigned to me."

"I know you'll call Doctor Adams and Mr. McDevitt. But don't forget Mr. Paradise. He did sound anxious."

"I'll call him first," I said.

"Yeah, sure," she said.

Well, she knows me too well. I called Doc Adams. I got his assistant, the delectable Susan Petri, who told me that Doc was conferring with a patient at the hospital. I told her to have him call me at home later in the evening. Then I phoned Charlie McDevitt's secretary, Shirley, and told her to confirm with Charlie our Friday golf date. She told me Charlie had cured his slice. I figured we'd read all about it in the papers, the way Charlie was spreading his joyous news.

Frank Paradise lives in Brewster on Cape Cod. He owns an old farmhouse with two centuries' worth of ells and dormers, a big barn converted to a workshop, an Olympic-sized swimming pool, a tennis court with a clay surface, a sailboat, a forty-eight-foot tuna-rigged boat, and a pair of hostile Dobermans.

Frank made a lot of money designing jet engines after the war, and since then he has devoted himself to his lucrative hobby of inventing things. Most of the stuff he dreams up I don't understand—computer innards, electronic doodads about the size of a B-B pellet, and elegant little gizmos that make space ships fly and weapons kill.

Once in a while, though, he comes up with something I can appreciate. For example, he concocted a super-strong instant-drying glue that bonds anything to anything else, but rubs right off human skin as slick as rubber cement. He sold the patent to a big drug company. Almost at the same time, he came up with another glue that bonds only human skin. He was negotiating the sale of that stuff with the CIA.

Frank sends me off to Washington about twice a year to conduct patent searches. I usually enjoy the trips, unless Frank happens to have invented something in August. There's a political science professor at Georgetown who insists that the restaurants in D.C. are better than those in Boston, and always likes to try to make her point. She also knows the Smithsonian inside out and enjoys showing off her expertise.

Frank answered the phone on the first ring. Judging by the static, I figured he was out in his barn. I said hello a couple times, and he yelled back, "Hang on. Gonna change phones." When he came back on, he sounded better. "This one's got my own receiver in it," he said. "The guys who make commercial cordless phones don't know beans about insulating. This salt air raises hell with 'em."

"What's up, Frank?"

"Brady, listen to me. I'm going batshit down here. Outta my mind. Somebody hijacked my boat."

"Hijacked?"

"Hijacked, whatever. They stole it, for chrissake. Woke up this morning and she's gone from her mooring."

"Sounds like she broke loose in the storm."

"Brady, I got this rig for mooring her—made it myself—"

"Okay, Frank. I believe you. She's hijacked. Did you tell the cops?"

"Yes I called the cops. And I called the Coast Guard and the insurance guy, too. She's a sweet little boat, Brady."

"This is the sailboat, right?"

"No. The *Egg Harbor.*"

Frank's "sweet little boat," I happened to know, was worth about a quarter of a million dollars. Frank had the teak varnished, the twin diesels overhauled, the brass polished, and the hull caulked and painted every winter. It came equipped with loran and sonar and every other piece of electronic gear imaginable. Frank and I had landed an eight-hundred-pound bluefin tuna off the tip of Provincetown in that boat back in eighty-three, not to mention the tons of bluefish and occasional striped bass we had hauled onto her decks from Casco Bay to Long Island Sound.

A sweet boat.

"I am saddened at your news," I told him truthfully. "But I don't know what you want me to do about it."

"I keep telling you about pirates. Now maybe you'll believe me."

"You were talking about guys swiping your ideas, not your property."

"Same difference."

"Frank, seriously, what do you want me to do?"

"Hell. Find my boat."

"I said seriously."

"Okay. Seriously? Seriously, if she doesn't turn up, there'll be insurance adjusters who'll want to screw me. If she does turn up, her hull all stove in, all that lovely stuff stripped off her, same thing. Mainly, I want her back, and I want to know that the Coast Guard is doing its thing.

"I'll make a call," I said. "And try to relax, Frank. It's only a boat."

"Like hell it's only a boat."

"I know, I know."

I finally hung up with Frank. I don't think he felt any better, but I did keep my promise to call the Coast Guard. I was shunted from the commander's office to the legal office to the search and emergencies group to intelligence and law enforcement before I found someone who would talk with me. He said they had the particulars on Frank's *Egg Harbor* and would keep an eye out for her. I supposed that was all they could do.

It occurred to me that twice in the same day the Coast Guard had entered into my conversations—first with Harry Cusick, in speculating about cocaine traffic on the North Shore, and then with Frank Paradise.

Maybe I'm unusual, but whole months go by when I don't even think about the Coast Guard. I suppose that means they're doing a good job at whatever it is they do. If they didn't come up with Frank Paradise's *Egg Harbor,* I suspected I'd be giving the Coast Guard more thought.

I got back to my apartment a little after six. Except for the dishes that had been cleared and stacked in the washer, and my bed, which had been made, it was as if Sylvie had never been there. There are times when living alone is downright lonely, and none more so than coming home to a neatly made bed in an empty apartment.

I climbed into my jeans and sweatshirt and slid a frozen pizza into the oven. I sloshed some Jack Daniel's into a glass, dropped in three or four ice cubes, and settled down in front of the television to catch the evening news.

The weatherman was cautiously predicting clearing and cooler—he didn't seem too certain as to when this weather would actually arrive—when the phone rang. I hoisted myself off the sofa and padded in stockinged feet into the kitchen to answer it.

"Mr. Coyne?" said a voice I didn't recognize.

"Yes?"

"This is Buddy Baron. I heard you wanted to talk to me."

six

"BUDDY," I SAID. "WHERE THE HELL have you been?"

"Around."

"Where are you now?"

"I'm in town."

"Here? In Boston?"

"Yes."

"Well, tell me where and I'll come and get you. We've got to talk."

"No, I'll come to your place. Is that okay? Are you busy?"

"I just put a pizza in the oven. I'll throw together a salad. You can join me."

"Yum, yum," he said. "All right. I'll be right over. And Mr. Coyne?"

"What?"

"I know they want to arrest me. I hope you don't plan to play games with me."

"No games, Buddy. We'll talk. I'll have to take you to the police."

"That's what I figured. Okay. Fifteen minutes."

"Wait," I said. "Have you talked to your parents?"

"No. Should I?"

"They're worried about you."

"You mean they're worried about scandal. I don't want to talk to them."

"I intend to, then."

"Go ahead," he said. "Tell them I'm all right."

"Is it true?"

"Sure. I'm fine. Never better."

After I hung up with Buddy, I called Tom Baron's house. Joanie answered. Her voice was soft and slurry. She had been taking brandy in her morning coffee. I supposed it was martini time, now.

"It's Brady," I said. "I just talked to Buddy. He's okay."

"He's not okay," she said. "They want to arrest him. They think . . . Brady, it was nice to see you this morning. You should have stayed longer."

"Listen to me, Joanie. I'm going to bring Buddy to the police, do you understand? Is Tom there?"

"Tom's on the road. On the road again. Dum dum. Hit the road, Jack. He's, let's see. Springfield, I think. Yes. If today's Thursday Tom's in Sprinfield. Whatever today is. Meeting with bigwigs. Plotting and planning. Him and Eddy Curry. They wanna figure out what to do with a son who's gonna get arrested for murder. What they're gonna do with the campaign, I mean. Why doesn't Buddy call his mother, huh?"

"Joanie, take it easy, will you? Just listen to me. When Tom gets in, tell him I've found Buddy. Okay?"

"Tom's getting in late. It's just me in my big old house, my son and my husband gone, sitting here in the dark in my nightgown waiting to get tired. Lonely, Brady. You ever get lonely?"

"Sometimes, yes. Look. I'm going to hang up now. You understand that Buddy is all right?"

"Yes," she said softly. "Thank you. I understand."

"Take it easy on the booze."

"Sure. Excellent advice. I'll just sip. Ladylike sips. I'll be sleepy pretty soon."

"Good night, Joanie," I said, and hung up.

I was tearing a head of lettuce into a wooden bowl when the buzzer rang. It was the new night man, a skinny Puerto Rican man in his mid-twenties named Hector, telling me I had a visitor. I told him to send Buddy up, and a few minutes later there was a knock at the door.

Buddy was wearing gray corduroys and a blue sweatshirt, the same outfit he had been wearing the night of Alice Sylvester's murder. He hadn't shaved since then, either, I judged. He had his mother's soft, undefined facial features and his father's lanky frame.

"Come on in," I said to him. "Pizza's ready. Oil and vinegar on the salad suit you?"

"Great," he said without enthusiasm.

He went over to the big window and stared at the dots of light out on the ocean. I went to stand beside him. "How you doing?" I said.

He turned to look at me. He shrugged. "I'm doing."

"About Alice."

"I'm working on it."

"We've got some problems," I said.

He nodded. "Sure. I know. You got a beer?"

"I've got Pepsi," I said. I went to the kitchen.

Buddy followed me. "You shitting me?" he said. "I drink beer at home. I drink beer all the time."

"Good for you. But you're not legal age, and you're not my kid, and I'm not going to give you a beer."

He sat at the table. "I always thought you were fairly cool, Mr. Coyne."

"Oh, I am. I'm wicked cool. But I don't give booze to underage kids. I don't consider that cool."

I slid a plate and a salad bowl in front of him. I retrieved the pizza from the oven, sliced it, and put it on the table. From the refrigerator I got a beer for myself and a can of Pepsi for him. Then I sat down across from him.

"I didn't realize you were such a Puritan," he said.

"You need a beer that bad?"

He shrugged. "It's the principle."

"Exactly," I said.

He took a sip from the can of Pepsi.

"I think," I said, "we have more important principles to talk about, anyway."

"Well, yeah. I know. It's just that I'm old enough to vote against my father, I'm old enough to go to prison, but I'm not old enough to have a beer."

"That's right. That's the law."

"I get it. You're a lawyer."

"Being a lawyer has precious little to do with it, actually," I said, sliding a wedge of pizza onto my plate. "Anyhow, that's what we need to discuss. Your being old enough to go to prison. Will you be straight with me?"

He looked at me for a moment, then nodded. "Sure. What do you want to know?"

"Did you kill Alice Sylvester?"

He stared at me, open-faced and childlike. "No, Mr. Coyne. Honest to God, I didn't. I loved Alice."

"I want to know everything that happened night before last."

Buddy picked up a triangle of pizza and took a tiny bite from the pointed end. Then he put it back on his plate. "I didn't kill her," he said softly. He looked beseechingly up at me. There was a smudged look around his eyes, as if he needed sleep. "I met her after dinner. We didn't have any particular plans. We usually just drove around, talked, maybe got ice cream or something. But that night, the first thing she told me was that she had plans for later, she could only see me for an hour or so. She was uptight about it. Like she was trying to pick a fight, get a rise out of me. Which, of course, she did. She knew all the buttons and switches on me. Like nobody ever did. I asked her what she had to do that was so important, and she said I didn't own her. Anyway, we went and got ice cream, and then I let her off downtown. That was it. That was the last time I saw her."

"That's all?"

He shrugged. "Sure."

"Did you make love with her?"

"Why would you say that?"

"Did you?"

"No."

"Did you use cocaine with her?"

"Of course not. I'm off that stuff."

"What did you do after you let her off?"

He poked at his slice of pizza with his forefinger. "I was upset. I didn't feel like going home. It was early. My mother would still be up, and I didn't want to deal with her. I come home late, she worries about what I've been doing. I come home early, it means something's wrong, that I'm depressed. So I drove around for a while. I *was* depressed, I'll admit that. Arguing with Alice. I was worried I was losing her." He smiled crookedly. "Pretty funny, huh? Anyway, after a while I said the hell with it. I drove to Cambridge. Walked around the Square for a while. I met a girl. We went back to her apartment. I ended up staying there for the night."

"Who was the girl?"

"Bonnie something."

"You don't know her last name?"

He cocked his head at me. "To tell you the truth, I don't know anything about her. She lives in a grungy apartment down near Central Square. She's old. Twenty-five or something like that."

I sipped my beer. "Why didn't you go to work the next day? Yesterday?"

He shrugged. "I would've been late. I didn't care. Bob wouldn't mind, I knew that. I was still depressed about Alice. Fighting with her, I mean."

"You didn't know what happened to her?"

He shook his head. "Not then. Not till later."

"So what did you do all day?"

"Nothing. Hung around."

"And last night?"

"I stayed in a hotel room. Had room service. They brought me a beer."

"What hotel?"

He looked at me and shrugged. I decided not to press the point. "What about today?"

"Nothing." Buddy got up and went over to the glass doors. He stared out a moment, then bowed his head and leaned his forehead against the glass. Then he turned to face me. "Look, I know this doesn't sound very good. But it's the truth. I was depressed about Alice. She was the only thing in my life that was any good. And I was getting the brush-off from her. I saw it clearly. She was seeing some other guy."

"Do you know that?"

"I could just tell."

"Who was the other guy?"

He shrugged. "No idea whatsoever. That's what we argued about. I accused her of seeing someone else. She denied it. I begged her to tell me. She said there was nobody. She tried to be jolly about it. Like I had nothing to worry about. I knew she was lying. I told her that. That's when she got pissed."

The pizza tasted like cardboard, but the sour taste in my mouth came from Buddy. I lit a cigarette. It didn't taste any better. "Listen to me," I said carefully. "For the time being, I'm your attorney. And you are in serious trouble. You've got to tell me the truth. Your story doesn't hang together. You're trying to make me believe that an argument with your girl friend caused you to hole up in a hotel for a couple days. You were with some woman named Bonnie who you can't identify, so she won't be able to verify what might be an alibi for you. You said you and Alice didn't make love, and you said you didn't do any drugs, and I don't believe you. Look," I said, as he stared out at the night, "pay attention here. You can tell me the truth. You have to tell me the truth, because right now you need me."

Buddy didn't speak, nor did he look at me. I got up and went to where he was standing. I grabbed his shoulder. He tensed and twisted away from me. But he looked at me. "Why don't you believe me?" he said.

"You left some things out of your story."

"Like what?"

"How did you know I was looking for you? How did you find out what happened to Alice?"

He nodded. "I called a friend this afternoon. A girl I know."

"And she told you about Alice?"

"Yes. I called her because she and Alice were friends. To find out if she knew anything about what was going on with Alice. A boy or whatever. She told me. That Alice had been killed. And she said a guy was at the school asking about me. She heard Mr. Speer talking on the phone. She heard him say your name and mine and Alice's. My friend remembered your name and described you. I figured I'd better call you."

"And that was the first you knew about the murder?"

He nodded. "Yeah. Here I am, being mad at her, feeling sorry for myself, and she's dead." He stared at me. "I did lie to you about one thing. I can't see how it matters, though."

"Well?"

"We did make love. After we got ice cream we went to a place we go to and—and she seduced me, I guess you'd say."

"Where did you go? To the school?"

He frowned. "No. We have a place. It's by the ocean. There's a development going in. A road goes right down to the beach, and a lot of half-finished houses. It's very private. Sometimes we take a blanket down by the ocean. That night it was a little chilly. We stayed in the car."

"Why would you lie to me about that?"

I saw tears well up in his eyes. He turned back to stare out at the ocean for a moment. Then he wiped his eyes on his forearm and looked back at me. "Because after we—we had sex—we argued again. She said she had to get going, as if that should hold me for a while, see? Like it was a little favor she was doing for me to appease me. It hadn't been like that before. I was confused, my feelings were hurt. I was angry. I—I slapped her. I mean, not hard, not to hurt her. I didn't want to hurt her. But I might've left a mark on her face, I don't know. I didn't mean to hit her as hard as I did. She laughed at me. She called me a baby. It was like—like she was somebody I didn't know, like some kind of monster, almost. She was cruel. She mocked me. Called me a loser, a druggie. It wasn't her at all. There was something going on with Alice, and I don't know what it was."

"What about cocaine, Buddy? Did you tell me the truth about that?"

He nodded. "Oh, yes. I've been clean for nine months. Almost ten."

"What about her?"

"What do you mean?"

"Did Alice do drugs?"

"Alice?" He hesitated. "She . . "

I waited. He was staring out at the sea again. When he didn't say anything, I said, "What, Buddy? What are you thinking?"

He turned. He had a different look. I couldn't read it. "Yeah," he said. "Alice had a little problem. Thing is, she was okay last night. I mean, when I was with her."

He stared hard at me for a moment. "Buddy—"

He shook his head. "I don't want to talk about it. Okay?"

I shrugged. "For now it's okay. Come on. Let's finish eating."

We went back to the table. Buddy picked languidly at his salad. I ate another wedge of cold reheated frozen pizza. "This other guy . . . ," I began.

"If there was one," he said. "She never admitted there was. I just suspected there was."

"Oh, there was one, all right," I said.

"I know she was murdered, but . . ."

I looked at him. "You think you're old enough to drink beer, I guess you're old enough to be talked straight to. Somebody murdered Alice. You know that. Before he killed her, he had sex with her."

Buddy's eyes widened. "Raped her, you mean?"

I shook my head. "They don't think it happened that way."

"How do you know?"

"The autopsy report. It also showed that she smoked cocaine."

"Crack. Yeah. It figures. Shit!" Buddy pounded his thigh with his fist.

"Who was it, Buddy? You must have some suspicion."

He looked hard at me. "No," he said. "I have no idea."

"Listen—"

"I don't know who it was," he said. His tone told me to back off. I decided to comply.

"Okay," I said after a moment. "Speculate."

He shook his head. "No. I can't. I can't think about it. I don't know."

"Have it your way," I said.

We finished eating in silence. Buddy ate a few bites of salad. I polished off most of the pizza. When we were done and had stacked the dishes in the sink, I said, "Now we go to the police. Ready?"

Buddy's head snapped around. "Now?" he said. I detected a hysterical edge to his tone. "Now? Wait a minute. Hey! Just wait a minute."

"There's a warrant for your arrest," I said mildly. "You've got to go."

"I'm not going now. No way, Mister." Buddy's eyes darted wildly around the room, as if he were seeking escape. I moved toward him, and he backed away as if I were attacking him. "Stay away from me, Mr. Coyne. You're not taking me anywhere. Not tonight."

I leaned back against the wall, hoping my example would relax him. He remained standing in the middle of the living room, half crouched. "Listen, Buddy," I began in soft tones.

"No. You listen. I know how this works, see. You take me in now. They book me, or whatever you call it. Then they stick me in a cell, because my old man can't get bail for me until the morning. And there's no fucking way I'm going to spend a night in a cell. I still get nightmares. Sometimes I think I'm over the edge and not coming back. Walls close in. The floor drops out from under my feet. The old hallucinations. From the bad shit I used to take. If you think I'm going to spend a night in a jail cell—listen. Jesus Christ, please listen to me! I'll beg you, if that's what you want. I'll do anything. But I'm telling you, I'm not going. Not tonight."

"Buddy, you don't understand. It's my duty. I've got to take you."

"Now? Can't it wait till morning? Look. I didn't have to come here. So what's the big deal? Just wait till morning. When the sun's shining. That's all I'm asking." He was pleading, his eyes wide. He held his hands out to me as if I could give him salvation. They were trembling.

He sensed my hesitation. "Look," he said. "We can go in the morning. Let me stay here with you. I'll be okay here. Then tomorrow take me in."

Unstable young people hang themselves in Massachusetts jail cells with alarming frequency. And Buddy Baron was an unstable young person. I decided I'd rather have a minor professional dereliction on my conscience than the possible tragic consequence of a hard-nosed adherence to the very letter of my duty. Another ten or twelve hours wouldn't matter.

I nodded. "Okay. Tomorrow morning. Without fail. You won't give me a hard time?"

He sighed, then managed a small smile. "Oh, Jesus, Mr. Coyne. Thank you. Oh, man."

"I hope the sofa is okay," I said. "I've got an extra bedroom, but there's no bed in it. It's full of junk."

He nodded. "The sofa is great. I owe you, Mr. Coyne. You have no idea."

I rinsed off the dishes and loaded up the dishwasher. Buddy wandered over to the television. He flicked it on and watched it for a few minutes. Then he came over to me.

"Can I help?" he said.

"I'm done. Thanks."

"Want me to pick up a little?"

I glanced around my apartment. Sylvie always teased me about my preference for disarray. She was right—it was a leftover from a marriage to a compulsively neat woman. "No," I said. "Everything's where it belongs. Thanks for the thought, though."

He shrugged. "What do you do, then?"

"What do you mean?"

"At night. Alone."

"I'm not always alone."

He nodded with mock sagacity. "Of course. Sure. How about when you are alone?"

"I read. Tie flies. Daydream. Study chess problems."

"You play chess?"

"Rarely. Badly. Under duress. When I have an opponent."

"Well?"

"You'd probably find me no challenge," I said.

He grinned. "Chicken?"

"No," I said. "I am not chicken."

"Let's play for a beer."

"No dice, kid," I said. "We will play for the sheer joy of the competition. Thrill of victory, agony of defeat. The chess pieces are in the drawer." I gestured at the kitchen sink, and he went and pulled open the drawer next to it, while I swept the magazines, newspapers, beer cans, and socks off the coffee table in the living room. A moment later I heard Buddy laugh.

"Mr. Coyne," he said from the kitchen, "this drawer is unbelievable. There's all kinds of junk in here. The chessmen are loose."

"I think there are two or three sets in there."

"You ought to organize things a little."

"I don't need to organize it," I said. "I know everything that's in there. Batteries, a set of socket wrenches, spare keys for everything, screwdrivers . . ."

"Fishhooks, a broken transistor radio, cassettes, dollar bills, golf tees, about three gross of pencils. Jeez! Anyway, you're right about the chess pieces. More than enough here, for sure."

We set up the board on the coffee table. Buddy played a cautious, defensive game, which I didn't expect. Most young chess players are impulsive, looking for the quick kill. That, in fact, more accurately described my style, which, I supposed, signified something important. Buddy declined most of the exchanges I offered, and he erected a wall of knights and pawns in front of his king that appeared impregnable. What I thought might be a crack in that defense cost me a pawn. It looked like enough of an advantage for Buddy to wear me down.

I smoked a lot of Winstons. Buddy drank a lot of Pepsi. We didn't talk much while we played. He was very intense about it. I had trouble concentrating.

We were well into what promised to be a long, tedious end game, advantage Buddy, when Doc Adams called.

"Bluefish!" he shouted at me. "Bluefish, Coyne. Can't you taste 'em, still flipping and flopping when we toss 'em onto the skillet?"

"PCB's," I intoned. "Mercury. Red tide."

"What's a little adventure in your life? Take a chance. No risk, no reward."

"I don't call consuming poison adventure, old buddy. Anyway, whose boat?"

"Your friend Frank. I thought he let you take it whenever you want."

"He used to."

"You've got to take better care of your friends. Especially those with boats. Bad form, getting on the outs with Frank. Damn bad form. Call him. Make up with him. Send him a bouquet of posies. Another week or two, the blues'll be all gone."

"Frank's boat got stolen."

"Ah, nuts." Doc hesitated. "You don't feel like renting one, do you?"

"Me? Not especially."

"Me neither. Let me think. We could go up to Plum Island and cast for them from the beach. Hit or miss, but fun."

"Okay," I said. "Let's do that. What's the tide going to be?"

"Hang on." While I waited for Doc to come back on the phone, I glanced at the chess game. Buddy was sitting back, grinning at a bishop move he had made. He mouthed the word "Check." I slapped my forehead.

"Here we go," said Doc a minute later. "Tide's up at four-thirty Saturday. We want to catch it coming in, we ought to get there around one. That's a nice time of day."

"I'll pick you up in Concord," I said. "Little before noon?"

"Good. I'll see if Mary will let me snitch a couple thermoses full of that homemade minestrone I smell. I'll build some sandwiches."

I told Doc to give Mary a big wet kiss for me, which he said would be a pleasure, and we hung up. I went back and sat across from Buddy.

"Check," he said.

"I know, I know." I studied the board. It was a long way off, but I finally saw it. The inevitable checkmate. I might avoid it. But to do so, Buddy would have to make a major blunder. I decided to give him credit for not doing that. I tipped over my king. "Nice game," I said.

"You're too aggressive," Buddy said. "No backup. You tried something and it didn't work and you had nothing to fall back on."

"Yeah," I said. "The story of my life. I'm going to bed."

"I don't think I'm going to sleep much," he said.

Buddy insisted on putting away my chess pieces properly. I found the felt-lined wooden box they belonged in under some papers on my desk. I emptied the bass flies out of it and gave it to him.

I found some sheets and a pillow and blankets for him. He said he could make up the sofa himself. I said good night to him, and he said, "Thanks for everything, Mr. Coyne. I'm glad I called you."

"Busy day tomorrow," I said. "Try and get some rest."

"About that beer," said Buddy. "I gotta admit it. You were right. It's kinda nice to know where you stand with somebody."

I awakened even earlier than usual the next morning. I lay in my bed for a minute or two before I remembered why I was feeling a little wired. Buddy Baron was sleeping in my living room. I was going to take him through the first steps of what probably would prove to be a long legal process. It would be painful for him and his parents, regardless of the outcome.

I slipped into my jeans and crept out to the kitchen. I was careful not to awaken Buddy.

I needn't have bothered.

He wasn't there.

seven

THE BEDCLOTHES I HAD GIVEN HIM the night before were stacked on the sofa, neatly folded. I couldn't tell whether he had used them and refolded them or not. I looked out on the balcony, in the spare bedroom, in the bathroom, without much expectation of finding him. And I didn't.

Buddy had left.

I sat at the table, listening to the coffee machine chug and gurgle. The police wanted Buddy Baron, and I had him, and I let him go. I had blown it. Cusick would be rightfully furious. I wasn't sure how Joanie or Tom would react. For my part, I was embarrassed. I had misjudged him.

When the coffee was ready, I poured a mugful and took it out onto the balcony to wait for the sun to come up. The question that nagged at me was this: If he intended to run away, why did Buddy bother to come to me in the first place? He knew what had happened to Alice. He knew there was an arrest warrant out for him. So why come to me? Did he hope for something that I failed to give him? Or did he get what he wanted?

Or did he just change his mind and chicken out?

Although I do some excellent thinking out there in the cool of the predawn morning on occasion, no answers were forthcoming this time. I finished my coffee, went in to shower and shave, got dressed, and headed for my car.

I stopped in the lobby downstairs and spoke with the security guard at the desk. He was a former Boston patrolman named Reilly who had retired early on a disability. Heart condition. He had himself a cushy job in my building now, but judging by the way his shirt stretched across his belly and the capillaries were exploding across his cheeks, I didn't figure his condition was very much improved. He was no help anyway. He had just come on duty. He hadn't seen Buddy. I made a mental note to check with the night man later.

I got to the office before Julie. I signed some letters she had left on my desk, glanced through some documents she had word-processed, and when eight o'clock came around I called the Windsor Harbor police station. The desk officer put me through to Chief Cusick.

"I don't exactly know how to tell you this, Chief," I began.

"Obviously it isn't good news. Why don't you just spit it out, Mr. Coyne?"

"I have been in contact with Buddy Baron."

"Well, that's not bad."

"Right. He called me, and I persuaded him to come to my apartment." I hesitated, and he said, "Oh, oh. Don't tell me—"

"He spent the night. At least part of it. At least I think he did. But—"

"Godammit it. You lost him."

"He slipped away. He was going to spend the night, and then I was going to bring him to you this morning. It was agreed. When I woke up, he was gone."

Cusick didn't speak. It made me uncomfortable.

"Look," I said.

He sighed. It hissed into my ear from the telephone. "Never mind. Just do me a favor, will you?"

"I know what you're going to say. I'm embarrassed."

"I hope the hell you are." He paused. "Okay. I suppose no harm has been done. We're no worse off than we were if he hadn't contacted you in the first place. No better, but no worse. We're not exactly helpless without you, you know."

"You've learned something?"

"Of course. It's what we do. It's not, by the way, what attorneys do."

"Dare I ask?"

"On one condition."

"I know."

"Bow out. Back off."

"You already told me that."

"I'm reminding you."

"Tell Tom Baron you're done with it. It's not your job. You'll only screw it up."

"I already thought of that," I said lamely.

"Good." He paused, and I thought I could hear him riffling papers. "Okay. In the interest of good community relations and all, here's what you can tell Tom after you tell him you're through playing private detective. First, we found Buddy's car. The Cambridge cops found it, actually, parked behind an apartment building in Central Square. They've got it staked out. I assume eventually Buddy will return to it. Second, he's used a bank card to get cash three times in the past two days. A hundred bucks each time, which I guess is the maximum they allow per shot. Twice in the same bank in Cambridge, and once in the city. We've got the people in all the Shawmut banks alerted to keep an eye out for him. So one way or another, we'll get him." He paused. I imagined him tucking the papers neatly back into their proper manila folder and placing the folder on his blotter, lining the edges up. "Now it's your turn, Mr. Coyne."

"For whatever it may be worth," I said, "I don't think he killed the girl. He told me what happened. I think it was the truth."

"With all due respect, Mr. Coyne, and I know you're a very successful attorney and all, your judgment lacks credence just now. Why don't you just tell me what he told you, and let me draw my own conclusions."

I smiled to myself. Cusick was getting his money's worth out of my blunder. I related to him what Buddy had told me, and he said, "Why do you assume that's not a lie?"

"Intuition, I guess."

"Your intuition told you it would be okay for him to spend the night."

"You've made your point, Chief."

"Good. Well, when we catch Buddy we can get the details. I assume it can be checked out. But a few things trouble me about this tale."

"Why is he running, for example."

"Exactly."

"He's frightened," I said.

"Obviously possible. More likely he's lying."

"I don't think he's lying," I said.

"Not to belabor a point, but I do not value your opinion very highly just now. Thanks for the information."

On that note I hung up with Chief Cusick and called the Baron house. This time Tom answered.

"Brady," he said when he heard my voice. "I was about to call you."

There was something about Tom's tone that I couldn't identify. Anger. Anxiety. Resignation. "What's the matter?" I said.

"Did you see the *Globe* this morning?"

"No. I've had a busy morning."

"Front page, Brady. Big black letters. It says, 'Baron's Son Wanted for Murder.' Jesus Christ!"

"It's the truth," was all I could think of to say.

"You think if I were a Democrat they'd print that?"

"Yes. Of course."

"Ah, you're like all the rest of them," he said sadly. "You just don't understand how it is."

"Well, right now my concern is Buddy, not your campaign. Maybe that should be yours, too, Tom."

"I am concerned about Buddy. You don't need to tell me how to feel."

"He was with me last night, you know."

"Joanie told me. A big relief. I got in late. She was still up. Half in the bag. Make that entirely in the bag. But that's great that Buddy showed up. He's okay, huh? You're bringing him in this morning, I understand. I want to see him. Where—?"

"Tom," I interrupted.

"What? What's the matter?"

"Buddy scooted out sometime in the night. He's gone."

"What the hell do you mean, gone?"

"I mean gone. He ran away."

"Well, Jesus. What do we do now?

"Nothing to do. The police are looking for him. It was me who screwed up, Tom. Not Buddy. I should've taken him in when he first showed up. He just seemed so scared."

"Poor little bastard," muttered Tom. "Must be scared shitless." I heard him expel a loud breath. "I don't know, Brady."

"You don't know what?"

"Whether this is good news or bad news. It's great that Buddy's okay. And I can't say I like the idea of him in jail, or out on bail, even, or . . ."

Tom's voice trailed off. I finished his sentence for him. "Or you getting all those negative headlines."

"That's not—ah, hell. It *is* what I was thinking. This is damn confusing, Counselor."

"Well, this is bad news, Tom, to answer your question. I don't think Buddy did anything wrong. He's scared. That's natural. But the sooner we get him to the police, the sooner it'll all get straightened out. And your front page stories in the *Globe* will start sounding better to you."

"You make me sound like a monster."

"Sorry, Tom."

"Yeah. I had it coming. Tell me. How did he seem? He's not . . ."

"He's not doing any drugs. No. He seemed—well, scared, of course. And upset about Alice. Aside from overreacting to the idea of a night in jail, he seemed good. I enjoyed his company. He whipped my tail at the chessboard. He got mad when I refused to let him have a beer. He's a good kid, Tom. And I think he's pretty well put together, considering."

"Considering," muttered Tom. "Considering the horseshit job of fathering he's gotten. Well, then, what's next? Will you keep looking for Buddy?"

"Nope. No way. I gave you a day, like I said I would. I'm afraid I did more harm than good. Let the police take care of it. When they get him, let me know. I'll get my old assistant, Zerk Garrett, on the case."

Tom was silent for a moment. Finally he said, "Brady, about the *Globe.*"

"There's not a damn thing I or anyone else can do about newspapers printing the news. You're a public figure. This is news. You've just got to ride with it as best you can. Have a little faith in the fairness of the voting public."

He chuckled. "I don't know any politicians who have that kind of faith."

"And that," I said, "speaks volumes. How's Joanie taking it all?"

"She's dead to the world right now. She hasn't seen the paper. Far as she knows, you're bringing Buddy in and she's going to jail with me to bail him out."

"Give her my best. And keep the faith, Tom."

"You gotta get it before you can keep it," he said.

A few minutes later Julie came in. She presented herself in the doorway to my inner office and stood there, her hands on her shapely hips, glaring at me. "Now what did I do?" I said.

"It's what you didn't do. The coffee. You waiting for your secretary to make the coffee this morning?"

"Mea culpa," I intoned, pressing my palms together under my chin and bowing deeply to her. "I have sinned. But I have seen the error of my ways."

"Ah, forget it. I'll take care of the coffee. You might want to look at the paper. Article on the front page of interest."

While Julie put the coffee on I sat at her desk and read the *Globe* article. It contained the facts as I knew them except that it failed to mention the presence of cocaine in Alice Sylvester's blood, and it failed to suggest that she had engaged in intercourse with two men, and, if one was disposed to read between the lines, it implied that her sexual encounter had not been mutually consented to.

In other words, Buddy Baron had raped and murdered her.

I read the article twice. Both times I got the same implication. Oh, it was couched in euphemistic language, and it was peppered with words like "alleged," and it was buttressed with quotations from Harry Cusick, the Windsor Harbor police chief. Bottom line, though: The son of the Republican candidate for governor raped and murdered his girl friend.

I read it once more, this time as a lawyer, with an eye to the Bill of Rights. The article was entirely factual, and certainly not actionable. Newspapers' First Amendment rights are well protected, and the *Globe* lawyers knew the law better than I did anyway.

It was, nevertheless, a very damaging article for a candidate for public office. I didn't need legal training to tell me that.

Julie brought me a mug of coffee. I kissed her hand. She gave me a gentle slap on the cheek. "Masher," she said. "Don't forget the Fallons. Ten-thirty." And she eased me out of her chair so she could get to work.

I went back into my office and called Tom Baron.

"Me again," I said. "Just read the article in the *Globe*. Wanted you to know that there's nothing in it I can help you with. You've got yourself a political problem, not a legal one. Eddy Curry can help you, maybe. But not me."

"Appreciate the thought," he said dolefully. "Matter of fact, Eddy's on his way over. We're going to put our heads together. I got a summons from a bunch of party bigwigs. Eddy thinks they want to dump me. Trouble is, I got the feeling that Eddy may agree with them. That isn't bad enough, Joanie's semiberserk. Thinks something's happened to Buddy."

"Maybe you should," I said.

"Should what?"

"Bow out. Gracefully, now, before any harm is done."

"Can't," he said quickly. "Won't. I'll never get another shot like this one. Nope. Going to scrap it out. Wish the hell you'd come on the team."

"Well, I'm not."

I spent the next hour or so on the phone, doing the things that make the legal profession exciting. I set up two luncheon meetings with attorneys for the next week, I declined an invitation to serve on an ad hoc committee for the Bar Association. I checked back with the Coast Guard, which had not found Frank Paradise's boat. I reconfirmed my golf date with Charlie McDevitt. I called a travel agent about a junket to the Madison River in Montana. I touched base with a few clients.

A thrill a minute. Real Perry Mason stuff.

At ten-thirty Julie ushered three people into my office. Two of them turned out to be Steve and Cathy Fallon, an attractive young couple in their late twenties. The third was a younger woman with a weight problem named Eleanor Phelps.

The three of them sat on the sofa and I took the chair across from them. The Fallon couple sat close together. They seemed stiff, ill at ease, and they kept their hands folded in their laps. Eleanor Phelps slouched in the corner. I offered them coffee, which they declined.

"How can I help you?" I said.

Cathy and Steve Fallon looked at each other, and evidently succeeded in communicating something, because she said, "Dr. Segrue—he's our doctor, you know—suggested that we tell you our problem."

Doc Segrue had told me a lot of his problems. I had even solved some of them for him. I smiled and nodded encouragingly.

"Steve and I—we've been married for five years now. We want to have a child. We've tried everything." She looked down at her clasped hands, which were wrestling with each other in her lap. "We've had no luck at all. Anyway, we finally went to the doctor. He tested Steve. You know . . ."

I nodded. "Sperm count."

She smiled gratefully. "Yes. And he was fine. So then he tested me. It's my fault."

"It's not a matter of fault," said her husband quickly.

"Whatever," she said, "I've got this problem. It doesn't really matter what it is. It can't be fixed. I'm—I'm sterile." She blinked. "I hate the sound of that word. Anyhow, Steve and I can't have children. Together, that is. Doctor Segrue suggested adoption. We've looked into it. It's—we'd like to try something else. Use some of our genes. Surrogate motherhood. Eleanor—she's my sister, you see—she's willing."

"You want your sister to have a baby for you?" I said.

"Yes. Steve would be the father."

"By artificial insemination," interjected Steve quickly.

Eleanor Phelps, from her corner of the sofa, giggled. "Immaculate conception," she said. "Don't you love it?"

Steve and Cathy did not seem amused.

"I'll be happy to draw up a contract," I told them. "But you've got to understand that I can't make it legally binding."

"Why not?" said Steve. "I thought that case—"

"Baby M," I said. "New Jersey case. One case. A precedent, sure. But every case is different. No one knows how Massachusetts courts will go. Depends on the situation, the judge, the lawyers." I spread my hands. "I'll make the best contract for you that I can. But different case, different state, it could go to the biological mother."

"Hey," said Eleanor. "Don't sweat it. The last thing I want is a baby."

"Why have you agreed to this?" I asked her.

She shrugged. "Do my sister a favor. Have the experience." She grinned ironically. "Fulfill myself as a woman."

"Have you folks discussed a fee?"

"Fee?" said Steve.

"What you'll pay Ms. Phelps."

The three of them looked at each other. "I'm not doing it for the money," said Eleanor.

"I suggest," I said, "that you agree to a consideration. That will enhance the viability of the contract, should it end up in court."

"Gimme a buck. Gimme a bag of M&M's," said Eleanor.

"Look," I said. "I'll outline what's involved. You folks can go home and think about it, while I draw up a contract. Then if you decide to, you can sign it. Okay?"

They all nodded.

"You, Ms. Phelps, will agree to be artificially inseminated by Mr. Fallon's sperm. If you become pregnant, you will agree to carry the child to term and, upon delivery, turn it over to the Fallons. You must visit an obstetrician regularly. You must eat properly, refrain from all drugs, alcohol, or smoking except as specifically permitted by the doctor. You will agree to amniocentesis, and if the fetus is defective, you will agree to an abortion if the Fallons want it. You will do all of this for a monetary consideration, which will be held in escrow pending your fulfillment of the contract. How does that sound to you?"

Eleanor Phelps had been staring at me. When I was finished, she shook her head back and forth. "Wow," she breathed softly. "Does it have to be so complicated?"

I nodded. "We're trying to anticipate the contingencies. That's what lawyers are paid for." I turned to Steve and Cathy Fallon. "For your part, you will pay Ms. Phelps a sum of money for this service. You will pay all of her medical expenses, plus any other expenses, such as loss of work time. You will pay her if she miscarries. I will detail all of this in the contract I create."

"What should we pay her?" said Steve.

"More than a bag of candy. I'd suggest ten thousand dollars."

"Why that much?"

"It's a standard fee. If it comes to that, we want a judge to take your agreement seriously."

Eleanor Phelps had been staring at me. "Ms. Phelps, do you have any questions?" I said to her.

"No. I guess not. It's not all that romantic, is it?"

"It's a business proposition. It has to be."

Cathy Fallon reached over and took her sister's hand. "It's the most wonderful gift you could ever give us," she said. Eleanor looked softly at Cathy. She nodded.

"I don't get it," said Steve. "I mean, I suppose legally . . . ."

His voice trailed away in the unarticulated question. People who love and trust each other tend to belittle the value or power of the law to mediate their interactions. "Look," I said gently. "This is all new stuff. One case doesn't define the law. None of the questions has really been answered. Can a woman give up the rights to her child before conception? Can she change her mind? Does a contract such as I propose constitute baby-selling, which is illegal? Whose child is one created by artificial insemination? What are the rights of the sperm donor? Of his wife? Can those rights be altered by a contract? For that matter, what is motherhood? Or fatherhood? Do biological mothers and fathers have equal rights to the child? What are the rights of the fetus?"

I sat back and spread my hands. Steve and Cathy Fallon looked solemn. Eleanor Phelps was smiling. "I was thinking," she said. "All the teenage girls who get knocked up, and all the rest who are petrified of it happening. Here you have folks who just want a kid." She shook her head.

"I have no wisdom on that," I said.

We chatted for a while longer. I went over the terms of the proposed contract again for them. Cathy and Steve seemed animated, excited as they began to understand the steps. Their child was becoming a reality in their minds. They mentioned the room they would redecorate. They asked Eleanor if she would help them shop for furniture. When she shook her head and said, "No, I'm not sure I'd want to do that," Cathy cocked her head and frowned. But then Eleanor grinned and said she was more interested in getting the kid's stuffed animals.

When I finally ushered them out of my office, all three of them were discussing their favorite boys' and girls' names.

And I felt I was practicing the kind of law that suited me. I was helping ordinary people do positive things that they wanted to do. I was dealing with life, not death. There were no adversaries in this case, no aggrieved parties, no pain or tragedy, no anger or malice.

Of course, there was no challenge for the attorney, either. I did not feel especially short-changed. A worthwhile challenge is getting a big brown trout to rise to an artificial dry fly. I didn't enter the legal profession to be challenged.

I felt so good about it, in fact, that I took Julie to lunch at Marie's, my favorite little restaurant in Kenmore Square. And that afternoon I did the necessary research so that I could rough out a contract for the Fallons.

I hardly thought about Buddy Baron for the rest of the day.

Before I left the office, I called Sylvie at her Beacon Street condo, where she lives and writes children's books. Most of her stories are adaptations of old Hungarian folk tales and myths. She writes them quickly and easily and makes lots of money at it.

She was in a good mood when I arrived. She had just received a new contract from her publisher which would keep her busy and wealthy for six more books. She would be off to New York to visit her agent and do some bargaining over the weekend. She insisted we celebrate her good fortune. She would cook for me.

She fed me chicken in a cream sauce with mushrooms, accompanied by broccoli and long-grain wild rice. Paprika was the dominant spice. "Old Hungarian recipe?" I said.

"Got it out of Fanny Farmer," she answered, grinning.

Afterwards we had the champagne that I had brought to celebrate her contract.

She tried to persuade me to spend the night. I put up a good fight, but she wore me down.

The next afternoon I met Charlie McDevitt at the clubhouse at Stow Acres. When I arrived I found him arguing racehorses with Tommy Porter, one of the owners of the golf course. The debate, I gathered, concerned the relative merits of heredity versus environment in the making of a champion.

"Blood," said Tommy.

"Training," spat Charlie.

"Up yours," said Tommy, indisputably laying claim to the last word.

As we strolled to the first tee, Charlie grumbled, "The hell does he know about it."

"He owns horses, I understand," I said. "All you do is bet on them."

While Charlie was taking his practice swipes, he told me how he had finally conquered his slice. "I just aim the V's at the tip of my right shoulder and pronate my wrists this way." He showed me. "Presto. Today's the day, Counselor. Today I whip your tail."

"Probably will," I said. "I've been ignoring my V's and neglecting my pronation lately."

His tee shot sailed out straight, then began to leak off to the right. It dribbled near a small evergreen that marked the edge of the fairway. "That was a controlled fade, not a slice," said Charlie. But I thought he looked worried.

I hooked my tee shot into the left trap. Charlie brightened considerably. "Try moving your V's toward your left shoulder," he said. "It's all in the V's."

"Appreciate the advice," I muttered.

As we shouldered our clubs and headed toward our balls, Charlie said,

"I snuck out the other day to try out my grip. I joined up with a twosome. Guy and a lady. Turned out the guy was a priest and the gal, who had a pretty swing, she was a nun."

"You didn't tell me you'd played," I said.

"I wanted to see how the new grip was gonna work. Anyway, this priest was a pretty good golfer, you could tell. On the first tee he hits this monstrous drive. One of those low ones that just seem to keep rising? But it gets out there and all of a sudden it takes this quick left. Wicked hook. Rolls under a tree. The priest says, 'Aw, shit.' Not real loud, but he's definitely pissed off. The nun looks at him and says, 'Now, Father, you mustn't use such language.' Gentle, but she rebuked him. And he says, 'I am so sorry, Sister.' Anyway, the priest goes over to his ball. Tough lie, but he gets a good whack at it and it takes off right for the center of the green. Then, as it starts to come down, it takes this amazing hook to the left again. Buries itself in a trap. The priest is watching in amazement, and when his ball lands in the trap he flips his club and yells, 'Aw, shit!' Louder this time. The nun looks real embarrassed at me, and she whispers to the priest, but I can hear her, she says, 'Really, Father. God will surely punish you for such language.' And the priest shakes his head and says, 'Please accept my apology, Sister. May God strike me dead if I use profanity again.' Look, Brady. Go ahead and hit your ball. I'll meet you on the green."

Charlie and I each reached the green in three shots. I was away. As I lined up my putt, Charlie said, "I was going to give this priest the secret of the V's. But he was kinda steaming, so I figured maybe he wasn't in the most receptive mood. I mean, he scoops his ball out of that trap, looks like a great shot, and the ball hits the green and takes a ninety-degree roll to the left, like there was a magnet or something in it. And the priest, he can't help himself, he practically screams, 'Aw, shit!' The nun crosses herself, and the poor guy, he's really chagrined. He looks at the sky and says in his loud voice, 'Strike me down if I curse again.' Okay. I'm away, I roll it up close and tap in for my bogie. The nun, she's lying about the same distance as you are now, and she gets down in two also. Then it's the priest's turn. He lines it up and strikes it nice and firm. The ball rolls right for hole, and guess what?"

"It rolls to the left," I said.

"It sure as hell did. Straight as a die right up to the hole, then boom, it darts off to the left. The priest can't believe it. 'Shit!' he yells. Well, Brady, I'm standing there kinda stunned, you know, and suddenly overhead comes this huge black cloud. And there's the rumble of thunder, and the sun disappears, and then I hear this crack and a big bolt of lightning comes shooting down, straight for the poor priest. Suddenly it veers off to the left and zaps the nun, turning her into a smoldering cinder. And this deep, heavenly voice booms out, 'Aw, shit.' "

I stepped away from my putt and stared at Charlie. "Imagine there's a point to that story, somewhere."

"I don't know, Brady. It's just something that happened to me."

I squeaked out a one-up victory over Charlie and his newly aligned V's, and he bought the beers in the clubhouse. Tommy Porter joined us briefly, but when he realized Charlie had conceded the argument on racehorses he wandered away.

I told Charlie the sad tale of Alice Sylvester and about Buddy Baron's mysterious disappearance and reappearance and re-disappearance.

"Lot of crack around," observed Charlie. "It does things to people."

"You guys have any handle on what's going on in Boston?"

Charlie was a lawyer for the United States Justice Department's Boston office. He had prosecuted plenty of drug importers. He shook his head. "Not really, to be honest. The stuff is so portable, so easy to make. And the business is so damn sophisticated, now. We nailed one bunch, the head guy had an MBA from Harvard. We've mostly gotten the middlemen. There are links to New York, Providence, Newark, even Miami. But, truthfully, so far they've got the jump on us. This crack is bad stuff, believe me."

"I believe you," I said. "I don't like what I see happening in Windsor Harbor."

"It stinks," he agreed.

We talked baseball for a while, and Charlie invited me to his house for dinner, which I declined. Instead, I stopped at Bannister's in Stow for a thick hunk of tenderloin. I lingered over my coffee, and it was nearly eleven when I finally got home.

I parked in the basement garage and sat there for a moment. Friday night. Sylvie was in New York to confer with her agent. I'd get right to bed. Tomorrow would be Saturday. Bluefishing with Doc Adams.

I dragged my clubs from my car to the elevator, glided up to the sixth floor, and dragged them to my door. I unlocked it and snapped on the light.

The first thing I noticed was a strange odor in my apartment. It reminded me of burnt pork.

The second thing I noticed was Buddy Baron. He was seated at my kitchen table. His body was erect, but his chin was slumped on his chest.

Buddy looked dead.

eight

HE HAD BEEN TIED TO ONE OF MY high-backed kitchen chairs with a length of nylon fly line off one of my reels, several turns around his chest under his arms and half a dozen more turns around his throat, snug to the chair back. His face was the color of a ripe eggplant. A check of his pulse confirmed what I already knew. Buddy Baron was indeed dead.

I called the police and figured I would have ten or fifteen minutes alone with Buddy.

"You shouldn't have left," I told his body. I slammed my fist onto the top of the table. "Dammit. I should have taken you in the other night."

Buddy had nothing to say.

I sat down across from him. "You were afraid, weren't you? That's why you left. I guess you had good reason. And here we all are—yeah, me too —hell, even your old man—suspecting you of killing poor Alice. This is my fault. All I can do for you now is try to vindicate you. For what that may be worth."

Buddy did not answer me.

My toaster was on the table, its cord stretched to a wall socket. That was not where I kept it. I picked up one of Buddy's hands. His arms still hung limply at his sides. He couldn't have been dead for long. No rigor mortis yet. The fingers on his right hand were blackened and blistered. I could visualize what had happened. The toaster had been turned on and Buddy's fingers shoved inside of it. He had been tortured. I wondered what his killer had hoped to learn from him.

I wondered if he had been successful.

I went out onto my little balcony to stare at the night and see what answers lay out there. I found mostly questions.

Buddy had left two nights ago. I supposed he'd taken a key from the drawer where he'd found the chess pieces. He had left with the intention of returning. He'd left with a purpose, not just to avoid jail. But what had he been after? And had he found it? It seemed clear to me that he'd hoped to learn something about Alice Sylvester's murder. He'd had an idea he wanted to confirm, or to find evidence to support.

Had his killer followed him to my apartment? Or had he come here to wait for Buddy? Or—a sudden thought—had the murderer come to wait for me, making Buddy a tragic victim of circumstance?

But if the killer had come for me, why?

Questions. No answers.

The buzzer rang. I went to answer it. It was Hector, informing me that a gang of policemen were on their way up.

The next hour or so was a blur of questions, mostly the same questions over and over. And most of my answers were "I don't know."

The medical examiner deduced that Buddy had indeed been tortured by someone burning his fingers in the toaster, and that he had died by strangulation. The M.E. speculated that the pain in Buddy's fingers had caused him to strain against the fly line bound tightly around his throat, which, in turn, constricted his windpipe until he suffocated.

After photos were taken they untied Buddy's body, laid it into a plastic body bag, and took it away. Most of the cops departed, leaving only a team of forensics guys and a state police detective named Horowitz. Horowitz was a soft-spoken man about my age who ruminated nervously on a big wad of bubble gum. He wore wrinkled chino pants and a short-sleeved white shirt with a little blue bow tie. He looked like a travel agent, not a cop.

I had spent most of this time seated on the sofa in my living room smoking cigarettes. Horowitz came over and sat beside me.

"Who's Eddy Curry?" he said.

"Curry? He's Tom Baron's campaign manager. Why?"

Horwitz shifted his cud of gum from his left to his right cheek. "Why would Curry come here?" he said.

"As far as I know, Curry doesn't even know where I live. I can think of no reason why he'd come here. What's Curry got to do with this?"

Horowitz called over his shoulder to one of the forensics guys. "Get that guard in here, willya?"

A minute later the plainclothes cop returned with Hector. He wore a gray shirt and dark blue pants and a badge. He carried no weapon. Hector's eyes darted around the room. When they lit on me, he looked relieved.

"C'mere," said Horowitz.

Hector came and stood in front of us. "Sit down," said Horowitz.

Hector sat on the edge of the chair next to the sofa.

"Tell it again."

"The boy come back maybe eight o'clock," he said. His right knee jiggled as if he were trying to shake off a swarm of killer ants. "Same boy come the other night, okay? I call up, like always. This time you not home." Hector lifted his black eyebrows to me. "The boy, he say he wanna wait for you, you give him a key. I figure he was here before, he's okay, right? He show me his key, see, and I know he's your friend. I fuck up, huh?"

I waved my hand. "No. No problem. It's okay."

"Did you give the boy a key?" said Horowitz to me.

I shook my head. "No. No, I didn't. But I know where he got it, I think. I've got a drawer full of junk. Including spare keys. He must've seen them when he was getting the chess set. He probably grabbed a bunch of them after I went to bed and tried them. He must've been planning to come back all along."

"Why? Why leave and then come back?"

I shrugged. "I have no idea."

Horowitz turned to Hector. "Okay. What then?"

"I say this already. I'm sorry I do a bad job. A little later, maybe eight-thirty, nine, two guys come. Ask to see you, Mr. Coyne. I say you not home. They ask is the boy there yet. I tell them, yes, he's there waiting. They say they with him, they wanna wait, too, they all friends, they gonna have meeting with you. What do I know? I call up there, tell the boy they coming up."

"What did Buddy say?" I said.

"He say, who are they? I tell him the names."

"Eddy Curry?" I said.

"That one of 'em, yeah. Other one Tom Baron. I remember that."

"You're sure of those names," said Horowitz. "Curry and Baron?"

Hector nodded vigorously and grinned. "Sure. One of 'em got the same name as the man running for governor, right?"

Horowitz nodded.

"What did these two look like?" I said.

"One tall, skinny. Other big guy. Not so tall. Fat."

"Tom Baron's tall and thin," I told Horowitz. "Curry's fat."

"We're going to take Hector to the station to look at some pictures," said Horowitz.

"Can I ask a question?" I said.

Horowitz blew a bubble. "You've been asking questions right along. Go ahead."

"Did you see Buddy leave the other night?" I said to Hector.

He looked blank. "I send him up there, remember? I don't see him come down."

"He could've taken the elevator to the parking garage in the basement," I said to Horowitz.

"What about Curry and Baron? Did you see them leave tonight?"

Hector shook his head. "I tell you that. No. Maybe they use the elevator, too."

"Okay," said Horowitz. "You go back and wait. We'll be with you pretty soon."

Hector stood up and hesitated. He looked at me. "I'm sorry if I fuck up, Mr. Coyne. I'm trying to do a good job."

I waved at him. "Forget it."

After Hector left, a uniformed policeman approached Horowitz. "Sir?" he said.

"What is it?"

"We talked with all the neighbors. On this floor, and five and seven, too. Nobody heard nothing."

Horowitz shrugged. "They never do." He nodded to the cop, who walked away. Then he turned to me. "Well? What do you think?"

"I think," I said, "that if Tom Baron and Eddy Curry came here to kill Buddy, they wouldn't have walked in the front door, given Hector their correct names, let him see them, and then done it here."

"Supposing they didn't intend to kill him. Say they figured they'd just talk to him, and then when he didn't cooperate they tried to torture him a little. To get information. Whatever it was he went after. It backfired. They ran out when they realized what happened."

I shook my head. "Tom Baron wouldn't kill his own son. Not Tom. Curry's kind of a bag of shit sometimes, but he's not a murderer."

"What about you, Mr. Coyne?"

"I'm not a murderer, either."

"Nah," he said. " 'Course not." He glanced at his wristwatch. "You got somebody you can stay with tonight? The boys'll be here a while, vacuuming and dusting and all. It's pretty late. You're just gonna be in the way."

"I've got to use the phone," I said. "Is that okay?"

"Depends."

"On what?"

"Who you're gonna call."

"Tom and Joanie Baron. Buddy's parents."

Horowitz shook his head. "No. Don't."

"Why the hell not?"

He sighed and popped his gum inside his mouth. "We're better at that sort of thing than you are."

"Come off it, Horowitz."

"Okay. I want to handle it my way. And I'm in charge of this case. That good enough for you?"

"I owe it to Tom to tell him."

"Tom Baron is a name in this case."

"Tom didn't kill his own son, for Christ's sake. You don't believe that, do you?"

He shrugged. "I believe very little, one way or the other. I either know something, or I don't know. Belief has nothing to do with it." He put a hand on my shoulder. "Look. Call them tomorrow. I promise we'll handle it properly."

I nodded. "Not that it's something I exactly look forward to."

"Don't talk to anybody about what happened here, Mr. Coyne. That's an order."

"I hear you," I said."

Sylvie was still out of town, but I had a key to her Beacon Street condo. I told Horowitz where I'd be and promised to show up at the state police headquarters the next morning to give a deposition.

I spent a restless night alone in Sylvie's big bed watching old black-and-white movies on a UHF channel. The next morning I called Doc Adams to cancel our bluefishing expedition. Then I taxied over to Horowitz's office.

Horowitz was still jawing on his gum. I wondered if it was the same piece he'd been worrying the previous night.

He had me talk into a tape recorder, telling everything I knew about Buddy Baron and my involvement with him and Tom. He prodded me with gentle questions, and it took nearly two hours. When I was done, he snapped off the recorder and said, "Well, that's about it for now."

"What about Curry and Baron?" I said.

Horowitz shook his head. "It wasn't them. Your night man, there, we showed him photos, he was positive it wasn't them. He didn't find anything that struck his fancy in the mug book. We got a couple sketches. The guy was pretty hazy, though."

"Can I see the sketches?"

Horowitz popped a bubble inside his mouth. "I was going to show them to you, you give me a chance."

Horowitz was right. The sketches could have been anybody. One had a fatter face than the other. The hairlines were different. I handed the sketches back and shrugged. He nodded.

"You want to keep an eye out, you know?"

"What do you mean?"

"These two guys, they went to your place, right?"

"So?"

"Just take care. We never did find any key. Assume they're got it. Better change your lock. We're circulating the sketches, of course, but as you saw they're pretty nondescript."

"You think they might . . . ?"

He shrugged. "Can't tell what's going to happen, Mr. Coyne."

"What about Buddy's parents?"

"They've been told. They're coming to ID the body this morning. We'll be holding it for a while, get an autopsy. And I talked to the chief at Windsor Harbor. Harry Cusick. He and I will be coordinating. He's got that girl, I've got this boy, and we figure two kids from a dinky place like Windsor Harbor get themselves killed—both strangled, actually—there's a connection. This does not take a lot of brains. So we're working together. What they call good, professional police work. We'll see where it goes. Maybe the Feds'll get involved." He stood up. "Anyway, Mr. Coyne, we appreciate your help. If you think of something, be sure to let me know."

He escorted me out of his office. We paused in the doorway to shake hands. "You can go home now, if you want," he said. "We're all done there."

"Find anything?"

"I don't know yet. Forensics'll put together a report. There'll be some things to check out. May need your help on that later. I'll let you know."

Noontime on a crisp September Saturday and I had nowhere to go and nothing to do. I wandered up Commonwealth toward the Common, aiming more or less for Sylvie's place. Too late to change my mind about bluefishing with Doc. Too early to hit a bar. The Red Sox were playing out another futile season in Cleveland, so Fenway Park would be locked up. The Old Howard had been razed years before.

A hug from Sylvie would have helped. But she was still in New York.

With a little mental shrug, I cut over to Copley Square. Might as well hit the office for a few hours. I could write a few letters and clean up my perpetually tardy paperwork. Julie would be proud of me when she came in on Monday.

I picked up a ham and Swiss on pumpernickel and a can of Pepsi at the deli and took them up to the office. I spread everything out on Julie's desk and ate while I listened to the tape from the answering machine.

Frank Paradise had called. "I want my boat" was the entire, plaintive message.

Two attorneys called, both asking me to get back to them on Monday regarding cases of mutual interest.

I perked up my ears at the next message. It was Eddy Curry. "Tried your house," he said. "No answer there, either. Appreciate it if you'd call Monday." He left a phone number that I recognized as a Boston exchange.

The last call intrigued me even more. The caller identified herself as Ingrid Larsen. I remembered the green eyes and the blond hair and the way her knit dress had clung to her curves when I followed her through the corridors of her school. "I wasn't very civil with you the other day," she said, "and I wanted to apologize." She sounded breathless, in a hurry, as people often do when leaving messages on a tape. "I am considerably less hostile away from the office, honest. Like in elegant restaurants." She cleared her throat. "Anyway, just to say sorry."

She left no number, no request for me to return her call. I thought about looking it up and calling her anyway. But I didn't. I didn't need an adventure just then. And I wanted to be witty and charming the next time I saw Ingrid Larsen, qualities of which I felt utterly devoid at that moment.

I downed the warm dregs of my Pepsi and went into my office. On my desk were the notes I had made for the Fallon case. Just what I needed. A writing exercise in legalese.

I roughed out a draft of the agreement between Steve and Cathy Fallon and Eleanor Phelps regarding their respective obligations toward their as yet hypothetical child. When I finished, I went back over it, adding a few whereases and whereupons until it sounded right. Then I rolled a piece of paper into my typewriter and put it into a form that Julie would be able to read.

It was nearly five o'clock when I finished. I propped my feet up on my desk and smoked a Winston. Then I smoked another one. Then I did what I had known all day I had to do.

I called Tom Baron.

An unfamiliar female voice answered the phone. "The Baron residence," it said warily.

"I'd like to speak to Mr. Baron."

"May I ask who this is?"

"May I," I retorted cleverly, "ask who you are?"

She cleared her throat. "I happen to be a neighbor, and Mr. and Mrs. Baron—something has happened. They can't come to the phone." She paused, then added, "I'm sorry."

"My name is Coyne," I said. "I'm the family's attorney."

"Oh, well. Yes. Please hang on. I'll see if Mr. Baron can speak with you."

I heard voices in the background, and a minute or so later Tom came on the line. "Brady, Jesus Christ."

"I'm real sorry, Tom."

"This is unbelievable, Brady. It's . . ."

"Tom . . ."

"Nobody is blaming you. I had to go identify his body."

"How's Joanie?"

"The doctor gave her some pills. She's sleeping. He wanted to give me some, too. I told him I needed to feel it. Joanie, I don't know what's going to happen to her. Hell, I don't know what's going to happen to me. This is —it's a nightmare. It's worse than any nightmare. A nightmare, you know you're going to wake up."

"I should've brought him in when I had him," I said. "Tom, he was a good kid. I liked him."

"Yeah," he said. "He was a good kid. Some of us, we never gave him credit. He was—we thought of him as a pain in the ass. He screwed things up for us. I mean, you love your kid. But you wish he was different. You wish you could be proud of him, instead of wishing he wasn't around. Not Joanie, though. She always accepted him. No matter what he did, she was his mother, by Jesus, and she was right there. Behind him. Me, all I ever did was try to fix things up. Fix him. Make him the way I wanted him to be. Make him so I wouldn't have to think about him." I heard Tom sigh deeply. "Brady," he said softly, "you should have seen him."

"I did, Tom."

"Christ! I forgot. God, that must have been awful, walking in like that, seeing him there."

Here was Tom Baron, his son having been murdered, trying to make me feel better. It revealed more sensitivity than I had thought him capable of. "Tom," I said, "if there's anything I can do."

"One thing."

"Name it."

"Don't quit on me now."

"I don't intend to."

"No, listen. I mean, I want whoever did this. To Buddy and to Alice. I'm not talking about the campaign here. Hell, I don't know what I'm going to do about that. I just don't want this to get lost in some police file."

"I already decided that," I said. "I'm involved. Somebody kills somebody in my house, it's personal with me. I don't know what I'm going to do, but I'm in this. All the way." I hesitated, then added, "Tom, listen.

The guys who did this. There were two of them. They used your name. You and Curry. They gave the watchman at my place your names to get into my apartment."

"That explains something."

"What's that?"

"That policeman—Horowitz—he grilled Eddy. Where were we last night. Times, names, corroborating witnesses, all that. Probably would've liked to grill me, too. Guess he figured I just might be feeling some emotions, just hearing my son's been murdered and all. Hell. I was giving the speech in Weymouth last night. About five hundred witnesses. Place was packed. Eddy was with me. Horowitz wouldn't say what he was after, according to Eddy."

"Well, that's what it was. The watchman looked at your pictures. Told him it wasn't you guys."

Tom cleared his throat. I waited for him. Finally he said, "Brady, I don't want you to take this the wrong way."

"Go ahead."

"Eddy Curry's been great. With us all day. Handling things. Making arrangements. But he told me I'd have to be thinking about something."

"The campaign."

"Yes. Did I want to quit. I think some of the party boys are getting nervous. All the headlines. Eddy didn't actually say that. He just asked me. I told him I'd have to think about it. Talk to Joanie, when she's able to listen. What do you think?"

"Aw, Tom. That's a tough one for me."

"It's a helluva lot tougher for me. I need a rational mind. Someone with perspective. Not Eddy. Not Joanie. Shit, especially not me. I can't stop thinking. If I wasn't in this goddamn campaign . . ."

"I can't see how the campaign has anything to do with what happened to Buddy."

I heard him sigh. "That's what I mean. Perspective. I keep telling myself the same thing. But no matter what I think, it doesn't change how I feel."

"You feel guilty."

"Hell, yeah. I look back. A kid's whole lifetime. Eighteen years. Where did I fuck up? What did I do, that if I did it differently Buddy'd still be alive? I mean, it's hard not to blame yourself when your kid gets involved in drugs, right? And if he wasn't involved in drugs . . ."

"Cut it out, Tom. This isn't helping."

"Actually, it is helping. It makes me hurt. I feel like I ought to hurt. I deserve to hurt. When I hurt, it makes me feel better."

"Well, Jesus . . ."

"Life's got to go on, right? Isn't that what everyone says? What's done is done. So you've just got to push on."

"The campaign, you mean."

"The campaign. Brady. What the hell am I going to do?"

"You already said it. Push on."

Tom paused for a long time. "I need you, pal."

"I already told you—"

"No. I mean, I need you to talk to. You're the only goddamn person I can talk to that I can trust. Listen. Is there any sense in me quitting the campaign? Tell me the truth."

"I don't see any sense to it. There's nothing to be gained."

"Right. Yeah. Okay. Then how do I handle it?"

"What?"

"You know. Buddy. I mean, if I do decide to keep on with the campaign, there's going to be questions. Legitimate questions. People are going to want to know. The press, the public. There'll be stuff in the papers. About Buddy and me and the family. Buddy's problems."

"And that," I said, "is Eddy Curry's bailiwick. Not mine, if that's what you're suggesting. You want to continue your campaign—well, I guess you ought to. I'm your friend. I'll continue to be your friend. And your attorney. But—"

"I wish the hell you'd come aboard, Brady."

"I've told you a million times—"

"That was then. This is now."

"I don't think so, Tom."

"Will you think about it?"

"Sure. I'll think about it. What I was going to say was this. I talked with Buddy a lot the other night. I am absolutely convinced he committed no crime. For all I know, he was trying to solve one. I've got a feeling that whoever killed him thought he knew something about Alice's murder. It's for damn sure that he didn't kill Alice. All of this will make its way into the papers. Hell, Tom. Buddy was a victim here. I'll bet he turns out to be a hero. I don't know much about politics. But if you're worried about this hurting your campaign I think you can relax."

"I never said I was worried about that."

"Fine."

"I haven't been able to put my mind to it. But, yeah, okay. That's good."

"Curry knows more about it than I do, though."

"Brady, I need a legal adviser."

"We've been through that."

"You said you'd think about it."

"I will. Is that what Curry called me about?"

"I don't know. Yeah. Probably."

"Tom, are you okay?"

"I'm hurting. That's a good sign."

"Give my love to Joanie."

"She asked after you a couple times. Be nice, maybe you could come see her."

"I'll see what I can do."

Tom thanked me several times. He seemed reluctant to disconnect. I couldn't blame him. Not that I offered him much comfort, but his alternative was sitting in the house where he had raised his son and staring at the memories, with his wife's hysteria to deal with when she awakened from her drugged sleep.

After we finally hung up, I went over to the cabinet in my office and found my special bottle of Jack Daniel's. Normally it's for ceremonial occasions—the generous settlement of a lawsuit, a not-guilty verdict, the reconciliation of an estranged couple.

This time I poured myself a shot and downed it neat, just like a brassy lawman in a hostile saloon. For nerves, for courage. Whatever, it never works for me, but it always seems like a good idea.

I went to the closet. My old briefcase was on the floor in back. I took it out and put it on top of my desk. I brushed the dust off it.

It wasn't one of those sleek attaché cases that most of my colleagues fancy. This one was the size of a small suitcase. I could have fit a pair of six-packs into the bottom of it comfortably. It had accordion sides and opened from the top. My father had given it to me when I graduated from Yale Law. It hadn't been new, even then. It had the initials H.F.S. engraved in gold on the side. "Harlan Fiske Stone," my father told me. "A very great lawyer and Supreme Court Justice. This was his. I think you're ready at least to carry Stone's briefcase now."

Actually, I didn't carry the briefcase. I valued it the way I would an old classic car. I didn't want to get it soiled or rained on. It was to own, not to use. Anyway, I didn't have that many occasions when I needed to lug around big sheafs of legal papers. When I did, carrying them in that big old clunker would constitute some kind of overkill. I had a slender attaché case of my own for that.

This time, though, I decided to use Harlan Fiske Stone's old briefcase. I stuffed it with the papers that lay on my desk and added two lawbooks that contained precedents for the Fallon case.

Then I went over to my office safe, opened it, and took out my Smith and Wesson .38 revolver. I snapped open the cylinder to confirm that I had left it unloaded. There was a box of cartridges in there, too. I loaded the gun and put it into the briefcase.

Zerk Garrett, when he worked with me, used to shriek and giggle when I carried the weapon with me. He was right—I was uncomfortable with it. In my pocket it bagged noticeably and bumped awkwardly against my hip. Nor did it feel natural in my hand.

The one time that I had occasion to take it out and aim it at another man, it was taken away from me. It had, in fact, been used to kill a man. Since that time it had left my safe only once, and that was when I was invited by a policeman I knew to shoot with him at the police range. I was impressed, at that time, by the noise it made, and by the way it bucked and leaped in my hand. It felt alive and powerful and I did not shoot it particularly accurately.

I wasn't sure if I could ever fire it at a human being. But I could point it and threaten with it. And I figured there was no harm having it with me. It was, at least, a minor comfort, when I reflected on the fact that somebody had killed Buddy Baron at my kitchen table.

I wondered if perhaps there was one man I could actually shoot at.

nine

JULIE WAS AT HER DESK WHEN I GOT
to the office Monday morning.

"Nice weekend?" she said.

"Don't ask." I plunked my battered old briefcase onto her desk, un-
clasped the top, and reached inside. I fumbled for the sheaf of papers I had
worked on all day Sunday. My hand touched the cold metal of the Smith
and Wesson. Foolishness, I thought. I removed the papers and quickly
snapped shut the briefcase.

I flourished the papers at Julie and set them atop her desk.

"My, my," she said, picking them up and flipping through them. "No
fishing trips? On the outs with all your lady friends?"

"I found a little spare time."

"It was a bad weekend."

"You don't know the half of it."

"Going to tell me?"

"You bring me a cup of coffee, I'll tell you."

"I'll bring you coffee because it's my turn."

I went into my office and she followed a minute later, bearing two mugs
of coffee. We sat on the sofa. I told her about finding Buddy's body in my
kitchen Friday evening, and my subsequent conversations with the police
and Tom Baron. As I talked, Julie stared solemnly at me. When I was
done, I shrugged. "So that's how it was."

"How horrible," she whispered. "Those poor, poor people."

"I think Tom and Joanie expect some wisdom out of me. I don't seem to
have any."

She regarded me solemnly. "And you," she said after a minute. "How
are you doing?"

I shrugged. "I'm tough."

"Oh, right."

"I'm okay."

"Bullshit," said Julie.

"Okay, so I'm not all right. So I can't get Buddy Baron out of my mind. So I keep thinking about my own boys, and how it must be for Tom."

"You don't need to be tough, you know, Counselor. It's okay to be objective and rational for other people. You can still have your own feelings."

"Well, you're right. Thank you."

"You're welcome. So what are you going to do?"

"Do? Nothing. Nothing different. Life goes on, right?"

"Right." She stood up and smoothed the front of her skirt against her thighs. "Life goes on. You get to work now."

"I can't stop thinking about Buddy."

"Think about him. That's okay. But get to work."

I flipped her a mock salute. "Aye, aye, sir."

She went out to her desk and I moved wearily to mine. I owed myself a vacation, I decided. I had determined a long time ago to be a one-man office precisely so that I could take vacations whenever I wanted to. Things kept happening to get in the way. I should have been an oral surgeon like Doc Adams. He kept taking lengthy, tax-deductible boondoggles to exotic places, in the guise of medical conferences, where days were spent flycasting for bonefish and tarpon, and evenings were devoted to drinking expensive whiskey and listening to other medical folks discuss the states of their arts.

The Commonwealth of Massachusetts requires these sessions of medical folks licensed here. I made a mental note to see what the state's bar association might come up with for us barristers.

In the meantime, I didn't have Doc's self-righteous explanation for his periodic ten-day abandonments of his practice. "Professional development, old chum," he liked to say. "Must stay *au courant,* don't you know."

When I'd ask him how hearing about new techniques in bowel surgery helped him extract impacted wisdom teeth, he'd waggle an eyebrow at me and give me some double-talk about holistic medicine.

He knew I didn't buy it. And he always came back with a great tan and photos of the fish he had snagged. Made me sick.

I vowed to get away at least once before the snow flew.

I was enjoying a mental debate between the Florida Keys and Mexico when Julie buzzed me. "Mr. Curry for you," she said.

"You were supposed to call me," said Curry when he came on the line.

"Busy as hell," I lied. "You were on my agenda. What's up?"

"I want to buy you lunch."

"You want to buy me lunch, you want something. What is it?"

"Let's discuss it over lunch, okay? Say at the men's bar at Locke Ober's at twelve-thirty?"

"In the first place, I'm always game for lunch at Locke's, but it's not the men's bar anymore. Ladies are shown every courtesy. In the second place, I want to know what this is about."

"Good. See you then."

"Wait a minute. This about Tom's campaign? Because if it is—"

"Twelve-thirty," repeated Curry, and he hung up.

"Son of a bitch," I growled into the dead telephone.

I hate being hung up on. I found the Boston phone number I had jotted down from Curry's message on my answering machine and I punched it out. An efficient female voice answered. "Republican headquarters. Baron for governor. May I help you?"

I asked for Eddy Curry and was placed on hold. I expected to hear a tape of "Happy Days Are Here Again." Or was that Democratic music? All I got was empty static.

A minute later Curry's voice said, "Curry."

I paused before I replaced the receiver on the hook. I felt much better.

Locke Ober's is located down a little dead-end alley off one of the streets that connect Tremont with Washington Street, just across from the Common. I walked to it from my office, sniffing the sharp autumn air and reconfirming the importance of a vacation. I arrived, as intended, a fashionable—and, I hoped, an insulting—twenty minutes late. The maitre d' steered me to a table in the corner near the bar. Curry was already there, stirring a Manhattan. I guessed it wasn't his first.

He half rose when I was deposited smoothly at my seat. "Hey, Brady," he began.

I ignored the hand he held to me and turned instead to the waiter who had materialized at my elbow. "Bourbon old-fashioned on the rocks," I told him.

"You don't need to be pissed off at me," said Curry.

"Who said I was pissed off?"

"You had to call back and hang up on me, right?"

I shrugged. "I didn't do that."

Curry grinned. "Right."

I grinned back and lit a cigarette.

Curry settled his head into his jowls like a turtle retreating into its shell. He regarded me out of hooded eyes. "Okay," I said. "So what's this all about?"

His eyes shifted to the glass he was slowly rotating on top of the table. "The candidate thinks very highly of you," he said. "For that matter, so does the candidate's wife." He glanced up at me and grinned. It was not a grin that conveyed humor, or good nature. Curry's grin was the expression of a large fish—a Northern pike, perhaps—with its eye on a wounded minnow. "Matter of fact," he continued, "it wouldn't surprise me if the candidate's wife had the old-fashioned hots for you."

"I've already talked to Tom about all this," I said.

Curry shook his ponderous head. "I doubt that."

"He asked me to be legal adviser to his campaign."

"Did he, now." It was not a question.

"Yes. He did. I told him I'd think about it."

The waiter slid my drink in front of me and hesitated. "Bring us another round in about ten minutes," said Curry. "We'll order lunch then."

"Very good," murmured the waiter. He pronounced it "vezzy." He looked Greek, or maybe Turkish.

When the waiter slipped away, Curry leaned forward. "No one knows better than you how tough this whole business has been on Tom and Joanie," he said. "I've been with them most of the weekend. Tom's a zombie. Joanie's a total basket case. I'm no shrink, but I don't see Tom making any kind of sudden recovery." He lifted his eyebrows at me.

I nodded. "I'm beginning to get your drift."

"Well. That's good."

"But why don't you spell it out for me anyway."

He shrugged. "Why not. Sure. Here it is. Tom Baron's a loser. No way in the six weeks between now and election can he recoup. Shit, a campaign based on law and order, old-fashioned morality, targeting drug pushers, no less, and his kid gets these kinds of headlines? The papers are chuckling up their sleeves and rubbing their hands together. And the polls are already disastrous. He lost four percentage points over the weekend." Curry peered at me. "Now do you get it?"

"Keep going."

He sighed. "Okay." He spread his hands flat on the table. "We want him to resign. It could be done gracefully, with class. Nice speech on the television. Family reasons. Mourning, right? Doing the grief thing. Wants to be with his wife. Everybody would understand. Tom would introduce his replacement. The party's got him all picked out. Perfect for the situation."

"Who?"

He shook his head. "Aw, I couldn't say right now."

"So you want Tom to resign. And Tom doesn't want to, right?"

"You got it."

"So where do I come in? How do I rate lunch at Locke Ober's? You think I'm important enough, you've got to let me in on all this smoke-filled-room stuff? Hell, you could have told me this on the phone. For that matter, you didn't have to tell me at all. None of my business. I never vote Republican anyway. Not since Frank Sargent. I wasn't going to vote for Tom Baron, and I'm not going to vote for his stand-in. So you don't have to feed me a fancy lunch."

"Come on, Coyne. Don't give me a hard time. You know what I want."

I shrugged. "I haven't heard it."

At this point our waiter returned with a manhattan for Curry and another old-fashioned for me. He slid menus in front of us, bowed, and moved discreetly away. I picked up the menu and scrutinized it. "What looks good to you?" I said.

"Dammit, Coyne. You wanna make me grovel, is that it?"

I nodded, very serious. "I want you to speak plainly. If that's groveling, okay. But first I think we should order."

Curry rolled his eyes.

I jerked my head at the waiter, who came over and said, "Sir?"

I ordered the swordfish, knowing it would still be twitching when they slid it under the broiler. Curry had something with a French name, which he pronounced badly.

After the waiter left, I said, "So why don't you fire him?"

"You can't just fire him. Christ, anybody knows that. He's gotta resign, and he's gotta resign gracefully, with dignity. And you're the only one who can talk him into it, dammit."

"What if I can't?"

Curry shrugged. "He loses."

"And what if I refuse to try?"

"Same damn thing."

"I'm a little slow," I said. "Let's see if I've finally got it. Tom Baron can't win. You want him to quit. But he doesn't want to. And you can't make him. So you want me to talk him into it. If I don't, he runs and loses. Right?"

"Exactly."

"We've got a problem, then."

Curry sighed.

"Because," I continued, "I'm not going to do it. He's been after me to be his legal adviser. I've been saying no. It's been selfish of me. I disagree with his politics. But then I see you. You're a useful example, Eddy. Know why?"

He shrugged his massive shoulders.

"Because you don't even have any politics, but you don't have a problem working with Tom. As far as I know, you do a good job. It doesn't matter what you believe or what kind of a human being you happen to be. You can help a candidate. Right?"

"If you say so."

"So it makes me realize there's no reason not to be Tom's legal adviser. I can vote any way I want and still work for him. And it happens that, among other advice I might offer him, one thing I'll say is to go ahead and run. Keep on with the campaign. The hell with your polls."

"So you're on, then."

"I'm on."

"Congratulations, I guess."

"You want to know why I'm on?"

Curry shrugged. "Go ahead. Tell me."

"Two reasons. One, I hate to see a man being treated like a piece of shit, kicked when he's down, abandoned when he needs support. I won't be a party to any of that. Second, Tom Baron has one compelling reason to continue his campaign, and becoming governor has nothing to do with it."

"And what could that be?"

"To clear his son's name. And his own. If he quits, people are going to assume that Buddy was a drug dealer and maybe a killer to boot."

Curry shrugged again. "Well . . ."

"See? You're assuming the same thing. Am I right?"

He spread his hands. "Who knows?"

"Guilty until proven innocent, right? Listen. I don't think Buddy Baron did anything wrong. I think he was a good kid who went through a bad time and had the spine to get through it. And then circumstances got him. If freedom and democracy and justice mean anything—if Tom's speeches mean anything at all—they mean that Buddy Baron shouldn't be tried and found guilty and punished after he's dead and can't defend himself. Tom can defend him. He'll have to, right? Now it's a campaign issue. See, I can help him with this. And I'm going to."

Curry stared at me for a minute, then hunched his neck. "This is a mistake," he said.

I shook my head. "I don't think so. I'm willing to live with it."

"Think it over. You'll change your mind."

"Nope."

"Well," he said, "we'll just have to try something else, then."

"You got any dirty tricks up your sleeve, you better think twice," I said. "Because Tom Baron's legal adviser is going to be on the alert for them."

Curry smiled placidly. "I don't think you wanna play hardball with us, Mr. Coyne."

"Oh, I don't know. I'm sort of looking forward to it." I pushed myself back from the table and stood up. "You can cancel my order. Or eat it yourself. Thanks for the drinks."

Curry waved his hand. "Aw, sit down. Relax. This is politics, for crissake, not anything serious. Hey, you win some, you lose some. For now, you win. It's okay. We can still have lunch together, some nice conversation. Come on. Sit."

I remained standing. "What do you want to talk about?"

"You follow the Patriots?"

I shrugged and sat. "Rather talk fishing."

Curry smiled. "I can talk anything. That's part of my charm."

The swordfish was, as expected, excellent, the Bibb lettuce salad crisp and cool. Curry regaled me with political stories. And he did turn out to have a sort of crude charm, at that.

"Never underestimate the importance of ethnics," he told me around a mouthful of lobster au-something.

"Ethics?" I said. "I wouldn't have thought ethics—"

"Ethnics," he interrupted, smiling. "Race. You know. This is a real issue with Tom Baron. Now, you and I know Tom's a Yankee. Good old WASP. But, see, the Irish, they think he's a Jew, and the WASPs, they've got him pegged for a wop who fixed up his name. The blacks assume he's some kind of Polack. The Hispanics, they don't trust anybody anyway. Nor do the Orientals. So what's he got? He's got nobody. He can't help it. And it ain't like he can go on the tube and explain himself. Candidates can't talk about stuff like this. Always somebody to offend. Everybody else talks about it, though."

While we waited for coffee, he told me about the candidate who participated in a charity bluefishing tournament a few years earlier. With the television cameras rolling, he barfed a couple of six-packs all over the microphone the interviewer was holding for him. There was some point about tactics Curry was trying to make with that tale. I wasn't sure I understood it.

On the subject of Tom Baron's wealth, Curry said, "The candidate can't win anyway. If he's rich, the voters figure he's a crook. If he's poor, they peg him for a loser. If he's rich and a lawyer, he's smart rich. If he's a real estate trader like Tom, he's dumb rich. Nobody likes either kind."

Later, Curry said, "What a political campaign is, it's a strategy, a bunch of tricks by which you take away as many reasons as you can for people to vote against your guy, and give them as many reasons as you can for them to vote against the opponent." He folded his arms across his big chest and smiled. "It's a helluva lot of fun."

As I walked back to my office from Locke Ober's, I figured out that Curry was trying to show me that a political campaign was no way to try to clear Buddy Baron's name with the public. Politics was shabby and petty and negative. It was dirty gutfighting, and I didn't know anything about it.

I had not intended to sign on as Tom's legal adviser. I had told him I'd think about it only to put him off until I could devise a graceful way to say no. Then Curry came at me like the bully I knew he was, and I reacted with my usual adolescent bravado. Kick sand in my face, eh? Not only do I refuse to talk Tom into resigning, but, by God, I'm going to help him win.

Showed that bully how tough I was.

And I could kiss that vacation good-bye, at least until after the first Tuesday after the first Monday in November.

By the time I got back to the office I was thoroughly depressed.

Julie greeted me with her usual sexy Irish smile. "Locke Ober's, huh? Have a nice time?"

"Great," I grumbled. "Pisser."

"Jeez," she said. "Good thing he didn't take you to Burger King."

I bent down and kissed the back of her neck. "Aw, I'm sorry, sweetheart."

I told her how I had stupidly committed myself to joining Tom Baron's campaign staff.

"I think that's lovely," she said. "I'm proud of you."

"Lovely," I said.

"No, really. Good for you." She paused and frowned. "You don't think he's going to win, do you?"

I laughed. "I hope not. That certainly isn't the point."

"Well, you going to tell him?"

"Suppose I ought to."

I went into my office and rang Tom's number. Joanie's slurry voice answered. "H'lo?"

"Joanie. It's Brady."

"My rock," she murmured. "Oh, Brady. Dear God."

"Joanie, I'm sorry. If there's something I can do . . ."

"Hold me," she whispered quickly. "Hold me, stroke me, hold me. Oh, dear, dear."

"Is Tom there?"

"You gonna come see me? Put your arms around me? Shut away all the bad? Hold me with your arms, those strong strong hands. . . ."

"I have to talk to Tom, Joanie. Is he there?"

I heard a man's voice in the background. Then Joanie suddenly shrieked. "Fucker!" A moment later Tom said, "Brady? Is that you?"

"It's me."

"Don't pay any attention to her. They've got her all doped up."

"It's okay."

"She'll be all right."

"Sure she will," I said.

"Did you think it over?"

"Yes," I said. "Yes, I did. If you still want me, I'm with you."

"Hey, that's tremendous. That's great news."

"Here's what I think," I said. "You've got to meet questions about Buddy head-on, okay? We cooperate with the police. We cooperate with the media. Buddy didn't do anything wrong. We both believe that. That's the message."

"I agree," said Tom.

I hesitated, then said, "Look, Tom. Just to make sure there's no misunderstanding. Our friendship is one thing. But I'm doing this for Buddy."

"I hear you. No problem. No conflict there."

"Winning isn't the point."

"Eddy Curry worries about that," said Tom. "She's blaming me, you know."

"Joanie."

"Yeah. You're the white knight, now."

"Why me?"

"It's got to be somebody. She thinks all this happened because I'm running for governor."

"She'll get over it," I said. "What about you, Tom? You blaming yourself, too?"

"I know it's irrational . . ."

"Whether it is or not, it's unproductive."

He sighed. "Tell it to Joanie."

"I'm not sure that's such a good idea. On the phone—"

"Yeah, I heard. Christ, Brady. She's sleeping in Buddy's bed now. Won't let me near her."

"Tom . . ."

"I'm sorry. Talk soon."

We said good-bye. I hung up the phone gently. I wondered what I had gotten myself into.

ten

THE YOUNG REPORTER TAPPED THE business end of the microphone and studied the portable cassette recorder, which rested atop the desk in my office. He sat in the chair beside me. I was behind my desk.

"Interview with Brady Coyle, October 3, ten A.M. in his office six floors above Copley Square in beautiful downtown Boston," he said, watching the little red bulb blink as he spoke. "Marv Adler, reporting."

"Coyne," I said.

He peered owlishly at me. "Huh?"

"Coyne. It's Brady Coyne. You said Coyle."

He shrugged. "Whatever. I'm confusing you with some guy from a novel. That one got shot to death, I think. I'll get it right when I write it up."

"You'd better get it right," I said.

I lit a cigarette and watched him examine the little pad of paper that lay open on the table beside the recorder. He wore a rumpled seersucker jacket over a blue button-down shirt. No tie. Jeans and sneakers. It looked like he had salvaged the jacket from the floor of his closet for the occasion.

"You ready, Mr. Coyne?"

"Shoot."

He cleared his throat. "Okay, then. For the record, sir, how would you describe your role in the Baron campaign?"

"I have no role in the campaign."

"But I have this press release—"

"I have been Tom Baron's personal lawyer for many years, and I continue to serve as his legal adviser. Since he has become a candidate for public office, some of the kinds of advice he may need will be different. That's all."

"Do you participate in strategy decisions?"

"No. Eddy Curry is his political strategist."

"But legal matters impinge on campaign strategy, don't they?"

"When and if they do, then I render advice."

"Can you give me an example of this?"

"Only hypothetical. It hasn't come up yet."

Marv Adler frowned. "Can you give me a hypothetical example?"

"Sure," I said. "Curry advises Tom to hire someone to assassinate his opponent. I tell him that it would violate a law and they shouldn't do it."

The reporter stared at me for a minute. "Look," he said after a minute, "I'm just trying to get a story here, okay? You agreed to the interview. Why are you being hostile?"

"I'm not being hostile. You haven't asked any good questions."

He sighed. "I was hoping you'd just sort of talk to me."

"I'm an attorney, Mr. Adler. I don't just sort of talk."

"Call me Marv, okay?"

"Happy to."

He flipped over a few pages in his notebook. "Well, then. Let's get to it. What about the Buddy Baron murder investigation? What's your role in that?"

"Like all good citizens, I am cooperating with the police."

"But as Baron's legal adviser—"

"I would have helped arrange Buddy's defense, had he lived and had he been arrested. Presently I am interested in seeing that he is not tried in the press."

Adler's eyes widened. "And do you feel that the press has dealt unfairly with the situation, Mr. Coyle?"

"It's Coyne, Marv. And no, I don't. So far the press has restrained itself."

"I'm glad we get high marks from you."

"I didn't say you got high marks. The press has had the sense to lay off for a while. Tom Baron's son was murdered. You people have given him a few days of space. But there's a juicy story there, and sooner or later you'll try to exploit it. That's probably what you're hoping for right now. When you do, my job will be to make sure nobody's rights get violated. Including those of Buddy Baron."

"So you think this is a juicy story." He narrowed his eyes.

I jabbed out my cigarette. I had chosen my words poorly. "What I meant," I said, "was that it's the kind of story the press thinks is juicy. I suppose the public laps that stuff up. That doesn't mean there's anything substantive to it."

"Do you think Buddy Baron killed the girl, Alice Sylvester?" he said, reading from his notes.

"No."

"Would you care to expand on that?"

"Sure," I said. "I don't think Buddy Baron killed Alice Sylvester. How's that?"

"Why? Is there some evidence, something that would prove . . ."

I hesitated. The germ of an idea crept into the edges of my consciousness. "I better not comment on that," I said.

Adler's face jerked as if I had spit in it. "What did you say?"

"I said, 'No comment.' "

"On the question about the evidence."

"Right."

He scribbled a note into the notebook, then peered up at me. "Can I ask why you refuse comment on that question?"

"You can ask. It would be pretty stupid for me to answer."

"Can I assume there may be some evidence?"

"I can't tell you what to assume, Marv."

He tightened his mouth. "Mr. Coyne, we're really just conversing here. If you want to say something off the record . . ."

"No, thank you."

"I can help you, you know."

I nodded. "I suppose you can."

"Let me ask you this," he said, staring intently at me. "Buddy Baron was murdered in your apartment. Why was he there that night?"

I lit another cigarette. "I'd better not answer that question, either."

"Another no comment?"

"Yes."

"But you had talked with him earlier, I understand."

"Yes. He came to me. He knew he had to turn himself in to the police. I was the family attorney."

"Then he ran away."

"He left my apartment, yes. The story's been in the paper's already."

"And then he came back again."

I nodded.

"To see you."

"I don't know why."

"To tell you something. Or give you something."

I stared at Adler. "I have no comment on that."

He frowned for an instant. Then he nodded quickly. "Right. No comment."

"You can quote me on that. No comment."

He cocked his head. "Sure," he said. "I probably will, at that. Let's go on. Do you think Tom Baron's going to win the election?"

"I have no idea."

"Do you intend to vote for him?"

"That's nobody's business."

"I know." He grinned. "Are you impressed with the way he has handled the issue of his son's murder in his recent speeches and press conferences?"

"He has handled it truthfully."

"But do you think it has been politically effective?"

"I have no expertise on what is politically effective."

"But as a citizen, what do you think?"

I shrugged. "It's not the sort of thing I think about very much."

"Was Buddy Baron a drug addict?"

I leaned forward. "Listen carefully, Marv. And you better not screw this up if you decide you have to write about it. A year and a half ago Buddy Baron had a drug problem. He was arrested for selling drugs. He used drugs. He had a dependency. I bet you knew that already."

Adler widened his eyes and nodded.

"He went to a rehabilitation facility in Pennsylvania for six weeks," I continued. "Since then, there was every indication that he was both drug-free and uninvolved in any drug dealing. All of this is well known, and I can't see how it's of any interest. But if you feel you've got to write about it, rest assured that I will read what you write. Very carefully. Do I make myself clear?"

He nodded. "Perfectly. But there are those who would say that when the boy was alive, he was a liability to Tom Baron's political aspirations, and that, now that he is dead, he is an asset. Would you care to comment?"

"Of course not."

"Why not?"

"If I told you, I'd be commenting, wouldn't I?"

He grinned. "Guess so."

"Let me say this, though. Buddy's death had nothing to do with politics."

"Really? What did it have to do with, then?"

I sat back and smiled broadly. "No comment, Marv."

He shook his head. "You're a very frustrating man to interview."

"Thank you."

"I thought you might like the chance to help me do a sympathetic story about the candidate and his son. Human interest. Profile in courage. Rising above adversity. Tragedy and triumph. See what I mean? But you're not being very cooperative, Mr. Coyne. How can I write this story if you won't cooperate?"

I shrugged. "I can't help you there, Marv."

"Don't you want me to write this story?"

"Not the story you want to write, no. It's a private matter. It shouldn't be a campaign issue, one way or the other."

"Correction," he said. "It is a campaign issue. Mr. Baron has made it a campaign issue. So it's fair game."

"Mr. Baron has not avoided the subject," I said. "But it was the press that made it a campaign issue."

"I won't concede that," he said. "And I think you don't really believe it, either. But regardless, Buddy Baron was the son of the candidate, and it would be irresponsible for the press not to point that out."

"Sure," I said. "And given that, it would be foolhardy for the candidate to ignore it. He didn't make it the issue. It has nothing to do with what kind of governor he'd make. But it's there. He's got to respond to it."

"You ask me," said the reporter, "it looks like he's making it *the* issue. Your man is running on a platform of his son's innocence."

"Is that a question, Marv?"

He smiled. "You got me excited, there. I'm supposed to be asking questions, aren't I? Sure. Make it a question. Is it fair to say that Mr. Baron is running on a single-issue platform—the innocence of his son? Is it fair to say that he is seeking the sympathy vote? Is it fair to say that he's trying to turn a disaster into something that will serve him?"

"I'm going to try to answer that for you," I said after a moment. "Not because I'm any expert. Just as an observer. First, in my opinion—and make it clear that I don't know for a fact if I'm right—Tom Baron has had to confront the issue of what happened to Buddy. That is political reality. He has said what he believes. That his son was a good kid who did nothing wrong. Which I happen to believe, too. Second, as to the sympathy vote, no, I don't think that's it, but you'd better check with Eddy Curry or Tom himself, because they're the ones who do the strategy. I think Tom would rather run on the issues. Third, I'm not aware of any disaster except that Tom Baron lost his son tragically. And that's a personal, not a political, disaster."

Adler nodded and wrote something onto his pad of paper. Then he looked up at me. "So who killed Buddy Baron?"

I laughed. "You think I know?"

"I bet you've got an idea."

"Off the record?"

He hesitated. "I'd rather not."

I shrugged.

"Okay," he said. "Off the record." He switched off the recorder, then looked up at me. "It's off. Here's the question. Who killed Buddy Baron?"

I leaned toward him. He bent to me. "I don't know," I whispered.

He sat back. "Well, thanks a shitload, Mr. Coyne."

"That was off the record, Marv."

"It was hardly worth recording."

"I didn't want it recorded."

He narrowed his eyes. "Are you . . . ?"

"Think about it, Marv."

He nodded slowly. "Okay. I think I get the picture. You ready to go back on the record now?"

"Yes," I said.

He turned on the machine. "For the record, Mr. Coyne. Do you know who killed Buddy Baron?"

"No comment, Marv."

His eyebrows twitched. "Are you working with the police on the Buddy Baron case?"

"No comment."

"What about the Alice Sylvester murder? Are you involved in that investigation?"

"No comment."

"Any link that you're aware of between the two cases?"

"No comment."

He sat back, frowned for an instant, then grinned. "Yeah, okay. I think I can use that."

"Good," I said. "End of interview."

I reached into my desk drawer and took out the tape recorder that had been quietly turning in there. I put it onto my desk and switched it off. The reporter stared at it for an instant, and then he grinned. "Good for you, Mr. Coyne," he said. "Nixon's got nothing on you."

He rewound the tape on his machine and played back part of it. Evidently satisfied that his equipment had functioned, he gathered up his gear. I led him to the door and shook his hand.

"Appreciate your time," he said.

"You're welcome."

"You're not an easy interview."

"Thanks."

*　　*　　*

The story appeared the next day on the page the *Globe* had begun to devote to campaign news. The headline read: "Murder a 'Juicy Story'— Baron Aide." I muttered "Jesus Christ" under my breath, folded the paper, and took it out onto my little balcony overlooking the harbor. I sat on one of the aluminum patio chairs, propped my feet up on the railing, and read on.

> Brady Coyne, a Boston attorney and the newly appointed legal adviser to the Republican gubernatorial candidate Thomas Baron, admitted in an interview yesterday that lurking beneath the facts was what he termed a "juicy story." "Tom Baron's son was murdered," said Coyne. "There's a juicy story there."
>
> Coyne, who said his role in the Baron campaign was "to make sure nobody's rights have been violated, including those of Buddy Baron," asserted, "I don't think Buddy Baron killed Alice Sylvester." When asked if he had evidence to support his belief, he declined comment.
>
> Coyne also refused comment on the question of whether he had somebody under suspicion for the murder of Baron's son, or whether he was conducting a private investigation. He further refused comment on the question of the relationship between the Baron murder and the earlier murder of Alice Sylvester. Both victims were teenagers from Windsor Harbor, hometown of Thomas Baron.
>
> Coyne also stated that the Baron murder was "a personal, not a political, tragedy."
>
> Boston Police also continue to decline comment on the Baron murder. Windsor Harbor Police Chief Harry Cusick announced in a press release: "The Alice Sylvester investigation is proceeding satisfactorily." He refused to answer reporter's questions.

I folded the newspaper and tucked it under the chair. The sun cracked the horizon, streaking the sky with spectacular red and orange patterns. Overhead hung purple globs of clouds, so dense that they looked as if they would fall to earth.

I went inside, showered, and shaved. I was munching a sugar doughnut out on the balcony again when the phone started ringing. I counted twelve rings before it stopped. A minute later it started again. Fourteen rings this time. I went back into the kitchen, poured myself some more coffee, and went on a necktie-hunting expedition, hoping to flush out one that wouldn't clash too badly with the gray herringbone suit I was wearing.

I found it on the floor beside the sofa under a stack of old *Field & Stream* magazines. A dark blue paisley pattern. Looked okay to me.

The phone rang again while I was fiddling with the knot. It stopped after seven. "Quitter," I said.

An hour later I answered the office phone myself, Julie having gone off to the ladies' room.

"Coyne, godammit," said the voice.

"You are persistent, Eddy, I'll give you that."

"Why don't you answer your telephone?"

"And interrupt my gourmet breakfast?"

"You mind telling me what's gotten into you? What's this 'juicy story' shit, anyway? You working for the bad guys here, or what?"

I sighed. "Not that I should have to explain myself to you, but that particular quote was yanked out of context, kicking and screaming."

"You said it, right?"

"I suppose I did. But from my point of view the interview served its purpose."

"And what the hell was that? To make sure McElroy wins?"

"All those no comments I got in there."

"Jesus," I heard Curry mutter. He paused, and I could hear the rustle of his newspaper. "I got it," he said. "Big fuckin' deal. What good do you think this is gonna do?"

"I haven't figured that out yet," I said cheerfully. "Can't do any harm, however."

"I gotta talk to our candidate," he growled.

"Listen," I said. "It's been great fun chitchatting with you like this. Perfect way to start my day. But you know how it is. Time is money. So, if all you wanted to do was schmooze a little . . ."

"It ain't," he said.

"It ain't?"

"You see the other story in the paper?"

"About the Patriots linebacker? Damn shame. Another knee. They've had more than their share—"

"The one that quotes the opponent, Coyne."

"What's McElroy saying now?"

"Get yourself a paper," growled Curry. "And next time save one of those no comments for when someone asks you to give an interview. 'Juicy story!' Good Christ!"

He hung up before I had the chance. He was good at that. I went out to the vestibule. Julie had returned to her desk. "Where's our paper?" I said.

She jerked her head at a side table. I gathered up the paper and brought it back into my office. I found the McElroy story on the same page as the one that quoted me. The headline read: "McElroy Charges Baron Hiding Behind Personal Tragedy."

I skimmed the article and got the gist of it. Tom Baron was refusing to confront the issues. Tom Baron was, by implication, daring his opponent to raise the question of Buddy's death. McElroy would have none of it. He had no intention of discussing what he called "my opponent's unfortunate family situation."

I thought the "unfortunate" was canny as hell.

McElroy went on to dare Baron to a television debate on what he termed "the real issues, not the phony issue of his son's death."

"When," asked McElroy rhetorically, "can we expect Mr. Baron to emerge from behind his veil of mourning? We are all sympathetic. Our hearts go out to Tom Baron and his family. But it is fair to the voters for him to continue to evade his responsibilities as a candidate for the highest political office in the Commonwealth? When will he become a candidate again? I am waiting for him. The voters are waiting for him."

McElroy, I decided, was a most formidable opponent. Probably had excellent advisers.

I put down the paper. Curry was blaming me for this? I called him at the Republican headquarters. When I was put through to him, I resisted the impulse to hang up on him.

"Don't lay this on me," I said to him. "Campaign strategy is your baby."

"Well, I am blaming you. Our esteemed candidate—who, by the way, has lost three more points since the funeral—is guilty as McElroy charges. All he wants to talk about is Buddy. Oh, he pretends he's after drug pushers, he talks about getting tough, shit like that. But it always comes back to these victims, as he calls them. And then he gets off on Buddy. 'Why, my own son,' he says, and we all groan, because we've heard it, we know what's coming. This is your doing, Coyne. The man's on a high horse and the voters ain't gonna put up with it. McElroy's making hay. Every time Tom opens his mouth, you can just see the votes drifting away. See, now the issue is that Tom's avoiding the issues. McElroy can't lose on that one. Because he's absolutely right."

"What do you want me to do?" I said, acknowledging to myself—but not to Curry, because he was too damn pompous for me to admit anything to, which, I was forced to admit, was pretty pompous of me—that he was right on all counts.

He chuckled. I recognized it. It was the same chuckle he had used to get me to sit down at the table at Locke Ober's when I threatened to walk out on him. "Hell, Brady," he said. "Talk to old Tom, willya? You're his friend here. He trusts you. Just tell him we need a little balance here. Tell him he's doing a helluva job on the Buddy thing, but now maybe he can start to get back to some of the other stuff. He don't listen to me. Just you. You and Joanie. Whaddya say?"

"Well," I said, awed by Curry's charm. "Maybe."

"He ain't gonna like that 'juicy story' crack of yours, either, you know."

"I told you. It was taken out of context."

"So sue the son of a bitch."

"I can't. I said it."

"Damn clever of you. Listen. Talk to our candidate, willya, Coyne?"

"Maybe. If I get a chance."

The chuckle again. "Terrific. Keep up the good work."

So I sipped my morning coffee and thought about it, and around eleven in the morning, finding myself with half an hour between appointments, I called the Baron house. I hoped Joanie wouldn't answer. Something else that didn't work out right.

"Oh, Brady," she said. "How nice."

The old lilt was back in her voice. I figured she had either been weaned from the tranquilizers, or else they had started her on a regimen of uppers.

"How are you doing, Joanie?"

"I am getting by. I am trying not to drink too much. I am off the pills, except for a Valium before bed to get a couple hours of nothing before the dreams come. I miss my boy so much that I feel like I swallowed a handful of razor blades and they're down there in my stomach churning around. But I am getting by. I've been to a few of Tom's things, and I find I can smile and shake hands without really thinking about it, and sometimes for whole minutes at a time I don't think about Buddy. Getting by. That's how I am."

"How's Tom?"

"Tom is—he's getting by, too." She laughed. I thought I detected an hysterical edge to it, as if it would change into a scream. But it didn't. "Everybody's getting by, Brady. Tom has the advantage over me, see. He's got things to do. Me? I'm putting in some bulbs. About the only thing to do this time of year. Tulips, daffs, crocus. It doesn't help that much. It doesn't exactly engage your mind. What you do, kneeling in the garden, is, you think. And then you cry. Everybody says it's good that I cry. I wish it felt good. Tom gets here and there, you know, making his speech, conferring, arguing with Eddy Curry. Keeps his mind off things, I guess." She took a long, deep breath, and I heard the hiss when she let it go. "Brady, I said things to you . . ."

"Forget it. It was those pills."

"Right," she said. "That's what it was." She hesitated. "Must've been the damn pills. You probably want to talk to Tom."

"Well, it's nice talking to you, but yes, if he's there."

"I'll get him. Hang on."

I heard her yell for Tom, and then he picked up the extension. "It's Brady," said Joanie. "I'm hanging up now." I said good-bye to her quickly before I heard the click.

"Tom?" I said.

"Hey, did you see the paper this morning?"

"Before you say anything," I said, "I was not misquoted, Tom. That line about a juicy story was taken out of context, but I said it. I'm damn sorry."

"I meant McElroy. What he said. About me hiding behind Buddy. Hell, I figured that juicy story line wasn't the old Brady Coyne, shrewd attorney, talking. Don't worry about it. But I've got to figure out what to do. I'd just as soon not give the damn election away."

"Listen to Curry, then. He understands politics."

"But you and I have a deal."

"I never said not to try to win."

"Look," he said earnestly. "It's not that I don't want to exonerate Buddy. You know that. But this isn't working."

"You've done what you can. Debate the bastard. Win the sucker."

"You almost sound like you're rooting for me." Tom sounded wistful, childlike, as if he really cared what I thought of him.

"I was never that impressed with McElroy," I said.

"You finding out anything? About the—the murder?"

"Nope. Not my job, Tom."

"But in that article, those no comments, it sounded as if—"

"You shouldn't pay too much attention to what you read in the papers. You know that."

He snorted. "For damn sure. Well, listen. Keep in touch, huh? You're still on the team, right?"

"Absolutely. I'm with you."

I spent most of that afternoon in court. More correctly, in the courthouse. I worked hard, did my job properly, and thereby managed to keep all of us out of the courtroom. My worthy adversary, an old-timer named Elliott Reynolds, with whom I've played poker a few times, and I worked out a settlement. We brought it to Her Honor, Judge Celia Hastings, in her chambers. She congratulated us for a job well done. Then we went back to our respective clients, shook hands all around, and reminded them how lucky they were to have clever barristers like us on their side.

Then Reynolds and I dropped in at Remington's on Boylston Street for a few celebratory martinis, which Reynolds insisted on paying for since he thought he'd gotten the better of me, which, of course, was a normal misperception, but one he felt so strongly about that I decided it would be unkind of me to disabuse him of his illusion. So I let him pay.

I took a cab back to the office. When I walked in, Julie cocked her head at me and said, "Woo-whee!" as she jumped up to grab my arm. "Where have you been?" she said, steering me toward a chair.

"Been to court. That's what we lawyers do. Go to court. Settled. Helluva job. That old bag Hastings loved it. Elliott Reynolds and me went to Remington's. Nice place. They got prints by that painter, Frederic Remington, on the walls. Cowboys and Indians. Cattle drives. Buffalo hunts. Wonderful stuff. That guy Elliott's a good shit. Bought me some martinis. They make a helluva martini at Remington's. Gonna take you and Edward there sometime, have martinis. Anybody call?"

"You are sloshed, Counselor. I'm getting you some coffee. Sit still."

"Rather have 'nother martini."

"Coffee," said Julie. It sounded like a command. Like "Sit," or "Roll over," or "Play dead."

She brought me a mug and sat with me while I drank it. Then she brought me another. I burned the roof of my mouth on it. When I complained, Julie said, "Well, good. It means you're not completely numb."

Then I got up and went to the lavatory. I urinated for a long time, splashed cold water onto my face, and then dared take a look at it in the mirror. "You old rogue, you," I said to my gray-eyed image. "You don't look like a drunk. You look like one helluva successful attorney, you do."

I didn't like the way I sounded, so I filled the sink with cold water and immersed my face in it. After doing that a few times, I began to feel worse. Which meant I had begun to sober up. So I dried off on a ream of paper towels and went back to the office.

Julie was putting on her coat. The dust cover was on the word processor. "You leaving?" I said, feeling self-conscious about my enunciation.

"You all right now?"

"Oh, yeah. The headache is right here—" I pointed with both forefingers at my temples "—meaning I am sober. Sober, hurting, regretful, depressed. Therefore, I'm fine."

"Good." She came over and brushed my cheek with a kiss. "You're so cute when you're loaded." She headed for the door. "You did have one call," she said over her shoulder.

"Only one?"

"Only one I couldn't handle myself."

"Who?"

"Somebody named Christie, no last name, from Windsor Harbor. She left a number. It's on your desk."

"So what's this Christie want?"

"These broads of yours. They never tell me."

"I don't know a Christie."

Julie rolled her eyes.

"I'll call her tomorrow."

"You've got to call her this afternoon. She's waiting near a pay phone. I told her I didn't know when you'd be back. She said she'd wait."

I looked at my watch. It was a little after five. "How long did she say she'd wait?"

"You better call her," said Julie. "She said she'd wait forever if she had to. It sounded like she was agitated."

"Christie, Christie . . . ," I mumbled, shaking my head at my alcohol-fuddled memory.

"She did sound kind of sexy," said Julie.

"And she'd wait forever, huh? Well, I guess I better call her."

eleven

I WENT INTO MY OFFICE. IN THE precise center of my blotter, squared with the corners, was Julie's note with the name "Christie" on it and a phone number. "You want to call this one," Julie had noted. "She sounds eager."

My secretary knew the difference between eager and anxious, so I was surprised at the distinct anxiety I heard in the voice that answered halfway through the second ring. "Mr. Coyne," she said when she picked up the phone. "Is that you?"

"It is I," I replied, with the careful attention to grammatical exactitude I typically employ when I am in the process of sobering up. "You are Christie?"

"Are you the same Mr. Coyne who was in the paper this morning? The one who knew Buddy Baron?"

"The same. And you—"

"Were you the guy who came to school a week or so ago? That I saw with Dr. Larsen and Mr. Speer?"

"Yes. That was me." So much for good grammar.

"I heard Mr. Speer on the phone use your name." She paused, as if she didn't know what to say next.

"How can I help you?"

"I'm—I need to talk to somebody."

"Tell me your last name, Christie."

"Oh. It's Christie Ayers. Look. Listen to me. I'm really like nervous here, Mr. Coyne. Can I talk to you?"

"About what?"

"About Buddy and Alice and stuff."

"What sort of stuff."

"I really don't want to do this on the phone. I was just hoping you could meet me somewhere."

"Of course. Where are you now?"

"Look. There's a little ice cream shop over in Essex. Shirley and Joe's. It's not far from here. No one knows me there. I've got my folks' car. I really need to talk to somebody. I'm kinda scared, truthfully. I can't think of anybody else."

"You haven't talked to anybody? What about your parents? Somebody at school? The police?"

"You don't understand. I'll try to explain. Will you come? Please?"

I said I would, and she gave me directions to the place in Essex.

"I'm on my way," I said.

"No. Make it seven-thirty. I've gotta—you know, set it up. With my folks."

"Fine," I said. "Just be careful."

"Anyway," she said, after I repeated her directions back to her, "you've got some ideas about who killed Buddy, huh?"

"What makes you say that?"

"That thing in the paper. When you wouldn't comment. That's like a hint, right? That's the way the cops do when they're just about ready to arrest some guy. They say, 'No comment.'"

"Christie, you can't believe everything you read."

"Whatever that's supposed to mean," she said.

After we hung up, I called Sylvie, who was now back in town. "Time to redeem that raincheck on monkfish," I said.

"Do you promise this time?"

"I promise."

I swung around to Sylvie's condo, double-parked on Beacon Street, and went in to get her. She buzzed me up, and when I got to her door I rapped lightly on it. She opened it a crack, gave me a green-eyed grin, unlatched the chain, and let me in. She was wearing one of those frilly little one-piece undergarments like Frederick's of Hollywood advertises in the backs of magazines. A teddy, I believe it's called. She put both arms around my neck and kissed me.

I reached up and gripped her arms. She pulled her head back to look at me. It caused her body to press harder against mine. "Not in the mood?" She smirked.

"It's amazing how the mood can unexpectedly come over a man."

She rotated her pelvis against me. "You," she said, "are in the mood."

"But I am also double-parked. And on a tight schedule. Throw something on, huh?"

She stepped back, stuck her tongue out at me, and disappeared into her bedroom. She emerged no more than two minutes later wearing a lime-green dress that picked up the color of her eyes. It had a scoop neck. She wore a single, thin gold chain around her neck. The heart-shaped pendant that dangled from it created the effect of an arrow pointing to her cleavage. Not that any arrow was needed.

She twirled around. "Like it?"

I nodded. "Not bad."

"Finish the zip."

She put her back to me and I zipped up her dress. I suspected she had managed to zip herself all the way up all by herself many times. She picked up her purse and a cream-colored jacket and said, "I'm ready. For anything."

When we got into the car, which miraculously had been neither tagged nor towed, I said, "Are you still wearing that little underwear thing?"

"My teddy?" She giggled. "No."

When we pulled into the parking garage under my apartment fifteen minutes later, Sylvie said, "I took it off."

"Huh?"

"My teddy. I took it off. It makes lines."

"Of course," I muttered.

We stopped at my place only long enough for me to exchange the herringbone suit for a pair of gray corduroy slacks and a Harris tweed sportcoat. Then we were back in the car and crossing over the Tobin Bridge, headed for Essex.

When we pulled onto Route 128, I said to Sylvie, "Are you naked under that dress?"

She touched the hair at the back of my neck. "We are all naked under our clothes, aren't we?"

Later, after we left the highway and were following a secondary road according to the directions Christie Ayers had given me, I said, "Dammit anyway, Sylvie. This is unfair."

"What is unfair?"

"Not wearing underwear."

"Does it show?"

"That's not the point. I know."

I pulled into the gravel parking lot of the little place called Shirley and Joe's. It was a low-slung shingled affair. A tidal inlet wandered through a marsh out back. There were half a dozen cars parked in the lot. I shut off the ignition and turned to Sylvie. While I was kissing her I ran my hand experimentally over her hip. Damned if she hadn't been telling the truth. No lines at all.

Shirley and Joe's was a pizza-hamburger-hot fudge sundae sort of place. Two walls lined with booths, a counter with a dozen stools, and an old-fashioned jukebox. To my delight, the song it was playing was an oldie by Pat Boone. Not that I liked Pat Boone especially. But all the contemporary alternatives were so much worse.

I blinked and looked around and saw a hand wave from one of the booths. I took Sylvie by the elbow and steered her over.

Christie Ayers looked vaguely familiar to me. When she lost her baby fat and decided how to handle her brown hair, which presently was allowed to hang in undisciplined strings around her ears and over her forehead, she might be pretty.

She wore a baggy blue sweatshirt with WHHS on it and too much green eyeshadow. She smiled nervously and motioned for me and Sylvie to sit across from her.

In this place Sylvie managed to be to both overdressed and underdressed at the same time.

"Well," said Christie, brushing the hair away from her eyes, "I'm Christie, in case you didn't figure it out. I know you're Mr. Coyne. You were at school."

"This is Sylvie Szabo," I said.

"Oh, hi. You're very beautiful."

Sylvie smiled. "Thank you."

"Christie," I began.

"You want something? Milk shake, sundae, like that? I'm gonna have a milk shake."

"Whatever," I said. "I remember now. You were in the computer room. The teacher—Speer, right?—was helping you."

A teenage boy wearing a white jacket stained liberally with pizza sauce and chocolate ice cream, his lips barely closing over a mouthful of braces, came over to us with a pencil poised above a pad. He frowned at the pad and mumbled, "Can I get you something?"

"Strawberry milk shake," said Christie.

Sylvie elbowed me in the ribs. "Brady promised monkfish."

"Not here," I said.

"Tea, please, then," said Sylvie. "With lemon."

"I'll just have coffee," I said.

The boy took meticulous notes, then looked up and said, "That's it?"

"Thank you," I said. When he walked away, I said to Christie, "Okay, then. What's on your mind?"

She stared at her hands, which lay on top of the table picking at each other. "I'm kinda nervous about this, to tell you the truth," she said without looking up. "My friends call me Christie Airhead. You know? Ayers? Airhead? They think it's funny." She appealed with her eyes to Sylvie. "It's not fair. But, jeez, I feel like an airhead right now. This was really dumb."

Sylvie reached across and patted her busy hands. "It's all right," she said. "Brady is a very good attorney. He will help you. You must relax. And stop doing that to your nails."

Christie stared at Sylvie. Then she smiled and nodded. She turned to me. "See, I stole something. That's why I can't talk to anybody."

"What did you steal?"

"Something at school. I mean, if my parents knew they'd kill me. Literally. And obviously I can't tell anybody at school. So I thought of you, naturally."

I shrugged. "Naturally."

"I mean, you being Buddy's lawyer and all."

"This isn't all that clear to me, Christie. What did you steal?"

"A file. Alice Sylvester's file."

"Her records, you mean."

"Right. Her file. If they find out, I'll get bounced. I don't need that. I'm just starting to get my act together, you know?"

I nodded. "Why don't you just tell me the whole thing. It's okay."

Christie glanced at Sylvie, who nodded to her. Then she looked at me. "From the beginning, you mean?"

"Yes. From the beginning."

"Well, okay." Her fingers began nibbling at each other again. "See, Alice and I were best friends. Were, I mean, up until the beginning of school this year. Before that, well, I guess we hung out together about all the time. She was real nice to me. Alice was so popular and pretty, and, well, I was sort of a loser, actually. It was flattering to me that she seemed to like me. She would tell me stuff—about boys, and what she did. Stuff she wouldn't tell to anybody else. Like she really trusted me. Alice did a lot of things I never did, believe me. Not that she was really wild or anything. Not then. It's just, she went to parties and everything. Stuff I never did. I don't want you to get me wrong, Mr. Coyne. I'm not saying Alice did bad things."

She looked up with her eyebrows arched, asking for understanding. I nodded to her.

"Anyway, she changed right after school started up in September. She started ignoring me, for one thing. She even said rude things to me. Told me to get lost, only not like that, if you know what I mean. And she started skipping classes. I know she wasn't doing any homework. And she was treating Buddy real bad."

"What about Buddy?"

"Oh, well, she was going with him. She had been since last spring some time. Her parents were like bullshit about it—pardon my French—but Alice didn't care. I mean, she did care, back at the beginning. She cared about her parents, I mean. But she really loved Buddy. She'd tell me what a nice boy he was, polite with her and all, how he respected her, and how sometimes she'd feel all sexy with him and it was Buddy who'd stop." Christie stopped and frowned at me. "This is just stuff she told me, Mr. Coyne. I mean, I don't really know . . ."

"That's fine. Keep going."

"Anyway, all that changed around the time school started. Like real suddenly. She was different to Buddy, different to me. Even to her parents. They called me once, asking me, like, what's the matter with Alice? I didn't know. What could I tell them? I didn't figure it out until later."

"Crack," I said.

She nodded. "Yeah. I didn't figure it out until I read something about it, and I looked at all the symptoms, and I said to myself, 'That's Alice,' I said. So I went to her. I told her. I said, you're killing yourself, what are you doing, we all love you, you gotta get help, look at yourself. She laughed at me. She told me to—to get lost, if you follow me. I talked to Buddy about it. He wouldn't believe me. He said she was just moody, she was nervous about college, had a lot of things on her mind, stuff like that. I mean, after everything Buddy went through, you'd think he'd be smarter. Now that I think about it, though, I think maybe he really did believe me, deep down inside of him. He just couldn't admit it. Because of his own problems. Anyway—"

The boy with the braces brought our order. Christie stirred her milk shake with a straw until he went away.

"Anyway," she continued, "then Alice died. I mean, okay, she was murdered. Wow, it's hard to even say it. And if you think I know who killed her or something, well, I don't. That's not it. Anyway, a few days after that I get this call from Buddy. He wants me to go into a cabinet and steal Alice's file. He tells me exactly where to go, when to go there, what to do. All of it. He says it's because he's figuring out who killed her, see, and if I was really her best friend I'd do this for him. For Alice."

Christie dipped and sucked on her straw. Then she looked up at me and shrugged. "So I did it. Just the way he said. Alice's guidance counselor leaves her door unlocked when she goes to the teachers' cafeteria for lunch. Same time every day. It was simple, just like Buddy said. Each kid has a folder with all kinds of stuff in it. Alphabetical. I just pulled open the drawer and found S and there was Sylvester, right near the end next to T. I took it and put it under my jacket, just like Buddy said."

"How did you get it to Buddy?"

She grinned. "I met him right here, at Shirley and Joe's. That same night. He called me at home around supper. I told him I got it. So we met here. In the parking lot, actually. He wouldn't come in. He said he didn't want anybody to see him. I figure he was trying to protect me, don't you think? I mean, so nobody would see me with him."

"That's very possible," I said.

"So I gave him Alice's file, with all the stuff in it."

"Did he tell you what he was looking for in the file?"

She frowned. "No. When I gave it to him, he went through it, kind of holding it in front of him sort of half open and flipping through the papers. He found what he wanted, though."

"How do you know?"

"He took out this one paper and he kinda studied it. And then he looked at me and said, 'bull's-eye.' "

"He said 'bull's-eye'?"

"Yes. I figure that means he got what he was after. So he thanked me and drove away. Then, like the next day, I find out he was killed. And it happened at your house, right?"

I nodded. "Right."

"Well, I started thinking it had something to do with that file. I mean, I don't know, but the timing of it—you understand? It's very confusing to me."

"I understand," I said.

"But the thing was, I was so scared. I mean, not just that I stole the file. That was bad enough if I got caught. But somebody killed Buddy, and somebody killed Alice, and they were like my best friends, and that is really scary. Then I saw the paper today, and I remembered you at school, and I figured you were the same person, Buddy's lawyer, and I know how lawyers are supposed to, you know . . ."

"Client privilege, you mean," I said.

"Yes. That's it."

"Of course, technically, Christie, you're not my client."

She frowned. "Oh, jeez . . ."

"And," I continued, "as an officer of the court, it's my duty to report anything I learn about a murder case to the authorities."

"But you can't. That's not fair."

"Unless, of course, you had retained me."

"But . . ."

"Do you want to retain Brady?" said Sylvie.

"I'm not sure . . ."

"Hire him," said Sylvie gently. "Do you want him to be your lawyer?"

She nodded. "Well, yeah." She looked from Sylvie to me. "I mean, I didn't think I had to hire you or anything. I figured I could talk to you." Tears brimmed her eyes. "Oh, shit. I can't afford a lawyer. My parents would . . ."

"You don't have to pay me," I said. I ripped a page from the pocket-sized notebook I carried in my jacket. I pushed it across the table to her, along with a ball-point pen. "Just write on it that you are retaining Brady Coyne as your attorney, sign your name, and write the date."

"That's all? I don't have to pay you?"

"That's all," I said.

She hunched over the paper and frowned in concentration as she wrote. Then she handed me the paper and the pen. She had written: "I retane Brady Coyne as my lawyer." It was close enough.

"Now," I said, pocketing the slip of paper, "you are my client. You have just retained me. That means that I must protect you. I cannot tell anybody else what you tell me. You can tell me anything at all. You are a privileged client."

She smiled. I realized she hadn't really smiled since I had met her. She had a lovely smile. "Well, that's cool," she said.

I touched her hand. "Having said that," I said, "I have to say this now. We probably should tell the police."

She frowned. "But you just said—"

"Right. I am advising you, now."

"I thought I could trust you."

"Christie," I said. "Listen. There are two murders involved here. You wouldn't want to hinder the police, would you? You want them to get whoever killed Alice and Buddy, don't you?"

She was shaking her head. "I told you what I know. Now you want me to get in trouble."

"Listen to Brady, dear," said Sylvie.

"I shouldn'ta come here," she muttered. "My father was right."

"Your father?"

"He always says, you do what's right, and let other people worry about themselves. Mind your own business and you'll get along fine. I shouldn'ta taken the file and I shouldn'ta told you."

Tears began to overflow her eyes. I'm a sucker for any female who cries. I reached across the table and put my hand on her wrist. "I probably wouldn't have to tell all of this to the police. They won't be interested in the fact that you took the file."

Christie snuffled and looked up at me. "Really?"

I nodded. "But you should understand that sometimes doing what's right means you can't mind your own business. Sometimes you have to pay a price to do what's right. I think you know what's right. Taking that file, that was something you did for a friend. For a good reason. Nobody can get too upset about that. Not under these circumstances. It's not really the same as stealing. Especially if telling me about it helps to solve the case."

"Will it, do you think?" Her eyes were wide with hope. "Solve the case, I mean?"

I shrugged. "I don't know."

"Do you have to tell the cops?"

"I don't know that either. Let me ask you a different question. Okay?"

She wiped her nose on her sleeve. "Okay."

"Try to think. See if you can remember what it was that Buddy pulled out of that file. When he said 'bull's-eye.' "

She squinted, as if the unfocused picture was in front of her. Then she shrugged. "It was on computer paper, that's all I can say. That wide kind with the green-and-white stripes."

"Did it remind you of any kind of document you're familiar with?"

"Oh, jeez, they print everything on that stuff. Letters, report cards, progress reports."

"So you have no idea."

"I'm sorry, Mr. Coyne. No idea."

I picked up my coffee cup. My coffee was cold. Then I felt Sylvie's hand creep onto my thigh, where she began scratching gently with one long fingernail. I glanced at my watch. Christie sucked on her straw until it made gurgling noises in the bottom of the glass. I said, 'Christie, you did the right thing, calling me and telling me all of this. And don't worry. I will protect your confidentiality. I'll keep your name out of it. Okay?"

She smiled and nodded.

"The other thing is, I don't want you telling anybody else about it. Nobody. Not even your best friend."

"My best friend was Alice," she said softly.

I picked up the damp check the boy had left by my elbow. "Right now," I said to Christie, "Miss Szabo and I have an appointment."

The three of us walked out to the parking lot together. Christie climbed into a late-model Chrysler—Daddy's car, I assumed. He probably figured that his Christie was at the library searching for old books on the Civil War, instead of meeting strange attorneys at ice cream parlors.

Sylvie and I cut through the back roads, heading for Gert's, where the monkfish would be off today's boat, the vegetables fresh from local gardens, and the breads baked that afternoon. If Gert's were located in the city, and if it were discovered by the Bacon Hill crowd, you'd have to call a week in advance for reservations, and even then, you'd only get a table if you held office or if Gert knew you.

But Gert's is situated on Route 127 outside of Gloucester. It hasn't been discovered yet, though I fear its days are numbered. It's a simple, square, weathered building. The sign outside says only, "Good Food," which, for those of us who know better, is like saying Shakespeare wrote good sonnets. Gert's features red-and-white checked oilcloth tablecloths, cloth napkins the size of bath towels, candles in old Chianti bottles, fishing nets and lobster buoys hung from the knotty pine walls, and a view of thick woods beyond the parking lot and the big dumpster out back.

The waitresses are all local girls. They sweat a lot.

The music that drifts over the good speaker system is all Italian. It ranges from Verdi to Julius La Rosa.

People go to Gert's for the food. I know no one who has ever been disappointed.

I feel about Gert's the same way I feel about a certain trout stream in north-central Vermont. I only tell my closest friends about the place.

Sylvie and I shared a bowl mounded high with steamed mussels reeking of garlic and butter, which we washed down with several glasses of the dusty house white. Then came the monkfish, an exquisite white-fleshed fish, delicate almost—but not quite—to the point of blandness. Gert seasoned it with a little lemon juice and freshly cracked black peppercorns.

Sylvie and I ate earnestly. It was one of the things I loved about Sylvie. She knows when to eat and when to talk and when to make love, and she knows when not to mix up her priorities among them.

It was a little after ten when we left Gert's. As we crossed the parking lot heading for my car, Sylvie put her arm around my waist and leaned her head against my shoulder. Our hips bumped awkwardly as we walked. "I'm really tired," she mumbled.

"I'll take you right home and tuck you in."

"That's not what I had in mind."

"My house, then."

She chuckled deep in her throat. It reminded me of what she was wearing.

I couldn't wait to get my hands on her.

She dozed in the car. I played a Benny Goodman tape, happy that his music was outliving him. An hour later I pulled into my spot in the parking garage in the bowels of my apartment building.

In the elevator on the way up, apparently refreshed by her nap, Sylvie leaned against me, her mouth lifted, her eyes half shut. It was a long kiss, the full six floors, and it was accompanied by some preliminary groping and stroking, and we didn't break it off until the elevator door slid open.

We walked over to my door. Sylvie hung on to my arm while I patted my pockets for the key. "Want me to help look?" she said, slithering her hand into my pocket.

"Jesus, cut it out," I said.

I found the key, unlocked the door, and Sylvie and I stepped inside. I found the light switch and flicked it on.

"Welcome home," said a voice.

He was a jowly guy. He was wearing a rumpled suit, and he was sitting at my kitchen table. He held up both hands, like a priest blessing his congregation. "Come on in. Make yourselves comfortable."

"Yeah. Get over there and siddown." This was a different voice, and it came from behind us.

I pivoted around to look. A tall, gaunt man wearing a dark windbreaker stood inside the doorway. He kicked the door shut behind us, his eyes never leaving me and Sylvie.

He held a very large automatic pistol in his hand. It was aimed at my sternum.

twelve

"WHO THE HELL ARE YOU?" I SAID TO the fat guy at the table.

He had squinty, pig eyes, and when he smiled his cheeks bunched up and almost obscured them completely. "Mr. Curry, sir," he replied. The last word was a genuine Southern "suh." He gave a courtly dip of his head. "And this gentleman is Mr. Baron."

"Mr. Baron," the gaunt guy with the gun, grinned wolfishly at their joke. Then he waved at me and Sylvie with his gun. "G'wan," he grunted. "Get over there."

Sylvie and I moved toward the table where "Mr. Curry" was seated. He pushed himself out of his chair and held it, gesturing with a sweep of his hand that Sylvie should sit there. She looked at me. I nodded. She sat down. The thin man, "Mr. Baron," poked me again, and I sat at the table across from Sylvie.

"How'd you get into my apartment?" I said.

"Your young friend was kind enough to let us borrow his key," said "Mr. Curry."

"Buddy."

"A very courageous young man," said the fat man.

"Did you have to kill him?"

"An unfortunate accident, sir. Unfortunate in several respects. Unfortunate, of course, for poor young Mr. Baron. Also unfortunate for this Mr. Baron here, and for me. Because the young gentleman failed to disclose the information we sought from him. He had the lack of consideration to die too quickly."

I nodded. Sylvie was staring wide-eyed at me. "These are the men who killed Buddy Baron," I told her. "Their names aren't really Baron and Curry. They think it's a joke."

"Oh, it is," said Mr. Curry, puffing his cheeks again. "It's a good joke." He was standing at one side of the table, both hands flat upon it, leaning forward so he could talk confidentially with us. Mr. Baron was leaning against the kitchen sink across the room, one ankle crossed over the other. He kept his gun pointed at me.

Mr. Curry turned to Sylvie. "You're a pretty one," he said. "Stand up, sweetheart."

Sylvie frowned at him and didn't move.

"Come on, darlin'," he said. "Lemme have a look at you, like a good girl."

"Leave her alone," I said. "She's got nothing to do with any of this."

Mr. Curry whirled to face me. His pale pig eyes glittered. "You shut the fuck up, friend. I'm getting to you."

"Oh, dear," I said, fluttering my eyelids. "The mean man is threatening me."

Mr. Curry twitched his head at Mr. Baron, who slowly unlimbered himself and ambled across the kitchen toward me until he was standing beside my right shoulder. "Hey," he whispered. "Hey, asshole."

"Up yours," I said wearily, without turning around.

Mr. Curry grabbed a handful of Sylvie's blond hair and gave it a sudden yank. Her head snapped backwards. She started to say something, but the words were choked as her throat was constricted by the motion.

I instinctively put my hands on the table and began to push myself up when Mr. Baron hit me with his gun barrel. He did it casually, the way one might swipe at a pesky housefly, and he caught me across the bridge of my nose. I saw a white flash of pain, and I heard the familiar crunch that meant another broken nose. It's the sound you hear when you step on a pavement littered with acorns, and you'd swear it's just as loud. But in fact, it's a noise heard only inside your own head.

"Aw, shit," I said. Tears were running down my cheeks, mingling with the blood from the gash across my nose and all the ruptured blood vessels inside.

Mr. Curry had hoisted Sylvie out of her chair, and he held her pressed backwards against his fat body, one wrist against her throat, the other arm across her chest. Sylvie was looking at me. There was no fear in her expression.

"Brady," she said.

"I'm okay," I told her. To the fat guy, I said, "Why don't you let her go?"

"Because, sir, we need something from you, and we are perfectly willing to do whatever needs to be done to get it. And I am not sure you believe that quite yet. Now do you understand?"

"What do you want?"

"Why, sir, I believe you know that. I surely do."

"I don't know what you're talking about."

Mr. Curry moved his hand so that it cupped Sylvie's breast. She tried to move her mouth to bite the wrist that was levered against her throat. He increased the pressure, and Sylvie made a gagging sound. Suddenly Mr. Curry squeezed her breast. I could see his fingers dig in cruelly. Sylvie's scream was pure pain. I instinctively started up from my chair. Mr. Baron whacked the side of my neck with his gun, and for an instant my entire left arm went numb. I slumped back into my chair.

I looked helplessly at Sylvie. Tears ran down her cheeks, whether from pain or anger or humiliation I couldn't tell. "Do not hurt him," she said hoarsely.

"I'm okay," I managed to say, although I was sure I didn't look it, the way the blood continued to drip onto the front of my shirt from my poor nose.

"Well, Mr. Coyne? What do you say?" The fat man was panting, from the combination of exertion and sexual arousal, I judged.

"What are you after?"

The skinny guy was holding the muzzle of his gun against the back of my neck. I figured he'd enjoy using it. So I had to watch as Mr. Curry grabbed the neckline of Sylvie's dress and ripped it down, exposing both of her breasts.

"Hey, look," said the thin man with the gun. "Bare tits. She ain't got on any underwear."

I felt the muscles in my shoulders and back tense. The fat man took one of Sylvie's nipples between his thumb and forefinger and manipulated it experimentally. Suddenly he squeezed it hard. Sylvie screamed. I half rose in my chair, and Mr. Baron tapped me square on the top of my head with the butt of his gun. The pain shot straight down to my rectum.

I was drenched with sweat. My muscles were drained of strength. I could only slump there and watch as Mr. Curry's fat hand reached down to the hem of Sylvie's dress and lifted it up. "My heavens, look at this," he chortled.

From behind me I heard the skinny man's lewd laugh. "Blonde, by crackey!" he said.

The fat man's red suety face was all bunched up so that it looked like a ball of uncooked hamburg. His fingers moved over Sylvie's thighs and bare belly.

"How about my turn?" said the man with the gun.

"We shall take turns, Mr. Baron," said the fat one, his bulk shaking at the humor of it all. "I shall go first."

"Wait," I said.

"Excuse me, sir?"

"I said wait. I'll give you what you want. I have it."

"An intelligent young man after all."

"Take your hands off the lady."

"Not until we have what we came for, sir."

"It's in the other room."

"Where?" said the skinny one.

"I can get it."

Mr. Curry jerked his head at Mr. Baron. "Okay. Go with him."

"It's just in the bedroom," I said.

I felt the gun barrel prod at my kidneys. "Let's go, asshole."

I limped slowly into my bedroom, flipped on the light switch, and went to the corner where my Harlan Fiske Stone briefcase stood. I pointed to it. "It's in there," I told Mr. Baron.

"Pick it up," he said.

I reached down and grabbed the leather handle.

"Bring it out."

I lugged the briefcase back into the kitchen. Sylvie and Mr. Curry seemed to have arrived at a kind of stalemate. He had let the hem of her dress drop, and he was fondling her bare left breast mechanically, kneading it as if it were a wad of pizza dough, while Sylvie sagged back against him, her eyes closed, her mouth set in a grimace of resignation.

I hefted the briefcase onto the table. "Now will you let her go?" I said to the fat man.

Mr. Baron stood across the table from me, facing me, his gun pointing at my chest. Mr. Curry remained at my left, still holding Sylvie.

"We'll have to see what you have for us, first," he said. His hand remained on Sylvie's breast.

"It's in the briefcase."

"Take it out," said Mr. Curry.

"Hang on," said the man with the gun. "I'll do that."

I shrugged.

"No," said Mr. Curry. "I want him to do it. Slowly, now Mr. Coyne."

I unsnapped the top of the old briefcase, pulled open the accordion top, and leaned over to peer down into it. Then I reached my hand in. There was a stack of papers on top. Drafts of the contract for the young couple who wanted to have a baby. I snaked my hand under them until I felt the cold steel of my Smith and Wesson .38. The way it lay in the bottom of the briefcase, the barrel was aiming toward me. I felt for the handle, found it, and tried to turn the gun around.

"What the hell are you doing?" said Mr. Baron.

I leaned over the briefcase again, and pretended to look around. "It's in an envelope," I said.

"Just dump everything on the table."

"No, wait. I got it," I said. I held the revolver by its grip. My thumb found the hammer. I held my breath as I double-cocked it. The click was inaudible from inside the heavy leather briefcase. I barely touched the trigger. It had always been set too light for me. The report was muffled by the briefcase. It sounded like the cherry bombs we used to explode inside mailboxes when we were kids.

Mr. Baron looked surprised. His eyebrows went up. He lifted his gun slowly. Then he dropped it. His mouth opened, as if he were about to sing the opening lines of the national anthem. No words came out. Instead came a gurgling noise, followed by a rush of blood.

A red splotch spread across the front of his windbreaker. Mr. Baron stood there, looking surprised. Then he fell backwards.

Mr. Curry, considering his bulk, reacted with an athlete's reflexes. He shoved Sylvie at me, and I instinctively reached to catch her. But one of my hands still held my Smith and Wesson, which had become entangled inside the briefcase, so that when Sylvie hit me I fell sideways onto the floor, bringing Sylvie, the briefcase, and the revolver with me.

Mr. Curry ran for the door. I scrambled out from under Sylvie and wrenched the gun from the briefcase. Mr. Curry was at the door, not hesitating, yanking at the knob. I leveled the gun at him as he pulled the door open.

"Stop right there!" I yelled, squinting down the barrel at Mr. Curry's fat back.

He didn't pause. He opened the door, skittered out, and slammed the door behind him. I lowered the gun.

I sat there on the floor stupidly, staring down at the gun. Sylvie moved beside me. She put her hand on the back of my neck. "Why didn't you shoot that man?"

"I couldn't shoot a man, Sylvie."

"But you did."

"My God," I said. I stood up and sprinted out of my apartment. I stopped in the corridor, looking one way and then the other. I checked the elevator. According to the light, it was at the lobby. I went to the stairwell. I neither saw not heard anything.

The fat man had gotten away.

I returned to my apartment. I phoned down to Hector in the lobby. He hadn't noticed anybody either entering a while earlier or having just left. I told him to watch out for a fat guy, probably the same one he had seen the night Buddy was killed. Hector was apologetic, and expressed great enthusiasm for helping.

I went over to where the thin man who called himself Mr. Baron lay on my kitchen floor. He was on his back, his arms outthrust, his legs spread. The front of his windbreaker gleamed wetly with the blood that had not yet begun to dry. His eyes stared at the ceiling. His open mouth was red, and his chin and lips were stained bloody.

I put my ear to his mouth and then felt for a pulse in his neck. I turned to Sylvie, who hadn't moved. "He's dead."

She nodded. "Good."

"Are you all right?"

"I am all right. My breast is sore. That is all."

"Let me find you something to put on," I said.

She looked down at the front of her ruined dress. "Yes, please. I am very cold."

I went to her and hugged her close against me. I could feel her shake and twitch. "I was so frightened," she mumbled against my chest. Her entire body began to shudder. I squeezed her tight. I could feel her fingernails dig into my back.

"Me, too," I whispered. "I was very frightened."

She clung to me, heaving and shivering. I smoothed her hair against her head and moved my hand in small circles on her back and kissed her forehead and cheeks, and gradually she began to relax. She pulled her head back and looked up at me. Her face was wet and her eyes were red and swollen.

"I am very glad you killed that son of a bitch," she hissed. "But I wish you had killed the other one, too."

"We'll get him."

I helped her into the living room and sat her on the sofa. She hugged herself and pressed her knees together. "Sit tight," I told her. "I'll be right back."

I went into my bedroom and found an old flannel bathrobe hanging from a hook in the back of the closet. I brought it out and sat beside Sylvie. I put my arms across her shoulders, urging her to lean forward so that I could drape the robe around her. She cooperated passively. She was staring in the direction of the skinny man I had killed.

I found a pack of cigarettes and lit one. Then I went to the phone and dialed the police emergency number. Miraculously, I was not instructed to hold, please, and I was able to instruct the woman on the other end how to find my apartment. I made her understand that it contained a corpse, that it was I who had created this corpse, and that I would wait with it for the police to arrive.

She made me repeat it all, which I did. Then I told her to tell State Police Detective Horowitz what had happened, that he would want to know.

I went back to the kitchen, stepping carefully over Mr. Baron's body, and took down a bottle of Jack Daniel's. I poured two tumblers one-third full. I took one over to Sylvie and handed it to her. She accepted it and looked up at me.

"Do you want to toast something?" she said, trying to smile and not making it.

"To life," I said.

We touched glasses. I took a large swig into my mouth, let it roll around for a moment, and swallowed it. Tears came briefly to my eyes. Sylvie took a big gulp, coughed, then sipped again.

"This is better," she said.

The police got there in ten or fifteen minutes. Their arrival was heralded by a call from Hector. He said into the intercom, "More problems, huh, Mr. Coyne?"

"You sure you didn't see anything, Hector?"

"I see nothing. I'm sorry again, Mr. Coyne. The police, they are on their way, now. They wanna talk to me again, probably, huh?"

"Probably," I said.

A minute later there was a knock at the door. "It's open," I yelled.

Horowitz was accompanied by eight or ten cops, two in plainclothes, the rest uniformed, some city, some state. He glanced briefly at the dead body on the kitchen floor, then came over to where Sylvie and I were sitting. He looked down at us and smiled.

"What's so funny?" I said.

"Hey, are you okay there?" he said.

I touched my finger to my nose. "It's busted," I said. "Again. And it's not funny."

"It looks funny," said Horowitz. He wore the same blue bow tie he had on the other time he had been in my apartment. He still shifted a wad of bubble gum from one cheek to the other as he talked. "We'll get it looked at if you want. We ought to talk first, though." He turned his attention to Sylvia. "How about you, Miss? Are you injured?"

"I am all right," she whispered.

Horowitz cocked his head and frowned at her. "You sure?"

"Yes."

He shrugged. "Okay, then. What I'm going to do, if you don't mind, I'm going to separate you two. Nothing personal here, but we do want to hear the stories separately. Get all the details that way. Understand?"

I nodded. Sylvie said, "Yes."

Horowitz called a young black cop wearing a freshly pressed suit, which I estimated cost him a week's pay. He came over. "Interrogate the lady, Al, will you?"

"Certainly," said the cop.

"Come on," said Horowitz to me. "Let's move over there."

We went to the other side of the room and sat in a pair of soft chairs. "Okay, Mr. Coyne," said Horowitz. "Let's have it."

"These two clowns were waiting here when the lady and I got home. Must've been around eleven."

"Two?"

"Yes. That one—" I waved in the direction of the dead man "—and a fat guy. He got away. They called themselves Mr. Baron—he's the skinny one over there—and Mr. Curry."

"You say they were here when you got home. Inside, you mean?"

"Yes."

"How'd they get in?"

"A key. I guess they got the key that Buddy used."

"The boy who was killed here, you mean. The Baron boy."

"Right. They're the ones who killed him."

Horowitz frowned. "So you never did change that lock."

"I guess I forgot."

"Describe the fat one for me. The one who called himself Mr. Curry, who got away. What'd he look like?"

I did the best I could, including the faint traces of a Southern drawl and the way he called me "suh." When I finished, Horowitz excused himself. He went over and talked to one of the uniformed policemen. As he talked, he kept glancing back at me, as if he was worried I might try to escape. The policeman went to the telephone. Horowitz came back and sat beside me.

"We're getting a description out. See what we come up with. It seems to match the one your night man gave us of the guy who was here that other time. He's on his way up. See if he can ID that sack of bones on your kitchen floor." He blew a bubble. "Okay, now, Mr. Coyne. Tell me how the shooting went."

So I did, as well as I could reconstruct it. Horowitz listened carefully, interrupting frequently for clarification and detail. When I finished, he said, "So what were they after?"

I shrugged. "I don't know."

"No clue?"

"Maybe a clue," I said. So I told him what Christie Ayers had told me about stealing Alice Sylvester's school records and giving them to Buddy.

"You think these two creeps would kill a boy over a dead girl's school records?" said Horowitz.

"I have no idea. It's the only clue I have."

"Why would they think you'd have it, assuming it's what they were after?"

"There was this article in the paper this morning . . ."

Horowitz grinned. "I read it. You think all those 'no comments' would do it?"

"Maybe. Combine that with the fact that Buddy came here after he got those records from Christie. Logical to assume they were here. Or that Buddy had told me about them."

Horowitz looked doubtful. "Maybe," he said. He blew an enormous bubble, which he pinched between his thumb and forefinger to break. It reminded me of how Mr. Curry had pinched Sylvie's nipple, and the look of pain on her face.

Horowitz took his gum from his mouth, rolled it in his fingers, and looked around. His eyes lit on an ashtray, which was mounded with dead cigarettes butts. He dropped the gum on top. "Far as they know," he finally said, gazing across the room through my glass doors at the view of the night sky, "whatever they were after, you still got. Right?"

"Just Mr. Curry," I said. "Not Mr. Baron."

He glanced over at Mr. Baron's body. "Right. By 'they,' I mean that fat guy who got away plus the others. Bound to be others."

"I don't have anything," I said.

"But they think you do."

"Look—"

Horowitz held up his hand. "Here's how I figure it, Mr. Coyne. These bad guys, they think Buddy Baron got ahold of something incriminating. Something to do with the murder of the girl in Windsor Harbor. He came here, then he left to get it, whatever it is, and then he came back here. So they followed him here. Now, maybe all he got was this girl's school records, and maybe they don't mean diddly squat as far as her murder was concerned. But they must've meant something to the boy, and it's pretty obvious he wanted to share them with you, since he came back here."

Horowitz looked puzzled. "What I don't understand is, why would he hide them? He thought it was his own father coming up the stairs."

"I guess I was the one he trusted."

"So when he hears these guys at the door, he hides whatever he's got, if, indeed, it's these records."

"I think it is. The way they were asking me for them. They certainly believed that my briefcase might contain what they wanted."

"Okay," said Horowitz. He fumbled in his pockets and came out with a fresh chew of Bazooka gum. I took the opportunity to light a cigarette. "These two guys," he continued, "they may not know what they're after. But they know they want it. They're willing to torture the kid to get it. Only he dies before he tells them."

"Right. That's what the fat guy said."

"And they know you're snooping around, Mr. Coyne. No offense, but that's how it looks, if you think about it. Maybe they knew you were meeting that girl tonight. And—"

"Damn!" I said, punching my palm.

"What?" said Horowitz.

"Christie. She could be in trouble. Stupid of me."

Horowitz nodded. "Tell you what. I'll call Harry Cusick, tell him to keep a quiet eye on her. From what you've said, I can't see as the bad guys would have any reason to harm her. But you're right. Better to be safe."

"Thanks," I said.

Horowitz proved to be a man of his word. He went to my phone and punched out a number. He spoke into it for a couple minutes. I saw him nod and gesture with his hand as he talked. After he hung up he came back and sat beside me.

"All set," he said. "I talked with Cusick himself. Last thing he needs is another tragedy with a young kid in his town." He sighed. "Okay. Back to these bad guys. I figure hitting on you is worth a try for them. Nothing to lose. They would have killed you, probably, no skin off their nose. What's one more murder, more or less? Only now, the way I see it, this fat one, he's more convinced than ever that you've got what he's after."

"So?" I said.

"So," he said, glancing across the room to where Sylvie was talking with the black policeman in the expensive suit. "So you want to catch the bastard?"

I thought of Buddy Baron's face when I found him tied to my kitchen chair. I thought of the way Mr. Curry had squeezed Sylvie's nipple and lifted up her dress. "Hell, yes," I said. "I want to catch the bastard. What do you want me to do?"

At that moment, a policeman came in with Hector. Horowitz excused himself and got up to meet him.

He spoke to Hector for a moment. The young man nodded nervously, licking his lips and looking wide-eyed around the room. Then they went over to where the dead man lay sprawled on my kitchen floor. Hector stared down, looked up at Horowitz, nodded vigorously, and turned his face away. I saw Horowitz jut his jaw at Hector, who shook his head and continued to look away. Horowitz grabbed Hector's chin and jerked his face sideways, forcing him to look down again. Hector nodded quickly and tried to move his head. Horowitz let go of his chin. Then he strode over to me.

"He says it's the same guy who was here the other time. Which is what we figured."

"So," I repeated, "what do you want me to do?"

"Nothing, really. Just don't let on that you don't have this whatever it is. I know you talk to the newspapers, and after this there'll be more stories, and your boss, there, the real Mr. Tom Baron, he gets a lot of air time. It wouldn't hurt if you managed to say 'no comment' if you get asked what these guys were after, or if you have it."

"You want me to be a decoy, you mean."

He rolled his gum back and forth a few times. "A decoy," he said. "Nah. Not really. All I'm saying, Mr. Coyne, is, if you get some more unusual visitors, or strange phone calls, maybe you ought to let us know. Of course, it would help us if you did get these visitors or calls. And if you can manage to act just a little mysterious whenever somebody asks you what this was all about, so much the better."

"You want them to come after me again?"

Horowitz blew a bubble. "They might just do that, whether I want them to or not."

"And you're going to have a policeman or two nearby, right?"

Horowitz nodded. "I think you need protection."

"Cops at the door."

"We'll keep an eye on the place."

I shrugged. "And Sylvie."

Horowitz nodded. "Of course."

"Because she shouldn't even be involved in this. It's because of me—"

He put his hand on my arm. "Don't worry. We'll take good care of her."

"You better," I said.

thirteen

AFTER A SHORT TIME, THE BLACK detective brought Sylvie back to the sofa. He steered her politely with his hand just touching her elbow. She walked stiffly. When she sat beside me, I put my arm around her. We drank more Jack Daniel's and watched the police scurry busily around in my apartment.

The medical examiner arrived. He knelt beside the body of Mr. Baron for a few minutes, then stood up and nodded to a young woman, who proceeded to take some Polaroid flash pictures of it. Then she and the M.E. departed, and two men wearing white jackets rolled Mr. Baron into a black plastic body bag and lugged him away.

Horowitz came back to us and said, "If you don't mind, Mr. Coyne, we're going to have to ask you to find someplace else to stay tonight."

"We can go to Miss Szabo's place," I said. Sylvie looked up at me and nodded.

"I'm going to have to take your gun. You'll get it back. Assuming it's properly licensed."

"It is."

"And we'd appreciate it if you and the lady would come to the station tomorrow and look through the mug book. See if we can figure out who your Mr. Curry is."

"Sure."

"You want me to drive you?"

"I can drive," I said. "No problem."

He frowned at me. "You ought to get that beak of yours looked at."

"Not much they can do for a broken nose."

"Might need a few stitches."

I touched my nose gingerly. "I'm afraid of needles."

Sylvie wrapped my flannel bathrobe around herself and we went down the elevator to my car. She leaned against me, and I kept one arm around her shoulders. She scuffed her feet a little as she walked. She stumbled once. I didn't know whether it was from the shock of events or the Jack Daniel's she had consumed.

She huddled against the door of my car, her legs tucked up underneath her and her arms folded tightly across her chest. She stared out the window on her side as I negotiated the largely empty Boston streets that took us from my place on the waterfront to her condo on Beacon Street.

"You okay?" I said.

"I am okay," she said, her voice just a whisper.

"Do you want to talk about it? It might help to talk about it."

"I talked with the policeman. He was very nice. Now I do not want to think about it."

I shrugged. "Okay."

We were passing by the Common on Boylston Street when Sylvie said, "Stop the car, please."

"Why . . . ?"

But I heard her gag, so I braked quickly and reached across her to unlatch the door. Just in the nick of time.

I went around to her side and helped her get out. I held her while she purged herself of mussels, monkfish, Jack Daniel's, and ugly memories, right on the sidewalk. A pair of young men strolled by, arm in arm, and they whispered and giggled and turned around to watch Sylvie puke.

"Go bugger each other," I yelled at them.

They seemed to think this was an enormously witty thing for me to say. One of them shouted back at me, equally cleverly. "Fuck you, Charlie."

After a few minutes, Sylvie said, "I am better now." I gave her my handkerchief and she wiped her face with it. Then we got back into the car.

I found a slot on Beacon Street only two blocks from Sylvie's place. I parked and we walked up. Sylvie walked better. She said she was feeling fine.

It was about three in the morning. A megadose of adrenaline was zipping through my veins. I felt like a speed freak who had just shot up. I felt as if I would never sleep again. I sat in Sylvie's living room sucking at a bottle of Molson's ale and smoking a cigarette while she went into the bathroom. I heard the shower go on. I listened to it run while I finished my Winston. I drained the bottle of ale. The shower was still running. I got up and went to the bathroom. I opened the door and was greeted by a cloud of steam. I shucked off my clothes and tapped lightly on the opaque glass door of the shower stall.

"I need someone to scrub my back," I said.

"I have done that before."

I stepped in. Sylvie was slick as a seal. Her blond hair was pasted to her head and face. I moved it away from her mouth and kissed her. She held herself rigid. Then she quivered and moved away from me.

"Where's the soap?" I said.

"Turn around," she said.

I turned and she lathered my back. Then she put the soap into my hand. "Now do me," she said.

She turned her back to me. Her shoulders were hunched forward, her head bowed. I moved the soap in circles on her smooth back and down around her hips. She arched backwards toward me. "That feels good," she murmured.

I moved closer to her. Carefully, slowly, I lathered her throat and shoulders, standing close against her. One of her hands moved behind her and touched my hip, urging me closer. I moved the soap around her breasts. Her nipples hardened, and I heard her murmur something in her throat. I lathered her stomach. Her hand came down to touch mine, to urge it downwards.

She turned to face me, lifting her arms and offering her mouth. "You taste soapy," I said.

She pressed herself against me and laughed.

"What's funny?" I said.

"Your nose. And your eyes. They are both black. You look like a raccoon. Or a robber."

I kissed her again, and somewhere in her throat she said, "Oh," and she didn't laugh, and a moment later she said, "Oh, yes," quite distinctly, and the steamy water cascaded over us, washing away the evil of the evening, and Sylvie and I shuddered together. She clung to me that way for a long time, with her knees locked up around my hips and her mouth against the side of my neck.

Later we dried each other with big towels. We powdered each other's body and walked hand in hand to Sylvie's big bed. We held each other and we slept.

The next morning Sylvie and I went to the police station.

"You're a sight and a half," observed Horowitz.

I ruefully touched the Band-Aid Sylvie had stuck onto the bridge of my nose. "It's a bit tender," I said nasally.

Horowitz gave us big albums full of portraits of criminals. We pored over them for nearly two hours. I didn't find a single picture that looked like the fat man who called himself Mr. Curry.

Sylvie found eight.

Horowitz thanked us anyway. He said they would have word from the fingerprint computer in Washington within forty eight hours on the man I had killed. If his prints were on file, perhaps we'd know more.

He said they had searched my apartment thoroughly but did not find a file containing Alice Sylvester's school records. "Turned the place upside down" was the phrase he used.

He said he'd call to let me know when I could get my gun back. I told him I was in no particular hurry.

Sylvie and I had lunch at the Union Oyster House. She had a green salad and a glass of tomato juice. I had fish stew and a bottle of beer.

She said she wanted to be alone for a while. I told her I understood. I dropped her off at her place, and I went home.

The police may have done a thorough job of scouring my apartment for mysterious school records, latent fingerprints, specks of rare mud, stray pubic hairs, and whatever arcane clues they were looking for. But they did a lousy job of cleaning up.

Of course, most of the mess was there before they arrived.

My Harlan Fiske Stone briefcase was gone. I assumed the cops had taken it for evidence. I hoped I hadn't ruined it by shooting a bullet through it.

I called the office. When Julie answered, I said, "Before you say anything, I'm home and I'm all right."

"I wasn't worried," she said. "I was pissed off."

"Well, if you knew what happened to me, you'd have been worried."

"You're all right. So I can be pissed if I want. Are you coming to work, or what?"

"Or what, actually," I said. "Be in tomorrow. Just wanted to let you know. Common courtesy, that sort of thing."

"You probably have no interest in who's been calling, or which clients are looking around for new attorneys, or anything, huh?"

"Nope. It'll keep. Be in tomorrow."

"Fine. Maybe I won't."

"Julie, I'll need you tomorrow."

"I'll keep it in mind."

After I hung up, I went into the bathroom. I peeled the Band-Aid off my nose. The gash didn't look so bad, now that it wasn't bleeding. The rest of my face looked considerably worse. I took two aspirin for the vague throbbing behind my eyes, which I ascribed to the displacement of bone and cartilage, but which may have been an adrenaline hangover. Then I hooked a can of Tuborg from the refrigerator, found the new Thomas Jefferson biography I had just started, and lay on my bed.

The telephone jarred me awake. I fumbled for it, found it, and muttered, "Whozit?"

"Sylvie," came a small voice.

"You all right?"

"I am very lonely."

"I'll be right over."

"No," she said. "I must go to your place."

"Are you sure . . . ?"

"I am very sure. I want to see you. And I want to be in your house again."

"What time is it?"

"Five-thirty."

"Will you take a taxi?"

"Yes. If you are not busy."

"I'm not busy," I said. "I'll cook us dinner."

"I am not very hungry."

I took a quick shower, shaved, and slid into my comfortable jeans. I found a big can of Hungarian goulash on the back of the top shelf where I had been hiding it. I opened it up, dumped it into a pot, sprinkled some paprika and tabasco and garlic salt onto it, and put the heat on low. I carefully shoved the empty can down into the bottom of the trash basket. Sylvie wouldn't know the difference.

I put candles on the table. I decanted a nice Portuguese red wine. I found two linen napkins that matched.

I chopped a large onion, four strips of bacon, and a sweet red pepper into a frypan, added two garlic gloves, and stirred them over high heat for about three minutes. Then I peeled and halved a just-ripe avocado and dumped my stirfry into each half. I shook a little Italian salad dressing over the top, covered them with Saran Wrap, and shoved them into the refrigerator to chill.

When Sylvie arrived, I was lounging on my sofa looking at the newspaper. She kissed me shyly, then wrinkled her nose. "What do I smell?"

"You like?"

"Did you open a can again?"

"Would I do that?"

She giggled. I took her coat. She had worn a slick off-white blouse and a simple blue skirt. She looked smashing, and I told her so.

"I cannot stop feeling dirty," she said.

"Perhaps another shower . . . ?"

She grinned. "Perhaps. Later."

I served her with as much elegance as I could muster. She laughed at my fake Continental accent. When she praised the goulash, I thought I detected a smirk lurking in her eyes. I chose to ignore it. We did not talk about the events of the previous evening. But Sylvie cleaned her plate, which I took to be a good sign.

Afterwards we took coffee into the living room. We sat side by side on the sofa and watched the evening news. There was a brief clip of Governor McElroy on the subject of the sales tax. Tom Baron received his equal time, discoursing, as usual, on the evils of drugs.

Sylvie picked up the remote control device and snapped off the set. "Mr. Baron will fool many people," she muttered.

"Don't confuse Tom Baron with what happened last night."

"I am not stupid."

"You had a very traumatic experience."

She stood up abruptly. "I do not want to think about last night," she said. She wandered into the kitchen and began to clear off the table.

"Leave it," I said. "We'll do it later. Come on. Finish your coffee."

She shrugged and went over to the glass doors. It was murky and moonless outside, and the scattered ship lights that drifted by were blurry blots. Sylvie stared out for a few minutes. I watched her without speaking. Finally she turned. "Would you like to get beaten at chess?" she said.

She must have read something in my face, because she came over to me, reached down to touch my cheek, and said, "Did I say something wrong again?"

I pulled her down onto my lap. "No. Not really. It's just that the last time I played chess, it was with Buddy Baron. You reminded me of that."

She nuzzled my neck. "There are other games we can play."

"No. Let's play chess."

"You will pick out some music. I will find the chessman."

I went over to the stereo and shoved a Rolling Stones tape into the tape deck. Then I went to the kitchen to pour some brandy for us.

Sylvie was bent over the drawer. Suddenly she said, "What is this?"

"I forgot," I said. "Buddy insisted on putting the pieces away properly. They're in the wooden box where they belong."

"I found the box. There's a piece of paper in it."

She handed it to me. It was a sheet of perforated computer paper, the kind with alternating green-and-white horizontal stripes. It had been folded into a thick wad so that it would fit into the box. I unfolded it.

"Buddy left it," I said.

Sylvie stood close to me, looking over my shoulder. "It was on the bottom, under all the chess pieces. What is it?"

"It looks like a report card. Alice Sylvester's report card."

"From the file that Christie took," said Sylvie.

"Yes. It's what Mr. Baron and Mr. Curry were after."

"But why?"

I shrugged. "I don't know."

Sylvie huddled against me. "What does it mean?" she whispered.

"I have no idea," I said slowly, staring at the rows of words and letters and numbers. "But when I figure it out, I think I'll know why Buddy left here that night, and why he came back. And maybe I'll know why they killed him."

fourteen

I SAT ON A WOODEN BENCH OUTSIDE
Ingrid Larsen's office the next day, feeling a little like a miscreant school-
boy awaiting his sentence for a day of hooky. Phones jangled. Typewriters
clattered. Students and secretaries bustled. Everybody carefully ignored
me.

I had dropped in at my office first thing that morning to mollify Julie. I
read the mail, signed some letters, returned some calls, and canceled the
only appointment I had for the afternoon. Then I took off for Windsor
Harbor. By sheer good fortune I found myself motoring past Gert's at just
about noontime. Actually, I had to take an earlier exit off Route 128 to
pass by Gert's. But it was a scenic way to get to Windsor Harbor.

And it seemed silly to drive right on past Gert's. I had so few opportuni-
ties to slurp down a bowl of her seafood chowder. Fresh scallops. Big
hunks of lobster tail. Littlenecks. Oysters. Crabmeat. Fresh halibut.
Cream, butter, onion, potato, pepper. With a glass of ale to wash it down.

So I sat outside the principal's office at Windsor Harbor High School
burping quietly and feeling quite content, not at all offended that I had to
wait for Ingrid Larsen to become available.

When I had arrived, the white-haired one named Emma had said, "But
you don't have an appointment." She seemed quite flustered by my presence. Her words were an accusation.

"Yes, ma'am, it's true that I have no appointment. I am willing to wait
until Dr. Larsen has a spare moment." I gave her what ordinarily was a
foolproof winning smile. It worked infallibly with old ladies. Emma, however, appeared immune to its magic.

"Well"—she sniffed—"you'll just have to wait and take your chances."

"Please let her know I'm here."

"She's quite busy."

"I know you'll do your best for me." The smile, again, and I thought I detected a flicker in Emma's eyes.

So I waited. Alice Sylvester's computer-generated report card was in my pocket. With Sylvie the previous evening, I had speculated on its significance.

"Maybe Buddy wrote something on it," I said.

"There is no writing," said Sylvie.

"Hmm. No. There's not. Perhaps there's a microdot. One of the periods, a dot over an i."

"A microdot?" said Sylvie, leaning close to me and examining the report card.

"Just a joke."

I hugged her. We looked at the numbers and letters and words, all printed out in dot matrix. "This is from two years ago," I observed. "Alice's sophomore year."

"She was a good student."

"She was supposed to have been an excellent student."

"Except, look," said Sylvie, running her finger down a row of grades. "A D is not so good."

Alice Sylvester had received a final grade of D in biology from a teacher named Tarlow. "That is odd," I told Sylvie. "I saw Alice's records when I was at the school. I don't remember seeing any D's. She had mostly A's, as I remember it. I'm positive she didn't have a D on that record."

Sylvie put her hand on the back of my neck. "You have been hit on the head recently. Much has happened. Perhaps you don't remember so well."

"Mm. Maybe you're right. And it's true. I just glanced over Alice's record that day. Still . . ."

So I'd decided to check out my memory with Ingrid Larsen. Because unless I was mistaken, it was this report card that had gotten Buddy Baron killed, and had brought the two hoods who called themselves Mr. Curry and Mr. Baron back to my house for another attempt to find it. If these two guys wanted it so badly, there was a story in it. The story that told how Alice Sylvester was murdered, I guessed.

I just couldn't read the story.

As I sat there, I reviewed the pieces that seemed to fit together. The scenario, as I constructed it, went this way: Buddy appeared at my house when he heard Alice Sylvester had been murdered; when I told him the police wanted to arrest him, he ran away; he contacted Christie Ayers, a friend of Alice's and his, and persuaded her to filch Alice's file and hand it over to him; he removed the report card from the file, presumably because it was the only item in it he wanted; with the report card, Buddy felt he had evidence that would exonerate him, so he returned to my apartment, ready to face arrest, confident he would be cleared, and perhaps even convinced that he could identify the real murderer; the two guys calling themselves Mr. Curry and Mr. Baron somehow picked up his trail and followed him to my place; when Buddy heard them at the door, he hastily stuffed the report card into the box of chess pieces, assuming that no one else would find it there and that sooner or later I would.

He probably also assumed I would have the wit to figure out the significance of it all.

Which, thus far, I hadn't. But it was important enough for Buddy to withstand excruciating torture to protect, and I intended to try to vindicate his faith in me.

Still, aside from that D in biology, I had no clue.

The door to the principal's office opened. A man and a woman and a teenage boy appeared, followed by Ingrid Larsen. She was wearing a silky pale blue blouse and big dangly earrings of the same hue. She looked great.

The four of them paused at the doorway. The two adults, parents of the boy, I assumed, looked grim. The boy sulked. His hair looked as if he'd slept on it. He had a hoop in his left ear. Ingrid was talking to the three of them in a low voice. I saw the father shake his head, which caused Ingrid to frown and lean toward him to speak. He shrugged. He wore a gray suit, expensive, conservatively cut. He picked imaginary lint off his lapel. Then he touched his wife's arm and began to steer her away.

Ingrid spoke to the boy. He hesitated, then looked up at her, his eyebrows arched. She cocked her head, said something else, and smiled. He shrugged and nodded, then turned to catch up with his parents.

She looked around the open office area. Her eyes passed over me without registering. Then she went back into her sanctum.

I got up and walked to her door. Emma hurried over. "Oh, you can't go in there now."

"Will you please tell her I'm here, then."

"Now, I'm sorry, but—"

"You are forgiven." I walked through the door into Ingrid Larsen's office.

She was standing with her back to me, leaning with both hands on her desk, studying something on top of it. I cleared my throat.

"Yes? What is it?" She didn't bother to turn around.

"It's not Emma's fault. I trampled her."

She turned. "Oh," she said. "It's you."

"You don't have to pretend to be thrilled like that. I know seeing me is probably the highlight of your day, but—"

She smiled. "I'm sorry. My mind was somewhere else."

She came toward me with her hand extended. I grasped it. "I'll only take a minute," I said.

She gestured to a chair, and we both sat down. She sighed deeply. "Thank God I'm not a parent," she said.

"Rough session, huh?"

"Sometimes I think teenagers would be better off without parents entirely. Maybe I ought to be running a boarding school. Keep the bad influences away."

"Wasn't it Plato who said that children should be taken from their parents at birth and raised by experts?"

"In the *Republic*. Yes. Plato among others. Of course, Plato was a fascist." She smiled at me. "I'm not a fascist."

"No. I wouldn't have thought so."

"That boy misbehaves so that he can get his parents' attention. It's the only way he knows."

"It seems to be working."

"I told them to let the kid grow up in his own way. Let him make some mistakes. Ignore some of the behavior and it'll go away."

"Sounds risky," I said.

She shrugged. "It is. I think he still has a chance to become an autonomous human being. His parents have to give him a fair shot at it." She sat back and tilted her head at me. I suspected she was giving me what she thought was her best angle. It was an excellent angle, at that. "What can I do for you, Mr. Coyne?"

"First, is there any way you can check and see if Christie Ayers is in school today?"

She frowned at me, then shrugged. She went to her computer monitor and tapped at the keyboard. A minute later she turned to face me. "She's here. At least she was in homeroom this morning. Why?"

I shook my head. "Nothing you need to know about."

"Is that why you're here? To see if Christie's in school?"

"No, that wasn't it. You heard about Buddy Baron?"

"Yes. A horrible thing. It was at your apartment."

I nodded. I took Alice Sylvester's report card from my pocket, unfolded it, and handed it to her. "It is possible that the men who murdered Buddy were after this."

She frowned. "I don't see . . ."

"Me neither. The only thing is that D in biology. I don't remember seeing a D on her transcript."

"It is odd," she murmured, studying the paper. "Alice was elected to

National Honor Society her junior year. Usually you can't go into NHS with a D. She had Ira Tarlow for biology. I suppose he could have entered the wrong grade and had it changed later. Otherwise . . ."

"Otherwise what?"

She shrugged. "Otherwise, I don't know. Let's take another look at that transcript."

She stood up and again went to the computer terminal on a table in the corner of her office. She sat in front of it and began tapping on the keys. I moved so I could watch over her shoulder.

"What are you doing?"

"Entering the codes. There's a secret six-digit number, and then three separate code words, before you can get into the data base. Gil Speer changes the codes every week."

After several seconds the machine beeped. The words ACCESSING FILE appeared on the screen. "Takes a while," Ingrid muttered.

"Who knows these codes?"

"Gil and I are the only ones who can get into this particular file. There are other files open to some of the secretaries. Attendance, for example. There's a different set of codes for them. Ah," she said, as the machine beeped again. She typed Alice's name. The machine gave her a number. She hit the return key and typed the number. Alice Sylvester's transcript almost instantaneously appeared on the screen.

We both looked at it.

"Biology. Tarlow. A. She got an A in biology," said Ingrid.

"That's what I thought."

"Mr. Tarlow must have changed his mind."

"Does that happen often?"

She frowned. "With Mr. Tarlow, that never happens."

"Then . . ."

"I mean," she said, "it could happen. Theoretically. If the grade were improperly entered by someone in the computer center. Then the teacher could authorize it to be changed."

"But . . ."

"But Ira Tarlow is very precise. A singularly uninspiring teacher, perhaps. But precise as hell. And hardly susceptible to persuasion, if that's what you're thinking. I really just don't understand this."

"So where could this D have come from?"

"Maybe," said Ingrid, "the question is where the A came from."

"The real question," I said, "is what's the significance of it."

"If there is any," she said. "All I can say is that Alice would not have been pleased with a D. Not pleased at all."

"Are you suggesting . . . ?"

"What, that she managed to change it? Not likely. Gil says this system is absolutely hackerproof. And Alice was no whiz at computers."

"I'd like to talk to Mr. Tarlow."

Ingrid smiled. "You're welcome to try. He's not the most, ah, cordial individual."

"You forget. I am an attorney. Persuasion is my game."

She shrugged. "I'll introduce you. You might want to keep in mind a couple things, though."

"Like what?"

"Like, Ira Tarlow is not a popular teacher. His job, in fact, is in jeopardy, although I am handicapped by a contract that protects him by virtue of his seniority."

"Ah, yes. Tenure."

She shook her head. "No, not tenure. That does not protect an incompetent teacher, contrary to popular belief. It simply gives teachers access to due process. No, in this case I face declining student enrollments, which requires me to cut back on staff. My goal is to protect our best teachers, regardless of seniority. The teachers' union makes that difficult. In any case, my relationship with Mr. Tarlow is, ah, strained these days."

"You want to get rid of him because he's unpopular?"

"Oh, no. That's not it. I mean, his unpopularity is obviously linked to the fact that he's not very competent. Look. He's a very old-fashioned man. He has grown very bitter. He's hanging on here to sweeten his retirement benefits. He can't understand how kids today can be any different from kids in the fifties. He doesn't like them—or me—questioning his methods. And he has not kept up in his field. Take biology from Ira Tarlow, you'd never hear about DNA. I'm not so sure he's even up to date on Darwinian theory. He blushes when he uses the word 'reproduction.' Refuses to discuss it as it pertains to primates. He stammers when he talks about stamens."

"Oh, my virgin ears," I said.

She grinned at me.

"Actually, I love it when you talk dirty."

She shook her head in mock disgust. "Come on. I'll take you to the science wing. Last period is just about over."

I followed her out of her office and into the corridor. "Mr. Tarlow is one of those whose daily departure is signaled by the last bell. Most of our conscientious teachers hang around to confer with students, meet with committees, work on lessons, correct papers, whatever. The science teachers like to set up their labs and demonstrations before they leave. But not Ira. We should just catch him."

As we were walking a bell jangled. The doors along either side of the broad corridor opened and students poured out, bursting with that adolescent energy that translated itself into loud laughter, much punching of shoulders, obscene language, and acute sexual awareness. The kids ignored Ingrid and me. We ignored them. We pushed our way against the general direction of the tide, which reluctantly opened to let us pass.

She ducked into an open doorway. I followed her in. A chest-high counter ran across the front of the room. It was equipped with two sinks, a variety of pipes and spigots, and several knobs, which I figured were hookups for Bunsen burners. Papers were strewn on top of it. There was a rack of dirty test tubes and several empty beakers.

Behind the counter stood a man stuffing papers into a briefcase very similar to my ventilated Harlan Fiske Stone model. He was a trim little man, with round rimless spectacles and a narrow little white mustache. He peered up myopically at Ingrid and me.

"Dr. Larsen," he said tonelessly.

"Mr. Tarlow, I realize we may be detaining you, the bell having rung and all, but I have a gentleman here who would like to speak with you."

He looked at me, nodded once, and extended his hand. "Ira Tarlow, sir."

"Brady Coyne," I said.

Ingrid Larsen smiled quickly at me, as much as to say, "Don't be deceived. The man's a charmer. But evil." What she actually said was, "Stop in when you're done, if you'd like. I'll be here all afternoon."

I thanked her, and she turned and left, closing the door behind her. I turned to the biology teacher.

"I'm an attorney, Mr. Tarlow. I am involved in an indirect way with the murder investigation of Alice Sylvester and Buddy Baron. I'd like to ask you a few questions, if you don't mind."

"Of course not. Would you like to sit down?"

I shook my head. "Been sitting most of the day."

"You don't mind if I sit, do you?" he said. "We teachers spend most of our days on our feet. And mine happen to be killing me. Teachers and nurses and airline hostesses all suffer podiatric distress. Occupational hazards." He climbed upon a tall stool and hooked his short legs around it. "Ahh. Better. Young teachers, they do not seem to mind sitting while they teach. To me, a teacher ought to be standing. It conveys command. I do not agree with the informality of our new generation of teachers. It encourages disrespect. Disrespect for the teacher, disrespect for the subject. Disrespect for education."

I smiled. "I see your point."

"I do go on, sometimes. I know. Dr. Larsen loves to remind me of it. I apologize. How can I help you?"

"I'd like to talk about Alice Sylvester."

"Very well," he said. He folded his arms, propped his chin up on his fist, and regarded me expectantly.

I laughed. "What I meant was, I'd like for you to talk about Alice Sylvester."

"Oh. I'm sorry. I am a very literal man. Tell me what you'd like me to say."

I summarized the case for him. "So you see," I concluded, "this report card was for some reason very important to Buddy Baron. It got him killed, in fact. And the only interesting thing about it seems to be the D in biology. Your course."

He had begun nodding his head as soon as I mentioned the report card. When I finished talking, he put both elbows onto the counter and leaned toward me. "She did get a D," he said. "She probably should have failed, but, frankly, her reputation cowed me."

"She was an excellent student, I thought."

He shrugged. "She failed the final exam. She left it blank. A zero. It counted fifty percent of the year's grade. I don't know why she left it blank. She knew the material. When she handed it in I glanced at it and asked her. She said she didn't feel like doing it. She said it was a stupid test. It was not unlike her. She was fully aware that my job has been in jeopardy, that the administration has been pressuring me to retire. I suppose she thought I wouldn't dare to fail her. Well, she was right, in a sense. I gave her the D instead of the F she deserved. And now you tell me they have changed it. That, too, could have been predicted, I suppose."

"Dr. Larsen says that she doesn't know how it was done, if it wasn't ordered by you. It was not done officially."

Tarlow shrugged. "Or else she isn't telling you. Mr. Coyne, truly I cannot see how this can be related to her unfortunate murder or that of the Baron boy." He smiled shyly. "Or am I some sort of suspect?"

"Oh, I don't think so," I said. "I'm having trouble with it, too. But it seems to be the only link."

He held out his hands, palms up. "I'm an old-fashioned man, Mr. Coyne. Computers I do not understand. I would like to. But I don't have the energy for it. Now administrative prerogative, that I do understand."

"Are you saying that someone above you ordered the grade changed?"

He shrugged. "I see no other explanation. Do you?"

"I don't—"

He hitched himself forward on his stool. "Look, Mr. Coyne. Let me be frank with you. Alice Sylvester was a spoiled child. Rather pretty, in a pouty way. Fairly bursting with hormonal spirit, if you follow me. And she was, indeed, quite intelligent. But typical of her generation. Self-centered. Demanded recognition of her accomplishments. Figured the school—and the other parts of her world—existed for the sole purpose of serving her. Her teachers earned none of her respect. She cultivated them, like—like my dear wife cultivates her roses, snipping at their thorns, twisting them into the shapes she wants. Flattering them to their faces, criticizing them behind their backs. Oh, I don't mean to suggest that I felt anything but a horrible tragic loss when I heard she was murdered. She was no different from her peers. They do tend to grow into adults. Often they come back, oh, years later, and they thank me for having standards, for insisting on civility in my classroom, things like that." He paused and grinned. "You have to stop me, Mr. Coyne. I get off the track."

I shook my head. "It's all right. It's helping me to understand."

"My students see me as dry, humorless, one-dimensional. I don't care. My job is to teach them biology. I am very conscientious about it. I never try to become their friend, to make myself available to hear all their petty problems. Adolescence is the most carefree, irresponsible time of a person's life, or at least it is for those fortunate to live in a community like Windsor Harbor. But to hear these young people talk. The worries, the burdens, the pressures. My goodness, Mr. Coyne. Do you realize how important it is to get early admission to an Ivy League college? Not only to the children, but to their parents? I am not sympathetic to this. This is not life. These are not problems."

"Alice Sylvester and Buddy Baron had problems," I said mildly.

"Of course. They have been murdered. That is not what I meant."

I smiled. "I have two boys myself."

"I suspect from talking with you that they're nicer people than Alice Sylvester."

"You're suggesting that somebody pressured the administration to change Alice's grade, then."

He shrugged quickly. "It's the only explanation I have. It would be unethical. But such things happen."

"Dr. Larsen says that did not happen. But it is a thought." I straightened up and held out my hand to Ira Tarlow. "Mr. Tarlow, thank you for your time."

His eyebrows arched quickly. "Is that all?"

"Yes, I think so."

"I'm sorry I haven't helped you, sir."

"I don't know whether you have helped me or not, to tell you the truth."

We shook hands and I turned for the door. Tarlow followed me. "Mr. Coyne," he said.

I stopped. "Yes?"

"I did not murder the girl."

"I never thought you did."

He smiled at me. "Sure you did, Mr. Coyne."

fifteen

I FOUND MY WAY BACK TO THE MAIN office through the empty corridors. I strode past Emma, eyes forward, shoulders squared, and went directly into Ingrid Larsen's office.

She was reading from a sheet of pale green paper. She looked up when I cleared my throat, put the paper into her desk, and smiled. Dazzlingly.

"Please sit," she said.

I complied, and she came over and sat beside me.

"So what do you think of our Mr. Tarlow?"

"I liked him very much," I said.

She grinned. "He's quite good with adults."

"I can see how he might put kids off," I said. "They can't run into too many like him."

She nodded. "It's a problem. You're right."

"Yes. You need to find more like him."

She cocked her head at me to see if I was joking. I arched my brows and nodded once to indicate that I wasn't.

"I tried to call you after you were here last time," she said after a moment.

"I got your message. An apology, I believe it was. Unnecessary. Instantly accepted."

"It's just that pressure from people like Tom Baron—"

"I understand," I said.

"There was a hint in that message, too." She smiled. She had excellent teeth. In fact, she was altogether quite flawless.

"Yes, I got your hint. I've just been real busy lately, and with murders and whatnot . . ."

She frowned for an instant, then tossed her head. "Sure. Maybe sometime, huh?"

I nodded. "Sure. Maybe. Look, Ira Tarlow says he did not authorize any change of Alice Sylvester's grade. He gave her the D."

"Then," she said, "it's a mystery to me. I think you'd better talk to Gil Speer. It must be some kind of computer glitch, and he's the only one who understands that stuff."

"Can I see him now?"

"Let me give him a buzz." She went over to her desk and tapped out a number on the phone. "Mr. Speer, please," she said. After a pause, she said, "It's Dr. Larsen. . . . Well, I'll only take a minute of his time. . . . Thank you." She looked up at me. "His students are very protective of him." She waited, then said, "Gil. It's Ingrid. . . . Yes, I understand. The budget projections. I appreciate your position. But Mr. Coyne is here. . . . Brady Coyne. He's an attorney. You met with him after Alice Sylvester's . . . Right. We were hoping you'd have a minute . . . Of course. Perhaps a little later, then. . . . Well, why don't you give me a time and I'll . . ." She rolled her eyes for my benefit, then returned her attention to the phone. "Let me check," she said. She turned to me. "He's really tied up now. He says if you want to go to the computer room around six he should have a little time."

I nodded. "Six is okay."

"He says six will be fine," she said into the phone. She looked up at the ceiling and sighed. "Well, I do appreciate it, Gil. This could be important . . . It has to do with a grade that may have been changed on a student's transcript . . . Alice Sylvester, as a matter of fact. . . . No, nobody's accusing anybody. Mr. Coyne . . . Well, for that matter, I'm curious, too, Gil. . . . Well, good. Thank you. He'll be there at six."

She placed the receiver carefully back on its cradle. "A difficult man, sometimes. But irreplaceable. I'm sorry he couldn't see you sooner."

"That's all right," I said. "I appreciate your help."

"Well, it's true that I am more than a little curious myself. If some kid has gotten into those files, we've got major problems."

"My hunch is that Alice Sylvester's is the only grade that's been changed around here."

She shrugged. "I hope you're right."

I stood up. "Thanks for your help," I said.

We shook hands with excessive formality, and I left her office, wondering why I had failed to take her up on her suggestion that we have a drink together sometime. She was intelligent, gorgeous, sexy. My kind of lady. No harm in having a little drink with a lady like that. My own perversities confused me.

I had a leisurely cup of coffee in the little restaurant on the main drag in

Windsor Harbor, smoked a few cigarettes, accepted a refill of coffee, and scanned the previous day's *Herald* that I found on the chair beside me. A little after five customers began to trickle in, so I left. I still had an hour before my date with Gil Speer. I found an outdoor pay phone and called the Windsor Harbor police station. Chief Harry Cusick wasn't in, but I left a message for him. I was in town and would try to get back to him before I left. Had some possible new developments in the Sylvester case. Would be visiting Gil Speer, the computer expert in the high school. The on-duty cop read my message back to me. He had it exactly right.

Then I wandered down the street until I found myself standing in front of Computer City, the place where Buddy Baron had sold computers.

Through the front window I could see Bob Pritchard, the bearded guy who worked there, sitting at a computer monitor. He was alone in the store.

A bell on the door jangled when I went in, and Pritchard glanced over his shoulder at me for an instant before returning his attention to the screen. I went to him and looked over his shoulder.

He was playing a game that seemed to require the operator to shoot falling objects out of the sky before they landed on a fortress. He seemed very skilled at it. The computer made beeping and booming sounds, and the falling objects appeared to explode when struck.

"Can I sell you something?" he said to me without turning around.

"Nope."

He maneuvered the joystick rapidly. "Wanna look around, help yourself. Turn on the machines, play with them, if you want."

"I was hoping we could talk."

He grunted and muttered "Damn" under his breath. "What do you want to talk about?"

"Buddy Baron again."

He swiveled his head around. "Who're you?"

"Brady Coyne. We met before."

He scowled, then turned his body in his chair to face me. "You look familiar."

"I was in last week. I was looking for Buddy."

He nodded. "Oh, sure. Right. Guess you're not looking for Buddy now."

"No. He's been found."

He nodded and sighed. He pivoted around to face his machine. He switched it off, slid a disk out of the disk drive, inserted it into an envelope, and placed it in a rack. Then he stood up. "Come on over here. I got a few minutes. Got to be at the hotline at six-fifteen. Close up around six. Miss my dinner. Worth it, though."

He went over to a small desk near the front door and sat behind it. I pulled a metal chair alongside it.

"I want to ask you about crack," I said.

"Why me?"

"Last time we talked, I got the impression that you knew what was going on in this community. If you work at a drug hotline, you must be pretty concerned about it. And I've been led to believe that there's a problem here."

"Two kids dead, I guess we've got a problem. Though neither Buddy nor Alice OD'd."

"I think drugs are at the center of it, though."

He nodded. "I'd say you're probably right."

"What can you tell me?"

Pritchard rolled his shoulders, as if they were stiff from playing at the machine. "I volunteer at this hotline," he said. "Five nights a week. Sometimes I'm there all day Sunday. I figure I owe something to somebody. I had a bad problem once, and I called this place. I had a shotgun between my knees, and I was looking down the double barrels, and I called this place so there'd be somebody to listen when I pushed on the trigger with my toe. I had been high, and then I crashed, and I didn't have any money for more coke, and I couldn't stand it. And damned if the guy on the other end of the phone didn't talk me out of it. He came and got me and persuaded me to enroll in a program. And I climbed out of it. Similar to what happened to Buddy. So now, I figure there'll be a kid sometime with a gun in his mouth who'll call me." He shrugged. "I do it because it makes me feel good. It also makes me feel shitty. At least, so far nobody has made me listen to a gun going off."

"Lots of problems out there, huh?"

He nodded. "Even a small town like this. Bad problems. Especially lately."

"What's going on?"

"Crack, like you thought. Somebody's giving it away."

"Giving it away? Free, you mean?"

"Free," he repeated. "So far, free."

"To get kids hooked."

"Right. And it's damn effective. You understand about crack?"

"Very little."

"It's ninety, ninety-five percent pure cocaine, okay? Comes in these little hunks. They sell them in glass vials. When they smuggle them, they sometimes disguise them as firecrackers. Down in New York you can get a vial for ten bucks. Up here it'll go for twenty, twenty-five. Supply and demand, I suppose. Lots of competition in the Big Apple. So far around Boston the market is more closely controlled. Anyhow, you take one of these little hunks of coke and you put it into your water pipe and you light it and suck it into your lungs, and in about ten seconds—I'm not exaggerating, here— it hits your brain. The high is intense as hell. They say it's like nothing else. A million times better—if that's the word for it—than when you snort the stuff. It lasts only about ten minutes. Then comes the crash. And that's a million times worse. The kids tell me, they say, as soon as you crash you feel like you've absolutely got to have another hit. It's virtually instant addiction. That's why it's good business for these scumbags to give it away."

"I've got a question."

He peered at me with his eyebrows raised.

"Who?" I said. "Who's giving this stuff to the kids?"

"I don't know. If I knew, I'd have told the police. Chief Cusick keeps asking me what I hear. Hell, I'd tell him in a minute. I want it stopped as much as he does. But the kids won't say. They absolutely will not say where they're getting the stuff. I ask them straight out. I have no problem asking them. But, hey. The stuff is free, right? You don't rat on Santa Claus."

"Santa might kill them if they did," I said.

Pritchard shrugged. "There's that, too."

"But these kids know they've got a problem."

"Mainly, I hear from them because their problem is they don't have any more crack to smoke. They get more, their problem's solved."

"Pretty soon, though, they're going to have to buy it."

"Oh, absolutely. That's the scheme. See, I figure Windsor Harbor is like a trial market. You know, the way McDonald's might introduce spareribs or tofu sandwiches or something. They do their demographics and sell the new thing in a few stores, see how the folks take to it, try to project their profits. Windsor Harbor's like that. The new product is crack. If it looks like it's going to be a winner here, then the big boys'll move in. First here, then the whole North Shore. Crack, they say, is three times as profitable as snow. Foolproof to prepare, no special equipment needed." He shrugged. "Real bad news, crack."

I lit a cigarette and looked around for an ashtray. Pritchard opened a drawer in his desk and took one out. It was square glass with the logo of a computer company on it. "So how do you figure Alice Sylvester?" I said.

"Alice Sylvester got herself hooked on crack. I don't know, maybe she threatened to go to the cops. Whatever. They killed her. Object lesson, I suppose."

"Object lesson?"

"Sure. This is what happens if you even threaten to tell anybody where you're getting your crack. You get cut off. And then you get strangled to death. Only way to explain it."

"And that's why the kids are so close-mouthed."

"They're scared," he said. "Hooked and scared." Pritchard grinned at me. "You might have a small idea of what it's like."

"Huh?"

"You're hooked on those things, right?"

I looked at my cigarette. "I guess. It's hardly the same."

"It's closer than you think." He glanced at his watch. It prompted me to glance at mine. Ten of six.

I stood up, and he stood, too. He held out his hand to me. "Good luck, whatever it is you're up to."

I shook hands with him. "I appreciate your help," I said.

I got into my car and drove over to the high school. The long curving driveway was illuminated by tall lights, but the place looked abandoned. No cars in the big parking lot out front. No lights shone from inside. Just some floodlights up in the eaves of the sprawling brick schoolhouse, bathing the surrounding lawns and shrubbery in a surreal orange glow.

The driveway narrowed where it curved around the side of the building. This, Ingrid Larsen had told me, would take me to a direct entrance to the computer room. Here the drive was poorly illuminated. It ended in a little turnaround beside the building. One first-floor room was brightly lit. I parked beside a newish Volkswagen Golf and went to the doorway. I tried the handle, found it unlocked, and went inside.

I had entered directly into the large, air-conditioned computer room. The machines hummed almost sub-audibly. In a corner a printer was clattering. Gil Speer was sitting in front of it, watching the paper roll out of the machine. He was wearing well-faded jeans, cowboy boots, and a blue shirt with the sleeves rolled up to his elbows.

"Excuse me," I said after I walked up behind him.

He didn't turn. "Hang on a minute."

I hung on. A few minutes passed, during which the perforated paper slid out of the printer and folded itself neatly in a shallow box. Speer seemed mesmerized by the mechanics of it.

Abruptly the printer stopped. Speer tore the paper where it exited from the printer and picked up the folded stack. It looked to be about half an inch thick. Then he turned to look at me.

I was struck again by his youth and the softness of his appearance. A man of the future, all brain, vestigial body, with superior manual dexterity built into his genes in order to manipulate the machinery that would make civilization function. I felt awkward and out of proportion beside him, a crude throwback to a time when bulk and strength were survival tools.

Speer smiled. "I crunched some serious numbers, here. You want to decide whether you should repair roofs, build new schools, consolidate, whatever, all you've really got to do is know how to ask the machine. Lots of variables, of course, which makes it fun. Like the town's bond rating, demographics, enrollment projections, tax rates, state reimbursements. Factor all that stuff in there, turn on the switch, and this is what you get." He hefted the stack of paper in the palm of his hand as if he were weighing it.

I smiled. "I really don't know what you're talking about, Mr. Speer. But I think my question will sound pretty simple in comparison to all that."

He stood up, gestured for me to follow, and walked across the room to a large metal desk. He bent and slid open a drawer, placed his stack of papers into it, slammed it shut, and sat in the swivel chair behind the desk. I took a seat beside him.

"So," he said, "what can I do for you? Ingrid said it had something to do with a grade being changed?"

I took Alice Sylvester's report card from my pocket, unfolded it, and placed it on the desk facing him. He glanced at it and looked up. "How did you get ahold of this?"

"That's not important now—"

"These things are in the files. This is a copy, see? On this kind of cheap paper. It's a carbon. This is not the report card that went home. This came from a school file. How in hell did you get it?"

I shook my head. "Can I ask you a question?"

He picked up the paper. "This is two years old. All of this information is transferred to the permanent record section. It's printed out on transcripts. Then these files are erased. This was printed out year before last. Most of the stuff here—these term grades, the absences, that stuff—it all disappears. Only the final course grades stay."

"One of the final grades on this report card got changed along the way."

He shrugged. "Occasionally teachers will authorize that."

"Not in this case."

He shook his head. "You're wrong."

"Unless Mr. Tarlow is lying."

He cocked his head at me. "Ira Tarlow doesn't change grades. He doesn't lie, either."

"Then how did this D in biology end up as an A on the transcript?"

Speer gazed across the room toward the bank of computers, as if he were seeking answers there. "Alice was good," he said slowly. "Quick. But she was no hacker. She never could've broken the codes."

"That's one thing I wondered."

"Of course, it's possible somebody else . . ."

"Somebody else?"

He grinned at me. "I must admit, I've trained some pretty accomplished hackers over the past few years. Anything's possible."

"So you're saying that some kid changed this grade for Alice?"

He shook his head. "No. It's not really likely."

"I thought the system was supposed to be absolutely hackerproof. Dr. Larsen seemed quite certain of it."

"And this," he replied, tapping the green-and-white paper with his finger, "suggests to you that she is wrong. Am I right? Look. I change the codes every week. I don't write them down anywhere. They are only in my head. Mine and Ingrid's. Unless she writes them down."

"What if she did?"

He held his hands up in front of him in a gesture of surrender. "Then I cannot be held responsible. A janitor, a secretary, a student gets into her office, looks in her top drawer. The codes would be worth a lot of money to the person who knew how to use them."

"Who'd know how to use them?"

He smiled. "Anybody who has taken my course."

"Then—"

"Then, if Ingrid has been indiscreet, we've got a helluva problem. Imagine trying to verify every transcript. If Alice Sylvester's grade was changed, how many others?"

I nodded. "Supposing Ingrid Larsen did not write down the codes?"

"Look, Mr. Coyne. My codes are random numbers and words. Sometimes nonsense words. There is no pattern. It would take a skilled and patient hacker weeks to figure out one set of codes. Since I change them every week, there is only one explanation for this."

"It's Ingrid Larsen's fault."

He shrugged. "What else could it be?"

I smiled. "You."

He grinned. "True. I didn't think of that."

"You can see why I would, though."

"Well, frankly, what's missing here is a reason. You lawyers would call it a motive, huh?"

"I can think of several," I said.

He held up one finger. "Let me show you something, Mr. Coyne."

He pushed himself back from his desk. Then he bent over and slid open the bottom drawer. He reached in, fumbled for something, and then pulled it out and showed it to me.

It was a large square automatic pistol. Gil Speer was aiming it at my chest.

sixteen

"SO," I SAID.

Speer smiled. "So."

"Well, aren't you going to tell me to stick 'em up? Reach for the sky? You got me covered, pal."

He lounged back in his chair. The gun didn't waver. The bore was intimidating. "You pretty much have it figured out, don't you?" he said.

"Pretty much. I figure you changed Alice's grade. So she had something on you and you killed her. The rest of it's a little fuzzy, but I can see the outlines of it."

He nodded. "Let's go for a ride, Mr. Coyne."

"Aw, shucks. I was hoping we could play with your computers."

He stood up. "Come on." He gestured for me to go out the door I'd just entered. When I got to it I hesitated, and he said, "Open it. Slowly and carefully. Don't try anything funny."

"You get your dialogue from late-night movies?"

"Try not to be nervous."

We went out to the parking lot. Speer ordered me to open the door on the passenger side of my BMW. He stood there by the open door and told me to slide behind the wheel. Then he climbed into the passenger seat beside me.

"Nice wheels," he said. "Start it up." I obeyed. "Now head on out the way you came in. And whether you think the expression is hackneyed or not, I advise you not to try anything foolish. I am perfectly prepared to shoot you. If you drive too fast, or too slow, or try to blink your lights or something, I will shoot your knee. It will hurt like hell."

"I can imagine."

"Take a left down here at the end of the driveway."

I did as he instructed. "So why did you change the girl's biology grade?" I said as we drove north on the road, away from the center of town.

"Let's hear your guess."

"Okay," I said. "I figure it this way. She found out you were giving crack to high school kids. Probably heard it from Buddy Baron. So she went to you, threatened to tell. You asked her what her price was. You figured if she didn't have a price, she would've just told, and not bothered going to you. Her price was changing that biology grade."

"It was stupid of me," said Speer.

"Which," I said, "you soon realized. Your only out was to murder her. And since by then you figured Buddy knew about you, and would know that it was you who killed her, you had to murder him, too."

"I didn't murder Buddy," he said. "Take a right up there past the streetlight."

We turned down a narrow two-lane road that, if I was properly oriented, headed toward the ocean. There seemed to be very few houses along this road. It passed over a small saltwater creek, which looked as if it was at low tide. A vast marshland bordered it. It was illuminated brilliantly by the silver light of the full moon overhead.

"Slow down. It gets narrow and twisty up ahead. We wouldn't want to have an accident."

"I'm an excellent driver."

"I meant, we wouldn't want something happening to your knee."

"Oh," I said. "That kind of accident."

We drove on for a few minutes. The marsh gave way to low piney hills. Then more marshland. "Were you screwing Alice Sylvester?" I said.

"Moi?" said Speer. Then he laughed. "Sure. She was an absolutely stupendous piece of young flesh. Inventive, too. She did whatever I told her to do, and then found variations I'd never thought of. I can't imagine where a child like her learned all that. I like to think I inspired her. But I know better. She was a natural, I guess. I felt terrible when she died."

"When you killed her."

"Whatever."

"What happened?"

He laughed again. "I suppose you think my telling you will get you somewhere."

"I'm just curious."

"Sure you are." He said nothing for a minute or two. Then I heard him chuckle. The whole conversation was quite amusing to him. It was, I figured, the locker-room syndrome. Guess who I screwed? Alice Sylvester puts out. Gee, gosh. No kidding, Gil. What a stud.

"She came to me," he said in a softer voice, "all self-righteous and principled. Giving drugs to teenagers, Mr. Speer. How awful. What a naughty man. Really should just go right to the police. But . . . And I knew I had her. She wanted something. It wasn't hard to get it out of her, because it's what she wanted to say. She got this D from Mr. Tarlow. Totally unfair, but everybody knows he's a creep. Never get into Mount Holyoke with that D. Suppose I changed that grade for you, my dear? Oh, can you do that, Mr. Speer? Sure I can, young lady. But it would be very dishonest. But isn't giving drugs to kids dishonest, too? Well, I suppose it is. So I changed it, as you know. And we were even. She wouldn't tell on me, because then she'd have that awful D in biology. I couldn't tell on her, naturally, since I was the one breaking the rules, not to mention the law."

"But that's not where it ended," I prompted when he lapsed into silence.

"No. It's not. A few days—maybe a week—later she showed up in the computer room. It was late. I was getting ready to leave. I think she'd been lurking around, waiting to catch me alone, which isn't easy to do. She wanted to try crack. She knew I could get it for her. Said she just wanted to see what it was like. I told her it was bad for her. Nice kid like her shouldn't get mixed up with a bad drug. Told her to go ask her friends for some grass. She laughed. Said she knew all about grass. She came close to me. Put that soft little hand of hers on my cheek and said, 'Aw, please, Mr. Speer.' Look. I didn't want to get that chick involved with crack."

"I believe you," I said. "It would make her unstable, unreliable. No telling what she'd do."

He sighed. "Absolutely right. But then she put that soft little hand into my lap and rubbed her soft little body against me and said, 'Come on, Gil,' like that. Hey. What could I do? I gave her some crack." He paused. Then he laughed quietly. "She was extremely grateful to me, Mr. Coyne. And she had some marvelously unique ways of expressing her gratitude."

"I bet."

"Yes. Marvelous."

"So why did you kill her?"

"Slow down. There's a little driveway coming up on the left. There. By that birch tree."

"You want me to turn into that driveway?"

"Godammit, yes, I want you to turn into that driveway. Why'd you think I pointed it out to you? You think this is some kind of sightseeing tour? I killed her because she had started to become demanding as hell, and even a lovely piece of ass like her was beginning to get on my nerves. Crack does that. She was hooked bad. She was no longer reliable. I was pretty sure she had told Buddy Baron what was going on. I couldn't take the chance she'd tell others as well."

"But you screwed her that night before you killed her." I eased into the driveway. It turned out to be several hundred yards long, just a pair of ruts winding through a grove of pine trees. Ahead I could see some light.

"Pull up here," said Speer.

I stopped the car, turned off the ignition, and doused the lights. "Now what?" I said.

Speer just sat there. "Sure. Sure I screwed her. She had to screw for her hit of crack. That was our deal. Hell, I couldn't keep up with her. She would've banged me ten times a day. That's how bad she was hooked. The lass was insatiable. For the crack and for the cock. Want to hear something funny?"

"Right about now it would be welcome," I said.

"She had already screwed somebody else that night. I wasn't the first one."

"That was Buddy," I said.

"I was pretty sure it was. Anyway, we did it in the car, and afterwards I lit a pipe for her, and I waited for the rush to hit her, and when she was flying on that dope I strangled her. Believe me, it was painless for her."

"Considerate of you," I muttered.

"Oh, she was the best piece of ass I'll ever have."

"Explain to me now about Buddy Baron."

"God, was she good." Speer cleared his throat. "Baron? He knew. Alice let that slip. And then he got ahold of some evidence. Until today, I wasn't sure what the evidence was. I thought it was more than just that report card. I kept records, of course. We computer types, you know. Compulsive that way. I could've been careless, or Buddy might've been a better hacker than I thought. If anyone got their hands on my records . . . Shit. All he had was that damn report card. Thing was, though, Buddy knew what it meant. Alice told him enough for him to figure it out. Kid was too smart for his own good."

"So you sent those two goons to my house."

"I don't tell those goons what to do, Mr. Coyne. I'm just a peon."

"They work for the guy who supplies you with dope, right?"

Speer turned to me in the darkened car and nodded. "Yes."

"Who is it? Where are you getting this stuff?"

He laughed quickly through his nose. "I'm going to take you to meet him right now." He opened his door and slid out of the car. He crouched by the open door, his gun on me. "Okay. Slowly, now, Mr. Coyne. Open the door and get out. Be very careful. From here I might miss your knee and hit you in the balls or something."

I got out very carefully. Then I stood beside the car. Speer came around to my side. "Okay. We're going up to the cottage now."

The cottage, I saw by the bright moonlight when we got a little closer, stood on the edge of a saltwater creek. It appeared to be very isolated. There was a dark sedan parked in the shadows close to the little building. I couldn't tell the make or model. Behind the cottage stretched the marsh, and beyond the marsh, judging by the flat horizon, lay the Atlantic Ocean.

Beside the cottage the path descended to the riverbank, where a long dock jutted out. It stood on tall pilings with the tide at low ebb. Moored by the dock was a big ocean-going sportfishing boat. It was, I guessed, a thirty-six or thirty-eight footer. Not as big as the boat that had been stolen from Frank Paradise, but a substantial seaworthy craft, nonetheless.

The cottage was no more than that—a single-story shingled structure with a low wooden deck that appeared to encircle it on all four sides.

As we approached the door, I could hear the murmur of voices inside. It took me an instant to realize that the voices came from a television set.

Speer went to the screen door. The inside door was open. I stood beside him while Speer pushed his face against the screen and rapped on the wooden frame.

"Hey, it's me," he yelled over the sound of the television.

From inside a man's voice shouted, "That you, Speer?"

"Right," he said. "It's me, and—"

The blast from the shotgun lifted Gil Speer off his feet and slammed him backwards onto the ground beyond the deck.

The hole in the screen door was about the size and shape of a basketball. It would have been chest high on Gil Speer.

I may have stood rooted there for five seconds. No more than that. But during that brief time several thoughts presented themselves for my consideration.

I could crouch there and hide.

I could leap into the boat and speed away to safety.

I could pound on the door, present myself indignantly, and make a citizen's arrest.

I did the one other thing that occurred to me.

I started to run like hell.

I jumped off the edge of the wood deck and stumbled to my knees as I landed awkwardly in the dark. I stared frantically around. I had an open area to cross, about the size of a baseball infield, and then I'd reach the tree-lined driveway. Adrenaline pumped. My mind focused only on escape. I pushed myself to my feet. My right knee protested. The old football injury. I could ignore it. I began to run.

The sudden blinding light stopped me in my tracks. I turned and squinted back at the cottage. From under the eaves shone half a dozen floodlights. I made out the silhouette of a figure standing on the deck. He was training a gun on me.

"Mr. Coyne, sir," called a voice I recognized. It belonged to the fat man who called himself Mr. Curry. "Mr. Coyne, do come and join us inside."

I quickly weighed my options. At twenty yards, the shotgun Mr. Curry had trained on me would not miss, no matter how cleverly I might feint and dart toward the protection of the darkened forest. It might not kill me. I took no solace from that.

I shrugged and limped up the steps. Mr. Curry said, "What a pleasant surprise, sir."

I pulled open the mangled screen door. Mr. Curry followed me in.

I stopped abruptly and stared at the man who was sitting on the sofa, his legs crossed, a half-apologetic smile playing on his lips.

"Good evening, Mr. Coyne," said Harry Cusick, the Windsor Harbor police chief.

"I feel kind of stupid," I said.

"Oh, don't feel stupid," said Mr. Curry. "It's better if me'n Harry, here, feel smart. Right, Harry?"

"Sure. Absolutely. You're right as usual, Ralph." Cusick waggled his revolver at me. "Have a seat, Mr. Coyne."

"That's okay," I said. "I've been sitting all day."

"Sit!" said Cusick.

I sat. Cusick sat beside the other man on the sofa, facing me.

"Good," said the fat man. "We can try it again." He moved the barrel of his shotgun in little circles, crudely outlining my lung area.

"What's he talking about?" I said to Cusick.

Cusick shrugged. "You two know each other, I believe."

"The list," said Mr. Curry.

"Who are you, anyway?" I said to him.

He glanced at Harry Cusick. Cusick shrugged. "Tell him. It doesn't matter."

I decided I didn't like the sound of that.

"O'Keefe," he said. "Ralph O'Keefe."

"Never heard of you," I said. "No offense, of course."

He smiled broadly. "No offense taken," he said. "Now, sir, I'll give you another opportunity to tell me where the list is."

Cusick snorted. "There's no list, Ralph. That was Speer's hangup. All there was was a report card that Speer changed the grade on, for crissake. Maybe enough to bother Speer. Not enough to tie us in. We should have disposed of Speer a long time ago. Then we'd be clear right now, and poor Mr. Coyne here would be home sleeping in his bed."

O'Keefe smiled. "I figure we're clear anyhow."

Cusick looked at me. "I agree," he said. To O'Keefe he said, "You about ready?"

O'Keefe stood up. He still held the shotgun on me. "Let's go for a boat ride, Mr. Coyne. A beautiful night for it. Lovely moon, tide just turning—"

"Can it, Ralph," said Cusick wearily.

"Can I ask a question?" I said to Cusick.

"Why not?"

"Why Speer? I mean, the man's obviously a genius at what he does. How does a guy like that end up passing crack to teenagers and then getting his chest blown away by a shotgun?"

Cusick hunched his shoulders as if his neck was stiff, or he was bored by the subject. "I guess he was a genius. I don't know much about that. He had to've been pretty clever to put together the papers he did."

"What do you mean?"

"Speer, of course, wasn't his real name. MIT wasn't the place he spent his college days, either. The guy learned computers at an institution in Illinois where they don't have proms and you have to spend spring weekends in your room. And Gil Speer knew a hell of a lot about hooking kids on drugs long before I figured out who he was. He served his time, a model prisoner, and then went to work on a computer, putting together a nice new identity for himself. If he was as clever as me, of course, he'd probably still be doing what he wanted to do, which was to fart around with computers and screw high school girls."

"But you blackmailed him."

Cusick stifled a yawn. "Call it what you want. I persuaded him to join us in our fledgling little enterprise."

"You are a bastard," I said, shaking my head slowly.

He smiled. "Thank you very much."

"One more question," I said. "Why you, Cusick?"

He arched his eyebrows and grinned. "Why not?" was his answer.

"Come on, Harry," said O'Keefe. "Let's can the conversation."

Cusick nodded. "Right. You and Mr. Coyne, here, take Speer down to the boat."

O'Keefe started to protest and then, glancing at Cusick, changed his mind. We went out onto the deck. Speer lay sprawled on his back. The entire front of him, from throat to crotch, was stained dark. The blood that drenched his shirt and puddled on the wood planks glistened in the bright floodlights.

O'Keefe handed the shotgun to Cusick. Then he reached down and grabbed Speer by his armpits. "Get his legs," said Cusick to me. I bent and gripped Speer under his knees. Slowly, awkwardly, we lugged the limp, dead-weight body of Gil Speer down a rough path to the dock where the boat was moored.

Her name was painted on the transom. *Gretel.* Newburyport. A local boat.

We laid Speer on the dock while O'Keefe climbed aboard. Then he reached over and we heaved and shoved the corpse over the side. It fell into the bottom of the boat with a muffled thump.

Harry Cusick, who had followed us down the path, was standing on the dock behind me, the shotgun cradled casually under his arm. I thought of disarming him with a deft feint and jab and judo throw, grabbing the shotgun, and getting the drop on O'Keefe, just like on television.

What I actually did was nothing, just like in real life.

O'Keefe jumped back onto the dock and took the shotgun from Cusick, who then climbed aboard and ducked into the cabin. He started up the engines. They purred and burbled powerfully. Then he came out of the cabin. He held a revolver, which he was pointing at me. "Okay, Mr. Coyne. Come aboard. Step down. Mind the corpse, now. Be careful. Don't slip and fall on the blood."

I stepped into the boat. Gil Speer's body lay on its stomach. If it weren't for the impossibly awkward way one of his arms was twisted behind him, he could have been sleeping.

Cusick told me to go down below. There were three or four short steps. I had to duck my head. Below deck there was a small room with berths lined on either side. The boat would sleep six hunchbacked midgets in comfort. There was a door leading to what I assumed was the head.

"Sit," said Cusick.

I sat on one of the berths. Cusick remained standing, holding his revolver on me, until O'Keefe came below. "I undid the ropes," he said.

"Lines," said Cusick.

"Excuse me, sir?"

"Not ropes. Don't call them ropes. They're lines."

"Whatever. I undid them. Let's get going. Tally ho, or whatever you're supposed to say."

"Anchors aweigh," sang Cusick. He went topside. O'Keefe sat on the berth across from me, one fat leg crossed over the other, his shotgun resting on it, pointing at me.

"A sea cruise," I said. "Goody."

"You've got some sense of humor, Mr. Coyne."

I shrugged. "I just like boats. Can't help it."

"You ought to really like this trip."

"So who was your friend?"

"Which friend?"

"The dead guy. In my apartment."

"You mean Rat? Rat Benetti. You probably never heard of him."

"Never heard of you, for that matter. Which of you was the clever one who tortured Buddy Baron?"

"Oh, that was Rat. He was always creative at that sort of thing. The toaster was his idea. The kid died real fast."

"So you figured he had given me the report card."

"We actually thought he had Speer's list."

"Well, he didn't. And when you dropped in on me, I didn't have it, either."

O'Keefe yawned. "The sea air. Always makes me sleepy."

"It tends to make me sick," I said.

We had been moving for eight or ten minutes. Through the small porthole I could see coastal lights blinking in the distance. We seemed to be moving parallel to the coast, heading north.

It was what they call a medium sea. The boat bucked and rolled in the swells.

O'Keefe yawned again. He stood up, went to a cabinet, and pulled out a bag of potato chips. Then he sat down again. He rummaged in the bag and brought out a big handful of chips. He began to eat them. He ate delicately, taking little nips out of each chip.

He noticed me watching him. "You hungry? Want some chips?"

"Jesus, no," I said.

He cocked his head at me. "You all right?"

"Not really."

"You don't look that great, sir."

I swallowed hard and slumped back onto the berth.

"Listen," said O'Keefe. "You better the hell not puke."

"No promises," I mumbled.

"Aw, shit," he said. I felt his hands on me. "Hey. Come on. Get up. Let's go up there and get some air."

"Just leave me alone."

"Nossir, by Jesus, you ain't gonna stink up this boat. Not while I've got to ride in it." He grabbed my shoulder and yanked on it. "Get your ass up."

"Please be gentle," I moaned.

"Okay, okay. I'm gentle. Stand up."

I pushed myself to a standing position and remained there, swaying precariously with the motion of the boat. O'Keefe jabbed my back with the bore of his shotgun. "Go on. Up the stairs."

I pulled myself slowly up the steps. Topside, the fresh salt air tasted good. Cusick was in the cabin, steering. He swiveled his head around. "Hey, what the hell are you doing?" he yelled at O'Keefe over the roar of the engines.

"This bastard's threatening to blow lunch down there."

"Let him."

"Sure. Fine for you. You can stay up here and run the damn boat."

Cusick shrugged and turned his attention back to his navigation.

"Feel any better now?" said O'Keefe.

"No. Worse."

"Be easier if I just killed you right now."

"Do it," I said. "Please."

I made a gagging noise and stumbled for the side of the boat. Land appeared to be close, but I knew how deceiving distances can be over water. We were probably a couple miles out, still roughly paralleling the coastline.

I hung my head over the side. They were going to take me and Gil Speer's dead body out there someplace and dump us where the currents would carry us to Africa. Then they'd head back in and for them it would be business as usual. The disappearances of Gil Speer, computer specialist at a small North Shore high school, and Brady L. Coyne, mild-mannered Boston barrister, would be mysteries. Harry Cusick, the local police chief, would investigate thoroughly. He would give statements to the press. He would track down leads. He would discover that Coyne had been in town the evening he disappeared, that he had, in fact, had an appointment with Speer. The trail would end at Computer City, where Coyne was last seen alive.

Our bodies would never be found, at least not by human beings.

The sharks and other seagoing scavengers would undoubtedly find us.

I braced my hands against the side of the boat, tensed my legs, and pushed. I tumbled over the side into the dark, shockingly cold water.

seventeen

I WOULDN'T GLORIFY THE TUMBLE from boat to sea by calling it a dive, but it did the trick. I landed on my right shoulder, and in the same motion I aimed for the briny deep and kicked as hard as I could. I heard the muffled thrumming of the twin propellers pass overhead.

I stayed under until my lungs burned and lights began to flicker alarmingly in my head. It took an enormous effort of will to ease myself slowly to the surface and let just my face emerge. Air never tasted so sweet.

I found myself in the trough of a swell, a valley surrounded by smooth mountains of water. I could neither see nor hear *Gretel*. Nor could I see land.

I trod water for a few minutes, resting and replenishing my oxygen supply. I picked out the few constellations I recognized—both dippers, the three stars of Orion. They didn't help me get myself oriented at all.

I rode up onto the crest of a giant swell just in time to see *Gretel* coming straight at me. They had a spotlight, which they were playing around, first on one side then on the other. Since they hadn't centered me in it, I assumed they hadn't seen me.

I bobbed there for as long as I dared, waiting to see where the boat was going. It was about to pass just to the left of me when I let myself sink beneath the surface. From the way the sound moved under the water, I was able to determine when she had passed by, and I swam over to where her wake would be. It was, I figured, the last place they'd think to shine their light.

When I surfaced, I saw *Gretel* moving directly away from me. She was chugging along slowly. Cusick and O'Keefe were scanning the seas with the spotlight methodically. They'd probably turn soon and do another lap.

In the meantime, I realized I had other problems. I was an unknown but substantial distance from land. The water, while not frigid, was cold. I knew about hypothermia, and I knew that my allotted time to survive in the sea was limited. I probably had two hours. Three at the outside. Avoiding detection by the murderers aboard *Gretel* was one thing. But I also had to make it to land.

I floated to the top of another swell and found the glow of city lights in the night sky that located the coastline. I'd worry about the boat when it came near. But I had to start moving.

I set off, propelled by my inefficient crawl. Too much arm and shoulder, too little kick. I had never been completely comfortable in the water, and my lack of conditioning didn't help. I tired quickly, so I switched to a smoother sidestroke. That moved me more slowly, but it allowed me to regulate my breathing. After a few minutes I paused and tugged off my pants and shoes and let them sink. I found I could move better after that.

I kept oriented toward the coastline, and every once in a while I stopped swimming to check my progress.

It was discouraging. I didn't seem to be getting anywhere. The lights appeared to be as far away as they had when I started. I wondered if the tide was carrying me in the wrong direction, or if I was caught in a current.

And already I had begun to feel tired. My legs were growing numb from the cold water.

The good news was that *Gretel* had not made another appearance.

I realized that if I was to make it, I had to turn off my mind and put my body on automatic pilot. So I resumed my crawl stroke. After a few minutes I found a rhythm.

The rhythm came from an ancient work song I was taught in second-grade music class. "The Song of the Vulgar Boatman" was what I was certain old Miss Marselli named it. Something to do with big flat-bottomed barges on the Vulgar River somewhere in Europe, and it was several years before I learned that the river was in fact called the Volga.

But as a second-grader, the Vulgar Boatman had been a real, living presence. I pictured him vividly in my young imagination. He was tall, sinewy, and incredibly ugly. He had a scar on his cheek and rheumy red eyes. Long greasy hair, a scraggly beard, big, uneven, yellow-stained teeth. He poled that boat along, chanting his song, and interspersing it with all the colorful vulgarities my young ears had heard.

"Yo, ho, *heave,* ho," sang the Vulgar Boatman in my ear. "Swim, you asshole," he whispered.

"Yo, ho, *heave,* ho," went the song, and I stroked on the word "heave." Over and over again. "Yo, ho, *heave,* ho." I imagined myself pushing a barge up the Vulgar River. It was big and heavy, and we seemed to be heaving against a current, and I was the only one on it. I was the Vulgar Boatman. *"Heave,* you old shithead," I said to myself. I had a long pole, which I jammed onto the bottom and heaved, and that big old barge would inch forward a few feet before I had to plant the pole again.

And then my body was the barge, and setting that pole and heaving was my stroke, and the Vulgar Boatman had me moving. Right arm, heave. Deep breath. Heave.

I figured I had traveled all the way to the source of the Vulgar River before I lifted my head to check my progress.

It might have been my imagination, or exhaustion. But I seemed to be a little closer to land. But not much.

Yo, ho, *heave,* ho.

"Heave, shit-for-brains."

Left arm. Right arm. Breathe.

The current seemed to fight me. The barge was growing broader and heavier and more awkward. My pole seemed flimsy. After a while there was a roaring in my ears and a distant part of my mind warned me not to go to sleep.

The roaring became louder. It was not inside my head.

Gretel was coming up fast from my right. She would pass just in front of me. Her spotlight was sweeping, sweeping. Overhead, the full moon still shone brightly.

My mind snapped back. I figured Cusick and O'Keefe would have been smarter to work without the spotlight. The moon was bright enough to see by. The effect of the spotlight would actually be to render darker that part of the sea not directly illuminated by it.

I remember staying out on remote lakes in Maine after dark and trying to find the dock. Even without a bright moon, my night vision would do the trick just fine. Once, Charlie McDevitt had helpfully turned on a flashlight. Instantly, everything went black except what his flashlight showed. I told him to shut the damn thing off, and we found our way back easily.

So I figured all I had to do was watch the spotlight. The rest would be darkness to the guys abroad *Gretel.*

But *Gretel* was moving up fast now, and my reflexes must have been slow, because suddenly the spotlight was sweeping toward me, and I wasn't sure if I ducked under quickly enough. When I had to pop up for air, *Gretel* was making a big circle and heading back to me. I waited as long as I dared before I dipped under again.

If Cusick and O'Keefe had spotted me, it wouldn't matter whether they blasted me with O'Keefe's shotgun or not. By hanging around in the area, they would prevent me from making it to shore. My body temperature would fall. I would lapse into unconsciousness and eventually I'd slide under the surface of the sea and not pop up again. Ever.

I couldn't stay out there much longer and survive. I was too tired. The water was too cold. My body was too heavy. I was on a leaky barge, and that ferryman was the hideous Charon, poling me across the treacherous swamp of Styx toward a resting place from which I would never return. A rational piece of my brain warred with the delirium I distantly recognized. "No," it whispered. "Push on. Survive." Charon, my own Vulgar Boatman, urged me on.

So I pointed myself toward shore and took up the refrain. The Vulgar Boatman leered at me. *"Heave,* you stupid cocksucker. Yo, ho, *heave,* ho."

Yo, ho . . .

After what seemed like a long, long time I heard the roaring in my ears again, and someplace in my mind a warning bell rang for an instant. But I was too sleepy and too numb, and it was only when the roaring became louder and my body began to tumble that I realized it was the crash of the surf.

It lifted me and flipped me over. I gulped a mouthful of seawater and gagged. Back in the rational part of my brain that still operated, I thought how ironic it would be if I escaped all the bad guys and swam halfway across the Atlantic Ocean only to drown in the surf fifty yards from dry land.

I managed to get my legs under me. They felt like two hunks of driftwood, numb and useless. I stumbled and sprawled forward as a breaker knocked me down. But, by God, that was land underneath me.

I crawled up onto the beach until the surf couldn't reach me. I maneuvered myself into a sitting position. I looked back over the sea. I saw no boats out there. Only the white line where the surf was breaking, and beyond that the gray sea. It looked tranquil from my spot on the beach.

The moon had moved a long way since I had started. I glanced at my wrist. Somewhere along the way I had lost my watch. And, I remembered, my pants and shoes.

Then I began to shiver. Great racking convulsions came in waves, shaking me violently. I knew I couldn't sit there on the beach on this chilly October night for very long.

I punched and pounded on my legs. I struggled into a kneeling position. After an awkward minute or two I managed to stand. I staggered and stumbled around, and after a bit of that I found myself able to hobble in roughly the direction I aimed myself.

Then I looked around.

I was on a small sandy beach, no more than fifty yards wide. Big boulders had been piled to form breakwaters on either side. They extended far into the ocean. Beyond my beach there were other beaches, each demarcated by rock breakwaters. Opposite the ocean rose a small sandy cliff, which was fighting a losing battle against erosion. Wooden stairs led up from the beach.

I climbed the stairs. It took me a long time, taking one step at a time and resting after every three or four. But I made it.

At the top of the stairs was a wide sweep of lawn, a deep purple-green in the waning moonlight. It appeared impeccably manicured. A bed of rust-colored mums bloomed against a stockade fence that ran from the top of the stairs along the edge of the lawn to the house.

It was a big old year-round place, painted white. A glassed-in porch ran along the entire back side of it. There were no lights on.

I made my way around to the front. A peastone drive circled under a portico at the front door. A late model Mercedes was parked there.

I found a doorbell, jabbed it with my unsteady forefinger, and kept it pushed in. My legs were twitching and quivering and I felt the painful beginnings of cramps form in my calves. I leaned against the doorjamb and kept my finger on the bell.

After several minutes I heard a window go up. "If that's you, Peter, you can just turn around and go back to where you came from," came a woman's voice.

"It's not Peter, ma'am," I yelled hoarsely. "I need help."

There was a long moment of silence.

"Who is there?"

"I fell into the sea. I washed up on your beach. Please . . ."

Another pause. Then, "I shall call the police."

"Fine," I said. "But please let me in. I'm freezing."

"Are you drunk, young man?"

"No, ma'am. But I am nearly frozen to death. I can barely stand up."

"Did Peter send you?"

"I don't know Peter. Please, ma'am."

"Well. Wait a minute, then."

The window slammed. Then a light went on inside. Then there was the sound of somebody at the inside of the door.

The door opened a crack. "Uh, ma'am," I said, "I don't have any pants on."

She stuck her face out to look at me. She was, I guessed, around seventy. She had a deeply tanned and liberally wrinkled face with snow-white hair in a long braid that fell over the front of her shoulder. She had steely blue eyes and a warm, knowing smile.

"I've seen plenty of men without their pants," she said. "They all look pretty much the same to me. Mostly all shriveled up and vulnerable. Come on in here and get out of the cold."

"I'm not actually sure I can," I said. "My legs are cramping up pretty bad."

She came out and wedged herself under my armpit. She was surprisingly strong. She helped me inside, and together we stumbled into the kitchen. It opened onto the glassed-in porch. Beyond the glass, the ocean looked dark and secretive.

She put a pot of water on the stove and found a blanket for me to wrap myself in. I shucked off my wet underwear from inside the blanket.

"I'm Mary Watson," she said. "Who're you?"

"Brady Coyne," I stammered. I couldn't stop shivering.

The teapot began to whistle. Mary Watson dropped two teabags into a big mug, filled it with scalding water, added about four spoonfuls of sugar and a big dollop from a rum bottle, and handed it to me. I tried to take it from her, but my hands refused to cooperate.

So Mary pulled a chair beside me and held the mug for me so I could sip from it. She insisted I sip fast and get it into me. When it was empty she refilled it the same way, and this time I was able to hold it myself.

"Now, Brady Coyne, you tell me exactly what in hell you are doing creeping around people's houses at four o'clock in the morning without any pants on, or I will call the police for real."

I made up a story about a party aboard a boat, having a few beers, slipping off the deck while trying to untangle some lines, no one noticing. It sounded thin, and Mary stared at me with her head cocked to the side as she listened, a crooked, skeptical grin playing on her lips. But when I finished my tale, she only nodded a few times, as if to say that it might not be the truth, but it was good enough for her.

"I'll get you some clothes," she said. "Peter is about your size." I still had no clue who Peter was.

She disappeared from the kitchen. I sipped my tea. The rum formed a warm place in my gut, and I felt relaxed and tired. I yawned. The thick wool blanket scratched my bare skin, not an unpleasant sensation.

Mary returned a few minutes later with an armload. Corduroy pants (short in the leg, about right in the waist), flannel shirt (okay in the shoulders, arms a bit stingy), underwear, a wooly crew-neck sweater, and sneakers that were only half a size small. I dressed unashamedly in front of her, and she neither stared at me nor made a point of ignoring what I was doing, although I did turn my back to her out of principle.

"Seen plenty of men," she reminded me. "Some of 'em are hung a little better than others, though I never put much stock in that."

I was glad, nevertheless, that I had dressed with my back to her.

"What town am I in?" I asked.

"Why, this is Hampton."

"New Hampshire?"

"It sure isn't Wyoming."

"May I use your phone?"

"Of course."

There was a wall phone in the kitchen. Mary wandered out of the room. I called the Baron house.

On the third ring Joanie answered. "H'lo," she mumbled.

"Joanie, it's Brady. Is Tom there?"

"Juss minute."

I heard Joanie speak and a muttered reply. Then Tom came on the line. "Brady, for Christ's sake, do you have any idea what time it is?"

I checked the clock on the wall of Mary Watson's kitchen. "Five twenty-six. Approximately."

"Well, what the hell?"

"It's a very long story. And a very interesting one. I need you to come and get me."

"Right now?"

"Immediately."

He must have heard something in my voice. "Are you all right?"

"Yes. Hold on a second. I'll get directions for you." I called for Mary, and she came into the room. I told her what I wanted and put her on the phone. She told Tom how to find me. Then she handed the phone back to me.

"Now, Tom," I said.

"She sounds like quite a dame."

"Quite a dame, indeed," I said, glancing at Mary, who had taken a seat at the kitchen table. She rolled her eyes.

"So what's your hurry? You would seem to be in good hands."

"Just move it, please. I'll explain."

I hung up. Mary was staring at me. "Was that Tom Baron?"

"How'd you know?"

"You called him Tom. I recognized his voice. Is he a friend of yours?"

"Uh huh."

"If I lived in Massachusetts, I'd vote for him. Handsome fella."

"Mary, I need to make another call."

"Oh. Sure. I get it." She left the room.

I called state police headquarters and asked for Horowitz.

"He's not here now. Wanna leave a message?" The desk man sounded bored at the end of a long night shift.

"I've got to talk with him. Instantly. Can you patch me through to his house?"

"You kidding, Mister?"

"Look," I said. "My name is Brady Coyne. I'm an attorney. I have witnessed a murder. It is connected to two other murders that Horowitz is investigating. While you're sitting there arguing with me, the bad buys are getting away. It's Horowitz's case. I guarantee he'll have your ass if you don't find a way to connect me to him."

"How about Leary? He's right here."

"You didn't hear me, huh?"

"I heard you. Horowitz'll have my ass if I wake him up at five-thirty, I know that. I don't know about the other."

He seemed to be wavering. I decided to press my case. "What is your name, officer?"

"Bergin. Francis Bergin. Sergeant Francis Bergin."

"I assume, Sergeant, that you'd prefer not to become rookie Patrolman Bergin. So listen to me. I absolutely promise you that Detective Horowitz will thank you for waking him up. He will be very grateful. He may put you in for a promotion, or a citation, or a raise, or a shopping spree in the evidence locker. He will praise you for using excellent judgment in a crisis. And this, Sergeant Bergin, is a crisis. You could blow it. So come on. Be a hero. Connect me to Horowitz."

He hesitated. "It would take a few minutes."

"I'm not going away. Come on."

It took almost five minutes, and when Horowitz came on the line, he didn't sound in the mood for giving out citations. "What the fuck is this all about, Coyne?"

I gave him the chronology as concisely as I could. To his credit, he became instantly alert. He asked me the right questions at the right times. He made me repeat the directions to the cottage in Windsor Harbor where O'Keefe and Cusick kept *Gretel* moored. I told him to make sure that Christie Ayers was okay. He suggested I stay with Tom and Joanie Baron until he got in touch with me. "Keep out of sight. Don't let anyone know you're there."

"Play dead, huh?"

"Right. Play dead," he said.

When I hung up, Mary came back into the room. She looked at me out of the corner of her eye, and I knew she had been listening.

"Mary Watson," I said, making my voice gruff and stern.

She turned around with a wide-eyed innocent look. "Yes, Brady? What can I get you?"

I laughed. "Do you mind if I take a hot shower while I'm waiting for Tom?"

"Lord, no." She sounded relieved. "Come on. Follow me."

She led me upstairs, put out a big bath towel and razor, and showed me how to adjust the temperature of the water. I took my time at it, letting the heat and the steam soak deep into my flesh, and when I finished I dried myself and got dressed. I felt nearly normal. Tired, but that healthy tired that comes from good exercise.

A nap would have been perfect.

When I returned downstairs, Tom Baron was sitting with Mary Watson in the kitchen. They were sipping coffee and Mary was telling Tom how her Peter, at the age of seventy-eight, had gotten himself a widow lady, a mere girlchild of sixty-three and how about once a month he forgot to come home on time and Mary would lock him out of the house, and he'd stand on the lawn and cry and promise to be good until she let him in. Which, she was saying cheerfully, she always did, because he was losing some of his marbles and couldn't be held strictly accountable for his behavior.

He had, she said, become a horny old goat. She figured that his inhibitions were disappearing along with his memory. If he wanted to run around with that fat widow, it was no skin off her nose, one way or the other, she said.

She managed to get what she needed out of him anyway, Mary told Tom with a girlish giggle.

Tom Baron, I was forced to admit, had a way with people. Got them to tell him the damnedest things. My feelings were a little hurt that Mary had not chosen to confide in me.

I stood there, shifting my weight from one leg to the other. Tom barely glanced at me. Mary was talking a mile a minute. They both treated her tale as if it were utterly fascinating.

To Mary, at least, I supposed it was.

When she finally wound down, Tom stood politely. "I suppose I should rid you of this man," he said, jerking his head at me.

She smiled. "Oh, he's a nice enough man, even if he runs around without any pants on."

I thanked her profusely and promised to return Peter's clothes.

"Keep them. He won't know the difference," she said.

I tried to pay for the phone calls. She refused that, too. "It's been an adventure, Brady Coyne. I can't wait to tell Peter what he missed."

Tom and I went to his car. After we got started up, he said, "Now, for Christ's sake, will you tell me what happened?"

eighteen

IT TOOK ABOUT HALF AN HOUR TO drive from Mary Watson's place in Hampton, New Hampshire, to Windsor Harbor, Massachusetts. Just long enough for me to tell Tom the entire story.

He didn't interrupt me, even when I explained Buddy's part in it. When I finished, he was silent for a long time. Then he said in a soft voice, "Harry Cusick. How do you figure it?"

"Who knows?" I answered. "Greed, probably. Or jealousy, or love, or revenge. Pick your motive. You know him better than me."

Tom laughed sourly. "I thought I knew a lot of people. The thing about Cusick that gets me is this: I always thought he was *too* good a cop. A tough nut who took no shit from anybody. I couldn't budge him with Buddy."

"Everybody's got their price, Tom."

"Yeah," he said. "I'm learning that. I'm learning that about myself, even. It's a hard lesson."

Later, while he and Joanie and I were sprawled in his living room drinking coffee, Tom said, "I'm going to cancel out tonight. Supposed to be going to Taunton. Got a feeling that what's happening around here may be more important."

We had lunch. Tom and Joanie took a walk down along the beach. I opted to stick close to the phone. I ended up on the sofa in their living room.

I woke up when they came back in, rubbing their arms and stomping their feet. "Cold," said Joanie. "Winter's coming."

"So's the election," said Tom. "Thank God."

Around three in the afternoon Eddy Curry came by. Tom told him to call whomever he had to call to beg off the Taunton appearance. Curry began to argue, but Tom cut him off. So Curry shrugged and went to the phone in the den. He came back a few minutes later. "They don't like it," he said. "A state senator was going to be there. He wanted to be seen with you."

"He's probably better off," said Tom.

"He may well be, at that." Curry nodded.

A state police cruiser pulled into the driveway around five. Joanie got the door, and she came back a minute later leading Horowitz. He nodded to me, and I introduced him to Tom and Curry. They shook hands.

Joanie offered us drinks. Horowitz asked for coffee. I said that was what I wanted, too. While we waited, he said to Tom, "How goes the campaign?"

"We're going to lose," said Tom.

"Not necessarily," said Curry quickly.

Tom shrugged. "Oh, we're going to lose, all right. But it's okay. There are more important things."

Joanie brought our coffee. Horowitz spooned sugar into his, then bent and slurped it. "Mmm," he said. "No lunch today. Doughnut for breakfast. Long day."

"Let me get you something," said Joanie.

Horowitz waved his hand. "Naw. The coffee is great. Thanks."

"Did you check on Christie Ayers?" I asked.

Horowitz sipped his coffee and nodded. "She's fine."

"So are you going to tell me what happened?"

Horowitz peered up at me over the rim of his coffee mug. "Oh, we got 'em. Not very exciting. I had a dozen troopers with me. We snuck up on that little cottage. O'Keefe was sound asleep. Came without a squawk. All he's said so far is that this Rat Benetti—the guy you shot, Mr. Coyne— he's the one who killed your son—" he turned his head and nodded at Joanie "—and that you—" a nod to me "—jumped off his boat. He claims he never heard of Gil Speer. So then I went to visit Harry Cusick. He was at his desk, big as life. When I told him I was arresting him, all he said was, 'I'll be damned. He made it.' "

"Meaning me," I said.

Horowitz nodded. "Yes, sir. Meaning you."

"So what about Speer, anyway?" I said.

Horowitz shrugged. "Well, without a body . . . The old corpus delicti, you know. No trace of him on the boat. No blood, that I could see. They obviously swabbed it out. I'll have the boys go over it, and the cottage, too. They'll find traces, no doubt. And there is that big hole in the screen, of course. We can probably prove it was made by a shotgun. But that doesn't prove anybody got killed."

"I saw it," I said.

He nodded. "That helps. But it doesn't prove the man's dead. Therefore, it doesn't prove a murder."

"Jesus—"

"Look," said Horowitz. "Don't worry about it. All I'm saying is that it makes a murder conviction tough. Not necessarily impossible. Maybe we'll find a way to persuade one or the other of them to tell us about it. We have got some things. We'll put together a case."

"But," I said, "it was Speer who killed Alice. We can't get him. And we probably can't prove it wasn't Benetti who killed Buddy. Now, without Speer's body, what do we have?"

"We'll find something," he said. "The drugs, at least. I'm sure we'll find something at that cottage. And you'll testify to what happened to you, what you saw."

"Enthusiastically," I said. "So who are these guys, this O'Keefe and Rat Benetti, anyway?"

"Benetti was from Elizabeth, New Jersey. Smalltimer, according to his sheet. O'Keefe is out of New York and connected."

"The mob?"

Horowitz grinned at me. "Whatever you'd like to call it. O'Keefe is pretty high up in the drug department. He's got direct links to Colombia, Mexico, Guatemala. One of the main guys in the Big Apple, actually. We're real glad to have him. You do good work, for a lawyer."

I bowed my head modestly.

"But why Windsor Harbor?" asked Tom.

"Simple as pie," said Horowitz. "It's where Harry Cusick worked."

"They had something on him?"

Horowitz shrugged. "Maybe. Or maybe he just let it be known that he was greedy. Something else we'll find out soon enough."

"Anyway, you got them," said Joanie. "It's finally over."

Horowitz stood up and stretched. "I suppose it's over for you, Mrs. Baron. But it's not over. Not hardly. We got these two. A nice day's work. That's about all you can really say." He yawned and rolled his shoulders. "You coming, Mr. Coyne? We ought to get going. We both had a long day, huh?"

A few days later I got a call from Frank Paradise. "They found her," he announced in that booming voice of his.

"Who?"

"My baby. My *Egg Harbor*. She turned up in Sarasota, Florida. Stripped clean, of course, and in bad need of TLC. But she's afloat."

"That's good news, Frank."

"Wondered if you'd like to go down with me and bring her back. Might take three or four weeks, sorta cruise the inland waterway, catch some fish, drink some beer, tell some stories, polish her brass. You want, you can bring a lady."

"I know one who could use a little vacation," I said.

Sylvie had grown solemn since her encounter with the phony Messrs. Curry and Baron. She didn't tease me very often. She tended to cry after making love. She hardly ever wandered around the house undressed. She would enjoy the trip. We planned it for the third week in November, and Frank agreed that there was no reason on earth to get back to Massachusetts much before Christmas.

Cathy Fallon dropped by my office the morning after Halloween. She appeared very somber. She handed me an envelope. I opened it and took out the multiple copies of the contract between her and her husband and her sister, Eleanor Phelps. I glanced at them and then looked up at her.

"They're not signed."

She shook her head. "No. No, they're not. But thanks anyway. We will still pay you, of course."

I nodded and shrugged. "What happened?"

She sighed. "It was Eleanor. Basically, she started having second thoughts about becoming ugly and sick. She worried about stretch marks. Oh, she never said she wouldn't do it. But it was clear that she was unhappy about it. So Steve and I decided to forget it." She tried to smile. "We're going to adopt a South American child. Our name's on a list."

"That sounds wonderful," I said.

She nodded and gave the smile another try. This time it worked better. "Steve and I think so, yes."

On the evening of the first Tuesday after the first Monday of November, I drove Sylvie to the Elks lodge in Windsor Harbor. Most of the town had turned out. The folks were wearing red, white, and blue paper hats and were clutching little American flags. They waved them at each other by way of greeting.

The place was festooned with crepe paper and balloons and big BARON FOR GOVERNOR posters. Tom's smiling face peered down from the walls. Somehow the picture made him look a lot like Honest Abe. Eddy Curry was proud of those posters. He credited the advertising agency.

A band was set up in the corner, playing country and western tunes. The guy on the banjo was a dead ringer for Earl Scruggs, and played damn near as well. My feet stomped all by themselves. I always had a weakness for good bluegrass.

Against one wall a makeshift bar had been erected. There were a couple kegs of beer and several jugs of cheap wine, and Cokes for the kids.

I got us beers and Sylvie and I found seats. She hugged my arm and shouted into my ear, "American politics is so exciting."

I nodded vigorously. It was too noisy to attempt a real conversation.

I saw Eddy Curry bustling around at the podium that had been set up. It bristled with microphones. Television cameras were dollying around in front of it, jockeying for position. I touched Sylvie's arm and she got up to follow me.

"How's it look?" I shouted when I got Curry's attention.

"Shitty." He didn't seem too upset.

"The polls said he was catching up."

"Common phenomenon. He never had a chance."

"How's he taking it?"

Curry shrugged. "He'll be out in a minute. Judge for yourself."

Sylvie and I got refills on our beers and returned to our seats. A few minutes later the music stopped. There was some static over the PA system. People began to crowd around the podium. Sylvie and I stood up so we could see what was happening. Then a long applause began. The band played "God Bless America." The good folks of Windsor Harbor sang the words to it.

When the song ended, the applause began again. Over the heads of the crowd I could see that Tom Baron had made his way to the podium. He was smiling and waving and pointing to people he recognized, nodding and mouthing the words "Hi, there. Hello. How you doing?" Joanie was beside him. She wore a good, comfortable smile.

"My friends," came Tom's amplified voice.

More applause. Voices yelled "Way to go, Tom," and "Baron for governor."

"Dear friends," began Tom again, and when the applause drowned him out he shrugged and grinned and bent to kiss Joanie. The crowd loved it.

The band started up again. It played "Columbia the Gem of the Ocean." Nobody from Windsor Harbor seemed to know the words to that one.

After that, the crowd quieted. Tom tried it again.

"My good friends," he said. "I have just finished talking with Governor

McElroy on the telephone. I have congratulated him on his victory to-night."

Cries of "No, no!" went up from the crowd. Tom raised both of his hands over his head, urging them to stop.

"We have lost this election," he said. "It's all right. We fought hard and we lost. Somebody had to lose. This time it was us. Now it's time to come together, to heal old wounds. We have nothing to be ashamed of. We have raised the issues we wanted to raise. We have endured difficulties. We have had our tragedy. But we have persevered. We did not win this election. But Joanie and I have won much. We have met many wonderful people. We have a new feeling, a good feeling, for this grand state of ours."

The applause was loud and sustained and to my ears it sounded sincere. When it subsided, Tom continued, "Governor McElroy told me some-thing very interesting on the phone just now. He told me that he intended to assemble a special blue-ribbon, nonpartisan panel on drug abuse and enforcement in the Commonwealth. The governor has asked me to become the chairman of this panel. I have accepted."

During the applause that followed this announcement. Sylvie jabbed me in the ribs with her elbow. "Does this mean that you must become in-volved in Mr. Baron's blue-ribbon committee?" she said.

I pursed my mouth and arched my brows. "It might be interesting," I said.

She grabbed my ear and tugged my face down close to hers. "I want to know," she said, her breath warm on my cheek. "Did you vote for him?"

I kissed her on the mouth. She went with it for a long moment, then pulled her face away. I touched the tip of her nose with my forefinger.

"You should know better," I said. "I will never, ever tell."